She knew that look

She had once known the look of desire on a man's face—on many men's faces. But none of them had ever affected her like this.

Deep inside, some nether region of her innards rattled. Humming, vibrating, rattling—she couldn't tell which. It felt wonderful, like silver threads of pleasure were woven throughout her body and being plucked by some unseen hand like an angel playing a harp.

She felt a bit dizzy all of a sudden. Her eyelids felt heavy.

"It is less than a fortnight when we will be man and wife," Adam said thickly. He kept looking at her mouth, studying it intensely. Without seeming to move an inch, he somehow was closer. "Not long…"

"No. Soon."

He was going to kiss her, and she could do nothing but stand there, frozen on the spot, and wait for the touch of his mouth.…

* * *

The Sleeping Beauty
Harlequin Historical #578—September 2001

Praise for Jacqueline Navin's previous works

The Viking's Heart
"THE VIKING'S HEART is a beautifully
written medieval romance…
an entertaining and emotional read."
—*The Romance Reader*

A Rose at Midnight
"Nothing can prepare you for the pure love that flows
from Ms. Navin's writing. She gives warmth, humor,
tears of joy…her books are gifts to be treasured."
—*Bell, Book and Candle*

The Flower and the Sword
"…a touching tale of love's ability to heal
wounded souls."
—*Romantic Times Magazine*

The Maiden and the Warrior
"Ms. Navin has captured the essence of the time and
created a beautiful love story."
—*Rendezvous*

THE SLEEPING BEAUTY

JACQUELINE NAVIN

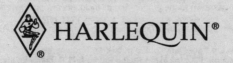

HARLEQUIN®

TORONTO • NEW YORK • LONDON
AMSTERDAM • PARIS • SYDNEY • HAMBURG
STOCKHOLM • ATHENS • TOKYO • MILAN • MADRID
PRAGUE • WARSAW • BUDAPEST • AUCKLAND

ISBN 0-373-29178-7

THE SLEEPING BEAUTY

Copyright © 2001 by Jacqueline Lepore Navin

Visit us at www.eHarlequin.com

Printed in U.S.A.

Please address questions and book requests to:
Harlequin Reader Service
U.S.: 3010 Walden Ave., P.O. Box 1325, Buffalo, NY 14269
Canadian: P.O. Box 609, Fort Erie, Ont. L2A 5X3

To Kelly.
The year this book was written was a tough one for you
and yet you have emerged from it with amazing benefit.
I admire your courage, your fortitude, your poise,
your sense of justice—just about everything about you
(except your hairstyle ☺). You have made your dad and
me proud and so very happy each and every day.

Chapter One

Northumberland, England 1852

Adam Mannion pulled his mount to a halt as the two of them rounded a bend in the packed-dirt road and stood staring at the sprawling mansion.

This was Rathford Manor?

His horse, a newly bought gelding with more spirit than sense, skittered sideways as if he, too, felt the sudden chill that seemed to hit once the house came into view. "Whoa, boy," Adam muttered, controlling the steed with a skillful jerk of the reins. The horse stilled and twitched his ears nervously as they both regarded the house.

Adam Mannion was nothing if not a practical man. In all of his thirty-two years, he had not seen anything to cause him to believe in anything outside the realm of the physical world other than a good, solid hunch one got at times when the turn of the cards was going one's way. Nevertheless, in this case he had to sympathize with the horse's skittishness. The place seemed…dead.

It appeared deserted. Not a single soul wandered in the gardens snipping herbs. No one trotted from the stables to greet him. The shrubbery that might have once lent grace to the noble facade was overgrown, ill tended and wild looking. Lichens grew on the stones, flourishing in the neglect that hung about the place like a pall. Many of the windows were shuttered, a strange sight when the weather was so mild. He supposed it indicated those rooms were shut up and unused.

"The Sleeping Beauty of Northumberland," Adam muttered, and huffed a short sound of amusement. Well, he was hardly Prince Charming set on cutting down the fence of thorns to rescue the princess, that was certain.

It was money that brought him to this godforsaken corner of England, up here where the wind came off the North Sea to blow across the lifeless moors. He would have preferred summering in Cornwall with his friends, or perhaps the south of France, or Italy as some of his more wealthy bows had. The difference was, he wasn't wealthy. Which was why he was here. Money. Oh, yes. And a wife.

The Sleeping Beauty of Northumberland, no less.

The horse nickered, a sure sign of derision, as if he could read minds, and Adam nodded sagely. "I agree. Silly stuff and nonsense, all of it." He shook his head and kicked his heels into the gelding's flanks. "We shall have to debunk the air of sorcery around here. It is pickling my brain."

However, his thoughts remained dark as he headed through the high grass and weeds growing on the terraced lawns. It was like heading into a mist-shrouded graveyard at midnight. The hairs on his arms stood up as though lightning were preparing to snap at his feet.

Dismounting, he brushed some of the dust off his trousers and smoothed his cravat, then laughed at his uncharacteristic fussiness. He supposed he was a bit nervous.

Going up to the door, he raised the thick verdigris wreath protruding from the mouth of an iron grotesque, and let it fall. The sound echoed like the low rumble of thunder. Nothing happened for a long time. Knocking again, he waited. He frowned back at the unsightly sentry and thought about his predicament.

Had his information been wrong? Or had he fallen victim to his friends' savage humor? The idea struck him like a blow. His "bosom bows" were rakehells and scoundrels, and it wouldn't be below them to play a cruel trick on one of their own. Maybe this was a prank, and they were right now gathered at White's by the wide front window, laughing themselves senseless as they thought of him traveling all the way up here for...for a fairy tale.

The Sleeping Beauty? He had been told fantastic tales of her beauty, of her charm and grace that had no equal, and— and this was the most important of all—of her fortune. A fortune he needed.

Money, beauty, a country miss whose reclusive preferences would pose no strings to his fast-paced lifestyle in the City. She was perfect.

How stupid of him. He was no green buck. Nothing was ever perfect. He should have known that by now.

Sighing, he silently admitted he had been duped. Thinking that if he left now he could make the inn in the nearby village of Strathmere by nightfall, he took a step down off the marble stoop.

He heard the door open behind him. Swinging around, he squinted. The figure inside was shrouded in deep shadows. He could only see it was a woman. A small, frail creature. Probably a servant girl. "What do you want?" she demanded.

Her impudence combined with his less-than-sublime mood at the moment served to annoy him. He said with an air of command, "I wish to see the mistress of the house. Lady Helena Rathford, if you please."

There was a short silence. "Who are you—" She broke off. In a more docile tone, she amended, "I mean, who may I say is calling?"

Her voice was cultured, not like a servant's at all. Then again, he was unfamiliar with this corner of England. Maybe the dialect was not as pronounced among the common folk as in other regions.

"Adam Mannion, Esquire." He folded his arms across his chest and waited to be asked in.

There was no response from the girl. "Go," Adam demanded, "and fetch her. Do not keep me waiting." He waved his hand at her in a shooing motion. Was she daft?

Her demanding tone was anything but. "What is it you want with her?"

"That is not your concern, girl."

"She doesn't wish to be disturbed. Go away."

To his utter astonishment, the door began to close. Two things spurred him into action. The first was his irritation at this annoying slip of a girl and the second was her unwitting admission that there *was* a Lady Helena Rathford in residence. He had doubted it when he had seen the poor condition of the house. He leaped back up the step and wedged his polished Hessian in the door frame just as she slammed the heavy oak portal closed.

"Lord, girl!" he cried, biting back some more vicious epithets he would have liked to employ as pain shot up his leg. "Are you trying to cripple me?"

"Move your leg."

"You impertinent chit. Get your mistress. I have important business with her that she…" He stopped. His foot throbbed. The pain edged his temper up. Pushing with one of his broad shoulders, he knocked into the door. The girl stumbled back and the oak panel crashed against the inside wall.

The intrepid servant was astonished, he saw. Her eyes were a startling blue—pale with a hint of green that made them almost turquoise. Grinning his most charming grin, he explained, "I've decided I'd prefer to wait inside."

She was taller that he had thought, probably because she had been hunched over before. Now she stood at her full height, looking brazen and outraged. Her hair was a mess, pulled back in a sloppy knot. Two hanks had worked out of the tether and shielded most of her features from view. Between those and the ubiquitous shadows clustering inside the house, he could barely discern what she looked like. All he could see was that she was thin, almost gaunt. A fine nose and a good chin impressed him as strong features in an otherwise frail mien.

Almost grudgingly, he acknowledged she was attractive. He was a man who enjoyed women, and he knew quality when he saw it. His objective observation of her good features disturbed him, for it was followed with a jolt of lust he found inexplicable. This girl was a hellcat. As a rule, easygoing misses with big bosoms were his favorite bedmates.

The girl retreated, melting back into the shadows. She called, "Get out of here immediately before I call my…my master."

"Call him then, I welcome it." Adam crept closer to the darkness. Really, the little idiot was a silly bit. He would have words with the Lady Helena when—or *if*—he was ever able to speak with her. "Where have you gone? Why are you hiding?"

"I am not hiding, you jackanapes. Get out now, I say!"

"Why, you imperious little snipe. How dare you refer so to your betters. Your behavior is reprehensible."

A snort was her response.

He went after her. She had him incensed. He had no idea

what he planned to do when he got her in hand. He didn't strike women, nor did he shake or manhandle them in any way. But still he stalked the shadows like an impatient predator.

"Where are you?" There was no answer. Perhaps she had grown frightened after realizing her wickedness, and fled. He straightened. He would just go and find her master himself, he decided.

Taking a few steps, he stopped, just now registering his surroundings. His eyes traveled in a slow circle and his breath came out in an appreciative whistle. The hall was a rotunda capped with what appeared to be a domed ceiling. Around him was artwork of magnificent proportion, all relief work in the neoclassical style that had become popular of late. Marble and painted wood and pure, white alabaster were all around him in various fashions of interior decoration. He walked about slowly, touching this and that, astounded by all that he saw.

He smiled. It was all he could do to keep from cackling and rubbing his hands together. The wealth displayed delighted him. He had come to the right place.

"Are you still here?"

He almost snarled. "I should say the same to you." He whipped around, scanning the darkened corners for some sign of her. In this hollow place where their voices echoed, the disembodied voice seemed eerie.

Another voice sounded. "My lady? What is it tha's goin' on? Who is come?"

My lady? "Lady Helena!" Adam called. "Are you here?"

Frantic whispers led him to the two figures huddled in the shadows. "Lady Helena?" he inquired, more urgently.

A flare of light startled all three of them. A man had joined them, coming up behind Adam with an oil lamp held

out before him in one huge, hamlike fist. He was large as
a bear and featured in the same fashion, his great bushy
brows drawn down in confusion. ''Helena, what the devil
is going on here?'' he demanded.

Adam turned back to the other two in front of him, which
he could see now with the aid of illumination. The girl
stared at him. Her features, bathed in the torchlight, were
startling. She seemed afraid, he noted. Well she should, for
this man who had just arrived was likely her master. No
doubt her atrocious behavior would win her a sound reprimand. Adam gave her a smug look before turning to her
companion, whom he expected to be the Lady Helena herself.

A woman stared back at him, her full mouth pursed in
irritation. She was at least two score and ten, her red hair
caught under a mobcap, with frizzled strands sticking
straight out from her head. Her face was lined, with a
healthy spattering of freckles over every inch. Both her age
and her obvious Irish heritage forbade her being the one he
sought.

Not Lady Helena.

With dawning dread, he turned back to the other female.
The servant who had taunted him. Lady Helena?

Helena blanched to see the look come over his face when
he realized who she was—a subtle blend of shock and war-
iness and…disgust?

Why should it hurt? Vanity, she supposed. It hadn't completely left her, despite the last five years.

This was a handsome man, after all. Dark eyes, dark hair,
well-dressed in expensive clothes straight from Savile
Row… A London dandy, no doubt. Although she tried to
strike a scornful pose, her insides were quivering too much
to make it effective. From the moment she had peered at

him through the slit in the door, there had been something about this man that had her stomach fluttering with a vague sense of apprehension.

She could easily guess why he was here—that didn't require any particular feat of brilliance. There was only one reason a man, any man, would travel to the northernmost regions of the country looking for her. A fortune hunter, then, ready with soft words and fawning praise. They had come before.

This one was different, however. He didn't seem the sly type who thought to win her with simpering compliments and false affections. This man had an edge to him, a hardness that wasn't completely tamed by his impeccable manners. He had dark hair, and eyes dark as sin that pierced her with incredulity, betraying his less than complimentary thoughts. His face was strong boned, with a square jaw and a straight, proud nose that gave him a certain presence. Not a pretty man, yet he exuded a virility that was indeed quite powerful.

That sensuously curved mouth said nothing, but she knew what he thought. Self-consciously she touched her wildly tousled hair and wondered if she had dirt on her face. The sudden anxiety over her appearance jarred her. It had been a long time since she had cared about such things.

Well, damn him! Dropping her hand, she told herself he was just a cheap swindler dressed in a nice coat.

"Father?" She forced out the words through a throat suddenly gone dry. "Please do not permit this man inside our home."

George Rathford looked at her, puzzled. "But he's already in, child. What are you about?"

"You can see I am in no condition to receive anyone," Helena protested. "Look at me! We were at work in the cellars."

The gentleman now turned to Lord Rathford and executed a correct bow. "My lord, I am honored to make your acquaintance. I am Adam Mannion, Esquire. At your service."

She narrowed her eyes critically as he paid respects to her father. Even as he bent at the waist in a cursory bow, he held his head at an arrogant angle. He had in him a reluctance to humble himself before a peer, as if there were a bit of a rebel residing behind those polite words.

She triumphantly awaited her father's response. If she had guessed this Adam Mannion's game, surely her father would be quicker to know it. George Rathford did not suffer fools.

"I have come to speak with your daughter—"

Her father cut him off. "My daughter? Helena, do you know this man?"

"No, Father. I was attempting to get him to leave when you came upon us."

Swinging around, the old man groused, "It's too damned dark in here. Why are all the windows shuttered? I can't see the fellow."

The Irishwoman spoke. "The sunshine makes dust motes, my lord. It is easier to keep the house this way."

"Damnation." Rathford peered again at Adam. "Want to see my daughter, eh?"

"If it is convenient," came the bland reply.

Helena saw her father chewing on the inside of his lip. It was a sign he was thinking. His rheumy eyes focused on her for a moment, then shifted back to the man. "It doesn't seem that the gel wants to see you."

"I...I noticed that, my lord."

"Women can be hard, Mannion. You know about women?"

Helena was stunned. This was not the curt dismissal she

had anticipated. There was even a glimmer of amusement on the old man's lined face.

Mr. Adam Mannion, Esquire relaxed. "Not enough, I'm afraid." What a clever response.

"Ah, who does?" Lord Rathford paused again, taking his time to consider the man before him. "Why don't you come into my study, since you've traveled all this way and Helena won't receive you? I'm of a mind to wet my throat a bit. You might be in need of a nip yourself."

Helen gasped. "Father!"

Mr. Mannion, Esquire, stopped and turned to peer at her over his shoulder as he followed Lord Rathford. His dark eyes nearly twinkled and the thick slashes above them lifted tauntingly. He said, "I'm afraid you'll have to await your turn, my lady."

And then he joined her father as they entered a paneled door off to the right, the one that led into her father's masculine retreat, the library.

She looked at Kimberly. The Irish servant's eyes were narrowed as she stared at the closed door. Helena grew frightened at that look. She was afraid of Kimberly.

To her utter dread, the servant turned that thoughtful gaze on Helena.

"Come upstairs," Kimberly ordered.

Chapter Two

"Sit down," Rathford ordered gruffly.

If Adam was bewildered by the man's abrupt change of mood, he knew he had better not show it. Selecting a chair, he slouched slightly and crossed his ankle on his knee. Propping his elbows on the armrests, he weaved his fingers together over his chest.

This room was only a bit more cheery than the cold hospitality offered in the shadow-shrouded hall. There was light, at least. Lots of books, gray as ghosts with thick layers of dust on them, lined every shelf. The furniture was comfortable, though, constructed of studded leather that softly absorbed the body's weight.

Rathford filled a tumbler with whiskey. "Are you of a mind for whiskey or port?"

"Whiskey will be fine." Adam looked around him. "Thank you for giving me your time and your hospitality. It's comfortable in here."

Rathford scowled at him and drawled sarcastically, "I am so glad you like it."

Adam took the jab without retort.

"I could ask you what you want with Helena, but you'd probably tell me a heap of manure." Handing him the whiskey, Rathford took a seat by the window and looked out at the ravaged garden. "So let me tell you what you want with Helena. You want her fortune."

Adam, who had been taking his first sip of the whiskey, nearly choked. Rathford smiled, never taking his gaze off the window. "She knows it, too. Do you think you're the first? Well, you ain't, boy. And you can forget trying to charm her. She'll have nothing to do with you."

Adam didn't reply at first. Running his forefinger across his top lip thoughtfully, he asked, "Then why not just send me away?"

"Because I may have some use for you, you arrogant pup."

The bitterness of the old man's response gave Adam pause. "What is it you want?"

Rathford started to laugh. Glancing at Adam, he raised his glass. "Why, the same goddamned thing as you do."

Adam puzzled over that one, but refused to rise to the bait and ask the old curmudgeon what he meant.

"I see you know when to shut up and listen," Rathford said after a while. "I like that. It's something, at least. A man hopes to have some respect for the man his daughter marries." Rathford glared at him. "You came here to marry her, didn't you?"

There was no sense in prevaricating. "Y-yes," he managed to reply.

"You need money?"

Adam tossed back a hearty gulp of the whiskey. "Yes."

"What is it? Demanding mistress? Gambling debts? Too much drinking?"

"The fickle blessings of Lady Luck have deserted me at this time," Adam said carefully. "My skill at the tables has proved inadequate without it."

"Cards? Horses? Or are you not particular?"

Adam shrugged. "Mostly cards. I'm usually good enough to live off my winnings, but lately I've run into a bit of trouble."

"How deep?"

"Four thousand."

"Good God. Well, it would have to be a goodly sum to hie you all the way up here." Rathford drew in a deep breath and expelled it, as if bracing himself for a particularly difficult duty. "You can have *five* thousand to cover your debts. I can give it to you today. Another fifteen hundred each quarter with which to amuse yourself. You might be able to use that if your 'bit of trouble' continues."

A hot flood of excitement spread through Adam like a stain on linen. "I could use it even so."

"And in return..." Rathford faltered. The whiskey hadn't dulled his senses enough that a dull gleam of pain wasn't detectable in his eyes. "In return, I shall require something of you."

"Yes, my lord. I understand."

"You want to marry my daughter. I will allow it. But for your part, you will promise me three things." He finished the whiskey. His sadness grew, it seemed, evident in the slump of his shoulders, the weary bow of his head.

Adam studied the man gazing dolefully into his empty glass. The whiskey he had just downed in a startlingly short amount of time was surely not his first today. Nor was his binge an unfamiliar activity. One could always tell by the bulbous nose, the tiny red spider veins tracing over the face, when a man was too fond of drink.

But there was a cunning here as well. And something else, something more...urgent. With his chin resting on his thumb and his forefinger caressing his top lip, Adam waited.

"The first," Rathford began, "is that you must not abandon Helena here. You will swear to visit at least twice a year, before and after the illustrious season, if you wish, so that your enjoyment of high society is not interrupted. You will stay for two months each visit.''

Adam frowned. He hadn't counted on so frequent a journey up to these cold climes. He hadn't necessarily intended to return at all.

''You will not leave her all alone—'' Rathford broke off, his voice choking a bit. ''You will come. The second promise is to be that you will do what you must as a husband to provide my daughter with a child. As many children as she desires. During these visits, you and she will be man and wife in all senses of the term.''

What it cost him to say this was evident in the rapid blinking of his eyes, in the way his jaw worked. His jowls began to tremble, so that his next words warbled more noticeably. ''The final promise is that you will always treat her with kindness. Never speak to her in anger, never raise a hand. I will have you not only cut off without a ha'penny to comfort you, but thrown in the darkest of cells in a place where no one will find you. And I'm not talking through legal means, boy. I will—'' His voice finally gave way.

This, at least, Adam had no compunctions about. ''My lord, I assure you your daughter will be met with kindness. Never will I do a thing to harm her, body or spirit. I am not a cruel or unkind man.''

''Money changes men,'' Rathford said prophetically. Bowing his head, he nodded, however, accepting Adam's vow. ''And the rest?''

Shifting in his chair, Adam admitted, ''I do not care for so frequent journeying. But I will do it. Twice a year, just as you request. I suppose.'' His lack of enthusiasm he didn't bother to hide. ''As for the other…I will provide my duty as husband as long as the girl is well. Her thinness may prevent—''

''No!'' Rathford slashed a hand through the air. ''No qualifications on it. You will…bed…her. You will give her children.''

Adam would have furthered the argument that the girl's health might make pregnancy a danger, but the man's countenance forbade it. Rathford's eyes blazed; his quivering lips were nearly palsied. ''I promise,'' Adam said.

Rathford froze for a moment, then like a wax doll held too close to a fire, he melted back into his chair. ''Very well. The bargain is done, pup. You shall have Helena as wife, and the bloody money, too.''

In the quiet of her bedchamber, Helena craned her neck to view the pattern of cards laid out before her. ''What do you see?'' she asked.

''Silence.'' Kimberly bowed her head. ''Don't ye be feelin' it? Yer mother, she's here.''

Helena froze. The mention of her mother brought an instant chill.

Kimberly opened her eyes and studied the three cards already laid out in front of Helena. ''Choose another.''

Helena obeyed, her icy fingers trembling as they selected from the deck. She placed the card where Kimberly indicated.

The servant frowned. ''Darkness. Very bad.'' She closed her eyes as she concentrated on communing with the long-dead Althea Rathford. ''She is very angry. Do ye not feel her anger?''

Helena had always been terrified of her mother, but Althea's rage when alive was nothing as terrible as the thought of her venom coming from beyond the grave.

Kimberly held her hands over the cards, palms down.

Her body stiffened and her head fell back. She was in communion with the other world. She moaned, then said, "Retribution."

Helena's breath accelerated, coming in rapid pants, her heart ready to tear out of her chest. Long, elegant fingers clung to the table.

Kimberly went limp. Helena waited with the dull echo of her heartbeat pounding in her ears.

Opening her eyes, Kimberly drilled Helena with her gaze. "This man is yer destiny."

"No! It can't be."

"Yer mother has called him here from across leagues of space."

"Does she wish to punish me? Is that why you said, 'Retribution'? Does she hate me?"

"A mother can never hate her child." Kimberly scooped the cards up, her crafty eyes staring into Helena's anxious ones. "She has great love for ye, just as she always did."

That was hardly reassuring. Helena had known all too well the yoke of her mother's love. She wrung her hands anxiously. "But he is a commoner. And..." She remembered his eyes. Dark, unfathomable and unforgiving. "And he seems so harsh."

Kimberly didn't argue further. Pressing her lips together—a sign that she had said all she was going to—she rose to place the cards back in their cupboard. Rising on shaky legs, Helena retreated to the other end of the room. She slid onto the window seat, her little corner where she always went to think.

Helena put no stock in Kimberly's predictions. She wasn't a believer. Not exactly. But guilt was a powerful thing. And the servant was clever, if nothing else. Kimberly's knowledge of the spirit world might or might not be accurate, but she certainly knew her way around the human soul.

How could Helena be expected to marry that arrogant peacock, a virtual stranger who was obviously seeking nothing but a nice fat purse? He did not hold any caring for her—how could he be her destiny?

Helena wrapped her arms around her chest and closed her eyes. She heard Kimberly leave.

Retribution.

It was time to pay for what she had done.

When she received a message from her father to change her dress, brush her hair and come to the conservatory, Helena was shocked. She had held out hope that her father had wished to annoy the man—this Adam Mannion—by playing along with his ''suit'' for a while. She couldn't believe that he would actually be interested in speaking to the man genuinely about the prospect of marriage.

But there was Kimberly's prophesy. And now this summons.

Going to the pier glass by her dressing table, she stared at her reflection as her numb brain assimilated the incredible events of this afternoon.

She had bathed as soon as she had come into her room, fetching the water herself and making do with a hip bath. Long soaks in the tub were a luxury of the past. Her hair was freshly washed, still damp, her face scrubbed clean.

Leaning forward, she concentrated on the stranger whose image she faced. Her hair, a wheat color, had once gleamed with rich luster, falling in a cascade of perfect curls. Each one had seemed to be made of pale ecru satin. Now it hung rather dry and dull, with only the tepid undulations of its natural wave to give it any style. Her skin was still good, but pale. No longer did the blush of roses flame in her cheeks. Her lips looked bloodless.

She was no longer a beauty. Which was how she liked it. She had never wanted to look in the mirror and see that other Helena, her mother's Helena, again. And yet this drab creature seemed a stranger. Perhaps a reflection of the true Helena she had never bothered to know.

For the first time since she'd pushed herself away from the strictures of beauty and grace that had been drilled into her as a child, she wanted something of her old self back. The thought of going to the conservatory and…and seeing *him* again was too daunting without it. Her mother had taught her how to use her looks to command attention, admiration. Power. She needed something of that skill now.

She took up her brush and began to pull it through her hair. Years of neglect weren't going to be cured in one sitting, but the slight sheen that came into the tresses gave her confidence. Pinning it up as best she could, she surveyed the effect. Not bad, she decided. Biting her lips and pinching her cheeks, she went to the wardrobe to inspect its contents.

The dresses were all heavy with dust, dull and limp with age, and in some places, moth-eaten. Even had they been in excellent condition, they were outdated. A yellow muslin wasn't too bad, she thought, pulling it out and brushing it off. The lace was still good and the stomacher in front boasted beautiful gold embroidery on ivory satin.

She flung it out before her, raising a cloud of dust. Then again and again. Each time it was as if she was shedding more than dirt. She was shedding the years. Her heart quickened. Destiny or not, she was going to give Mr. Adam Mannion a thing or two to reckon with. Namely, that she wasn't a treasure-laden galleon ripe for a pirate's plucking.

Her spirits lifted as she rushed about the rest of her toilette.

Chapter Three

The conservatory was magnificent. Adam looked around him, bouncing on his heels.

He wondered what his father would have thought to see him here, poised to marry an heiress. Not yet, he cautioned, checking the dangerous direction of his thoughts. The belle had yet to be won.

Lord Rathford, who had been nursing a drink while slumped in an old wicker settee, stood up when the sharp click of heeled slippers tapped upon the floor tiles. Adam looked over, mastering the sublime excitement that had stolen over him, and donned a sober mask.

The sight of Helena caused his jaw to drop. It gaped open for a moment before he recalled that it should be shut. He did so with such haste his teeth clicked together.

She was…incredibly different. Her hair was brushed and fixed into a neat twist. The simple style flattered her, revealing a face that was well-proportioned and delicate boned, with a pale complexion that needed no powder to enhance it. Her eyes were as vivid as a southern sea, her brow fair and arched, her mouth nicely pinked and prettily formed into a broad curve in the shape of a longbow laid on its side.

Her thinness, however, was disconcerting. In the soft fabric of the dress she now wore, he could see that the bones of her shoulders were acutely pronounced. The stomacher, meant to flatten a woman's chest and push her breasts upward, nearly sagged. The garment hung on her, even at the pinched waist, which was already shockingly narrow. Yet even in this faded finery, she made a palpable impact on the room as she entered, head held high, eyes straight ahead.

"Father," she said, pointedly ignoring Adam.

He grinned. She might have transformed her outward self, but she was still determined to bedevil him.

Rathford held out his arms to her. Adam's complacency vanished when he saw the older man's hands shaking visibly. Adam turned his head away.

Why all the melodrama? he thought testily. Christ, he wasn't a beast. And if they thought he was, why not throw him out and have done with it?

She breezed past him, into her father's embrace. Embarrassed at the intimate way they had their heads together, murmuring to one another, he looked out the dirty, multipaned windows.

"No!" he heard her say.

Rathford said something back. She protested; he overrode her.

Adam checked his nails. They could use a trim, he supposed. He sighed, waiting. Raising his eyes to the ceiling, he began to count the cobwebs.

A sharp cry and the rustle of skirts told him she had retreated from her father. Adam spied her sulking by some potted plant carcasses in the corner. She glared at him.

Turning to Rathford, Adam found the man red-faced. Biting his lips to hold back whatever emotions churned behind that ruddy facade, he gave Adam a curt nod and made for the door.

Adam supposed Rathford had told her the happy news. The rest was up to him.

Gritting his teeth, he approached Helena carefully, much as he would a skittish horse. Although he was certain she would not be delighted by the analogy, the situations were similar in that they both called for a gentle voice, a firm hand.

He was unprepared for the blaze of her eyes when she whirled on him. "My father says I am to wed you."

He halted in his tracks. It wasn't so much her anger—that he might have anticipated—but the stark blaze of fear he saw that stopped him. Holding up his hands in a gesture of peace, he said carefully, "I am certain the idea will be more agreeable to you when we know each other better."

"Why? Do you improve upon acquaintance?"

He bit back his temper. "I simply believe we got off to a bad start."

"When precisely was that? When you chased me into the shadows or when you pushed the door in and nearly knocked me down?"

He answered, "I believe it was when you called me a jackanapes."

Doing her best to flounce, she turned away from him with a sound of disgust. He reined in his mounting anger, reminding himself that he was supposed to be smoothing out their differences, not inflaming them.

He could coddle her pride. For five thousand and another six annually, he could do that. "I admit I thought you a servant," he said in a conciliatory tone. "It was unforgivable of me, but I can only plead the excuse of ignorance and poor lighting."

Her head came back around, slowly. Thoughtfully.

Encouraged, he continued. "You are no fool, that one can easily see." He took a step closer, glad she didn't skitter away from him. At this distance, he could see her prominent collarbone and the soft pulse that beat at the base of her throat. His gaze dipped lower to where the tiny breasts heaved under the too-large bodice. The slightest tremor stirred inside him. He swallowed, tearing his eyes away from the strangely exciting sight. "You don't trust me. I think this is fair. However, though I may be a cad, I am an honest one. If you don't believe me, consider that your father loves you too much to deceive you. He will no doubt share with you every facet of our conversation and the resultant bargain. Therefore, I have no choice but to be truthful."

She bit her lip with uncertainty, and he felt his stomach clench as the even, white teeth sank into tender flesh.

She said, "If all you want is money, I will pay you to go away."

"If money was the only consideration, I could pluck an heiress without going farther than the drawing rooms of Belgravia and Mayfair."

"Then why did you come?"

He hesitated. "There was talk. There was…a legend of sorts. Of a woman who lived in these parts, who was possessed of beauty and charm—"

The blue of her eyes grew icy when she cut him off. "If you wish to flatter me, you must think me indeed a fool."

"Of beauty and charm," he insisted, coming even closer, so that it seemed he towered over her. She was so petite, so fragile, like an exquisite doll made of porcelain. "That is the truth."

"And rich."

He didn't flinch. Almost, but he fought it. "And rich. Yes." There was an awkward silence.

She was the one who broke it. "I trust my father is compensating you well."

He didn't like that, not at all. Less so for it being the truth. "I have already admitted as much. You cannot wound me by taunting me with it."

"Can't I?"

He gritted his teeth. "You are very clever."

"Didn't they tell you that when they were extolling my beauty and wit?"

"Charm. It was beauty and charm. However, they clearly neglected to inform me of a few things."

Her lips twitched for a moment, then pressed together, extinguishing any hint of amusement. "You must be very angry at whoever sent you up here."

"Right now, I am concerned with you."

"Yes, of course. You can hardly kidnap me and force me to marry you."

"Your father thinks my suit to be a sound one. Should you not consider that?"

Tossing her head, she retorted, "My father is a drunkard whose affection for me has been lost in an intoxicated brain fever."

"He seemed quite clear thinking. He made me promise to treat you well, not to abandon you, and…to see to your needs."

"How wonderful." Her eyes blazed with a renewed flare of anger, blue-green fire coming straight for him. "It seems we're all set, then."

"That sort of sarcasm is unflattering." It wasn't true. Her features were alive and mobile with the play of emotions. His gaze once again dipped to those meager mounds of flesh, that miniature waist. What was coming over him, to wonder what that slender body would look like naked? Undressed, would it be hard angles and ungiving bone or would her breasts still rise to pinkened peaks and her hips flare with just the right sort of roundness to tempt a man's hand to slide along the contour?

She smirked. "Oh, heavens! And I do so wish to impress you."

He blinked, giving himself a mental shake. The direction of his thoughts surprised him. She was not the sort of woman he usually favored. She was haughty and brittle and far too thin. "You *are* making quite an impression."

With a brazen flourish, she squared off across from him. "Why should I care the impression you form of me? The days of my living for others' opinions are long since gone."

"That is obvious," he drawled.

"Nothing is obvious, Mr. Mannion. Nothing is what it seems here. If you knew what was best for you, you would leave this house, leave this place and count yourself fortunate to be gone."

He gritted his teeth. "I'm not leaving, Helena."

"And I didn't give you leave to address me by my name."

"It is only fitting, don't you agree, as you shall be my wife?"

"I have not agreed to marry you!" She exploded then, breaking away to pace. "You cannot possibly know what you are doing. You don't know things…. There may come a day when you consider your brilliant bargain not so attractive upon reflection."

"What don't I know? The reason why you and your father have chosen to molder here in this rotting mansion? I suppose I shall find the answer to that soon enough."

Startled, she whirled on him, eyes wide.

Strangely, he wanted to soothe her. Instead, his words came out sharp. "Do you truly want me to leave you to this dreary life? Do you love it so much?"

Her hand came to her throat. He could see it convulse under those long, thin fingers. He didn't relent. "Perhaps this is why your father accepted my suit, to get you out of this...." He waved his hands around, at a loss for words to describe the stagnant air around him. "So it remains, Helena, whether you will obey him in his wishes. Will you consent to marry me as your father commands? You are a dutiful daughter, aren't you?"

She looked up at him all of a sudden, startled. A doe cornered. Everything inside her was laid bare, raw and vulnerable. In a stinging moment of clarity, he understood something, something he couldn't even name, a feeling. That she needed him.

It was an intoxicating realization, filling him with a sense of power. Shoving aside the prickles of conscience, he pressed his advantage. "Will you consent to marry me?" His body tensed, awaiting her response.

Her shoulders weren't as squared. Her fear had edged out the burst of defiance and there was an air of resignation about her that curled his nostrils like a hound hot after the scent of a tired hare.

"Go away." It wasn't a command; it was a plea. "Leave me alone."

"I want an answer."

Her jaw worked rebelliously, but she lowered her eyes. Softly, she replied, "I do not believe I have a choice."

The surge of relief and triumph swept down from shoulders to heels, leaving him trembling with reaction. He'd done it. He'd gotten the money.

Slanting a glance up at him, her tone laced with contempt, she added, "If you are inclined to gloat, I would be grateful if you would do it somewhere else. And while you are congratulating yourself, Mr. Mannion, consider that you may find the fruit you have stolen may prove sour before too long.''

He ignored her, grinning as he snatched her hand. It was so cool. He touched his lips quickly to the slender back. ''You taste sweet enough to me.''

Snatching her hand back, she glared at him with prim affront. He laughed, buoyed by his great fortune today. ''Now, I am off to have my things brought up from the inn.''

''You are staying here?''

''At your father's invitation.'' He hiked his brows wickedly. ''Are you not happy to have me close? All the better to learn all those things a husband should know about a wife, wouldn't you say?''

She looked like she could claw his eyes out without a moment's hesitation. Without a word, she stormed off, her too-large dress gaping in the back. It should have made her look silly, like a twelve-year-old in her mother's gown, and yet she held herself with a dignity that would not allow anything so frivolous to be associated with her magnificent exit.

Narrowing his eyes as he stared after her, he wondered if she were going to prove difficult. He hadn't bargained on having to actually *contend* with his new wife.

Shrugging, he turned to other, more pleasant thoughts. Thoughts of money—six thousand a year! He laughed out loud as he jammed his hat on his head and exited the house.

Chapter Four

George Rathford was not nearly as drunk as he wanted to be. Maybe there wasn't enough whiskey in the world to take him to the oblivion he sought. Damnation, he was tired. Tired of the pain, tired of the hopelessness.

He blamed Althea, though it did him no good. It was useless to fault someone who was dead for one's problems. A cat chasing his tail was what he was—hating his deceased wife and helpless to do anything about the daughter whom he loved more than anything on this earth.

Had he done the right thing today? It was so hard to know. One rarely acted wisely when one was desperate.

There was little time left.

The housekeeper, Mrs. Kent, came in. "You wished to see me, my lord?"

"Instruct the servants that this man, this Mr. Mannion, is to be treated with all honor and courtesy. I want his room cleaned impeccably, his meals hot. I know there are precious little staff left, Mrs. Kent, but I must urge you to make the best impression possible."

"Will Kimberly also be expected to work, my lord?"

Rathford paused. The old Irishwoman was a blight on the house. Everyone was terrified of her, of her superstitions and her "powers." He considered it all foolishness, but he couldn't quite work up the courage to get rid of her. She was just a part of life in this old place—not a pleasant part, but a part just the same.

Perhaps Kimberly's presence was Althea's revenge on him for being happy she was gone.

"Kimberly has her own duties," he said, and swallowed a large gulp of whiskey to chase away his self-disgust.

Mrs. Kent's voice was stiff with disapproval. "Very well, my lord."

"One more thing. There is to be no...talk. That is, the reason for my daughter's seclusion may be of interest to Mr. Mannion. This might cause him to ask questions of the staff. No one is to speak of the accident. I cannot be more firm about this, Mrs. Kent. Any gossip on this topic will result in an immediate dismissal and no reference."

"That's harsh, sir."

"Indeed. So they will know how serious I am about this matter. My daughter's secret is to be kept."

"Very good, then. I'll tell them."

"And have Charles fetch another bottle, will you?"

Her frown creased her face. "Yes, my lord."

Adam spent the better part of the afternoon in the stables, as his room had to be "aired." Judging from the din coming from the house and the sight of several windows flung open to disgorge huge amounts of dust, the term "aired" was a euphemism for a full-fledged scrubbing.

While they worked, he enjoyed the company of horses and was surprised to find some astonishing specimens of horseflesh housed in the stalls. There were the work animals, and two fine Arabians whose sagging bellies bespoke of overfeeding and no exercise. With nothing better to do, he took them out to the paddock and trotted them a bit, then brushed them down when a quick-rolling thunderstorm drove them inside.

Tired and having worked up an appetite, Adam wandered into the house. The kitchens were deserted. Pilfering a smoked sausage from a string of links hanging on a peg, he munched as he sauntered out of the room and roamed the halls.

He smothered the smug sense of proprietorship that came over him. The place was nothing short of magnificent—underneath the dirt. It would be his someday. It felt good, and this surprised him. After all, he didn't even expect to be living in it, save those times he was obligated to visit.

Yet his mind couldn't help but create images of what the Romanesque busts would look like without their layer of grime, and just how brilliantly the gold leaf would glimmer if the filth-lined windows actually allowed in some light.

His good mood dwindled, however, as he passed through room after room of moth-eaten draperies and dust-dulled furniture. The Sleeping Beauty…yes, he felt like he was in an enchanted castle, and it was starting to send creeping tremors of disquiet up his spine.

The eerie effect was worsened by the loud patter of rain on the windowpanes. It sounded like bony fingers tapping, begging entry. It followed him as he wound his way through the house.

There was a music room, a portrait gallery, a column-lined portico overlooking a large ballroom that was now used for storage, apparently. In a small parlor, a painting caught his eye.

He moved closer, stopping when the sound of scurrying mice overrode the soft brush of his footsteps. Looking up, he studied the face framed above the fireplace.

It was her—Helena. Squinting, he looked again. Wasn't it?

The woman in the painting looked like her, but the eyes were colder. Empty, maybe, and devoid of fire. Her face was perfect, however, with high cheekbones blushed just right with the color of roses, and that pouting mouth that was slightly overfull and far too lush for her otherwise serious face. Her nose was perfection, her brow flawless. Dressed in an elaborate costume more suited to the last decade than to this, she was looking haughtily off into the distance, as if the laboring of the artist were of no consequence to her.

Oh, yes, this was Helena. That arrogance was unmistakable.

He let his eyes wander over the painted bustline, pushed up and flowing nicely over the straight line of the stomacher. It was a daring dress. Her breasts were exposed nearly to the nipples.

Low in his belly, a snake of desire stirred to life, coiling tightly like a cobra right before it struck. The artist had rendered her thin, but not as thin as she was now. The elegant length of her neck and the willowy repose of her bared arms showed enough flesh to make his mouth go dry. The difference in her face was also noticeable, fleshing out the promise of her otherworldly beauty.

This was undoubtedly an exquisite woman. Adam wondered if the artist had been flattering his subject, or had Helena once exuded that incredible blend of austere coolness and promised sensuality?

Immediately following these ponderings were the obvious questions, the questions that a man who had not come all the way to Northumberland for money alone would have asked first thing. Why?

Why did this incredible house resemble a tomb?

Why did the mistress dress and act like a common servant?

Why did a great and celebrated beauty shrink among the shadows and hide from the world?

He had told himself it didn't matter, but he was interested now.

"Mr. Mannion, sir," a woman's voice said from the doorway.

He started and spun around. A middle-aged woman in a checked muslin skirt and shawl knotted around her hunched shoulders smiled at him. She was pleasant looking, with bright eyes and a scooped nose that made her look a bit impish. "I am Mrs. Kent, the housekeeper," she said. "Your room is done and your things have arrived from the village. They've been unpacked. Would you like me to show you the way now?"

"Very well," he said, following Mrs. Kent out the door. Before he left, he cast one quick glance over his shoulder at the portrait and felt a renewed rush of curiosity.

What had happened?

Pausing at the threshold of the dining room, Helena took a bracing breath and squared her shoulders. But when she entered, she found only her father, seated at the head of the long polished table.

She was a bit taken aback by the fine linens and sparkling crystal and china settings. Looking about, she took in the improvements to the drafty place.

"Mrs. Kent has been busy today," she commented, taking one of the places set on either side of his.

"It is a time of great change," her father muttered into his glass. Although he had a wineglass at his place setting, he had his large fist wrapped around a tumbler.

"Indeed," she said, sitting stiffly and shaking out the linen napkin. "Here we are having dinner together, no more trays in our rooms. Just like civilized people."

"Helena, please. Not now."

"Of course, Father. Pardon me for troubling you. It's just that being bartered off to a complete stranger moments after setting eyes on him has put me a bit out of sorts...but, no, I must not speak of such things, mustn't I? I always should remember my manners."

"My God," he swore, and guzzled the drink down to the last drop.

"Isn't that what I was always taught—deportment above all things?"

"That was your mother."

"And where were you when I was being instructed in this treatise and all the rules of *haute société?* Off hunting?" Leaning forward, she gripped the edge of the table until it cut into her palm. "I remember wanting to go with you so badly. Once, when I was six years old, Mother had me dressed in a perfect white frock trimmed with delicate pink satin bows all along the hem. It was a beautiful dress, and costly. I know because she told me so, reminding me to take care, hounding me, really. I hated the thing, hated the prison I was in when I wore it. Trapped into being a lady when I wanted to run and jump and yell like a Red Indian.

"We were going to tea at a neighbor's. I always hated that, having to sit there perfectly still, perfectly silent, perfectly *deported.* When I saw you going to the stables, I ran out of the house and asked you to take me with you. I cried, 'Pick me up, Papa!' and held my arms out to you."

George Rathford hunched over in his seat, shielding himself from her words as if they were physical blows.

"You looked at me and smiled. I wonder if you remember. I thought for a moment you were going to lift me up and carry me off to a grand adventure. I knew at that moment you were my absolute hero and that you'd rescue me." She paused a moment before continuing, sotto voce. "And then Mother came. She scolded me and sent me inside, but I defied her, sure you would tell her that we were going hunting together, sure you would stand firm. Sure you would take me with you."

Her father looked despairingly at his empty glass, then glanced rather desperately at the sideboard where the decanters were situated.

Helena said, "When you didn't, I knew that you never would. You weren't my hero. Not at all. You were weak. You've always been weak, Papa. I don't blame you for it, it's just what you are, though I wish it could be different. And even with understanding that, I cannot see the reasoning you have to seal me to this devil's bargain. How could you?" Passionately, she strained forward, willing him to see her for once. "How could you do it?"

He just shook his head, his eyes downcast. He appeared miserable.

There was a long silence. Her father was not going to give her an answer, so Helena leaned against the back of the chair carved to depict an ornate shield and lifted her eyes to the ceiling.

Adam chose that moment to enter. Like a windup toy, Rathford sprang to his feet and lurched to the sideboard to pour himself another whiskey. Adam, coolly glancing at his host's jerky, nearly frantic movements, raised a brow and continued on without comment. "I do apologize for my lateness," he said, taking a seat, "but the accommodations, while wonderful, were a bit slow in coming."

She despised Adam for his smooth entrance and suave smile. Surely if a man had something to smile about, it was he—the victor triumphant and not above rubbing it in.

"We are not accustomed to guests."

His lips curled, cutting deeper into the lean lines on either side of his mouth. "You don't say."

She looked away quickly. He was impertinent and full of himself. She disliked him intensely. A footman entered with the soup.

"I saw your portrait in a parlor," Adam said in a nonchalant purr as he took up his spoon. "A remarkable likeness. It captures your mystery well."

"What were you doing in that room?" she demanded.

"Exploring a bit." He flashed her a smile that was all charm. She supposed he could be beguiling if he set his mind to it. But she wasn't misled. He was baiting her, there was no doubt about it. "I was curious about the house. It is quite lovely." Carefully, he skimmed the surface of the consommé with his spoon and tasted it.

"It is not yours. Yet."

His spoon stalled. "It is to be my home. Do you wish me to stay in my room?"

She gave him a snide smile to mock his. "I wish you would leave."

He shook his head as if thoroughly disappointed. "How shall we get to know one another, then?"

"I do not wish to know you."

"I see. You prefer your solitude. You like it here, moldering in this rotted out place—do excuse my frankness, Lord Rathford. You actually *adore* the dust and the dry rot and the mice." To his future father-in-law, he inclined his head. "Again, my apologies, my lord."

Helena spared her father a brief glance, to find he was fighting a smile. Amused, was he?

"Well, if the place is not good enough for you, perhaps you should leave."

Adam frowned and tapped his finger against his pursed lips. "Now, there is something happening here that is causing me to suspect…can it be? Is it that you *want me to leave?*''

''Your sarcasm, sir, betrays your lack of gentlemanly manners.''

''In response to your appalling breach of hospitality, I believe it most appropriate.''

''You are a bore!''

''And you are a skinny, waspish, miserable female who is allowing her soup to get cold.'' He nodded to the cooling liquid in front of her. ''If anyone ever needed all the sustenance she could find, it is you.''

She nearly came out of her chair. ''If you find me lacking, sir, then you may—''

''Leave,'' he finished for her, and blithely downed another spoonful.

Breathless, wordless, she gaped, her mouth working as her mind tried fitfully to formulate a suitable reply. There was a dry, wheezing sound in the room and it drew her attention to her father, who was shaking uncontrollably with his hands over his face.

For one brief moment, she thought perhaps he was weeping. He had seen the awful truth about Adam Mannion, realized his terrible misjudgment and now he was weeping!

Vindicated, Helena reached for her father, full of concern and ready to forgive. At her touch, Rathford raised his face and she saw that tears were streaming down the man's ruddy face, but he was *not* weeping.

He was laughing.

Dawning fury washed through her, leaving her electrified. She didn't dare cast even the briefest glance at Adam, sure he would be gloating. Throwing her napkin onto the table, she leaped to her feet and fled.

Chapter Five

Adam had a difficult time falling asleep. This was unusual for him. He usually experienced no trouble.

He had certainly gotten the best of Helena at dinner. Sent her out in a huff, he had, and it had felt good for exactly one-tenth of a second. Then he had felt mildly ashamed. After all, it was graceless of him, when he had obviously won everything so completely, to be snide about it.

Besides, it troubled him that she had missed dinner. She was so damned *thin*. He hoped she had eaten later, but doubted it.

Sitting up, he turned on his side and punched the pillow. The nights were certainly cool up in this corner of England. Tonight, however, the sheets felt clammy and his skin dry and hot.

A sound reached his ear, causing him to still his arm in midpunch.

It was music. It was a pianoforte, being played by an expert hand.

Maybe it was the completely moonless dark, or maybe it was this tomblike place finally getting the better of him, but the hair on his arms stood straight up and cold fingers traced a chill across the back of his neck. It was a sensation that had nothing to do with the plunging temperatures.

The strains were lilting, but faint. Carefully, he climbed out of bed and grabbed his trousers as he tiptoed to the door. Pressing his ear to the crack, he heard the music better.

On the dressing table lay his watch and fob. He fumbled for them after he had secured his trousers, and retrieved a flint box and small candelabra. Striking a flame, he lit three tapers and checked his watch. Half past one.

Who was playing the pianoforte at this hour?

Quickly, silently, he undid the latch to the door and entered the hall. The candlelight threw up shadows along the wall. They looked like undulating wraiths that melted into the darkness as he passed. Fanciful nonesuch, he scoffed, and padded barefoot down the corridor.

He didn't yet have his bearings in the house. Upon reaching the stairs, he wasn't certain whether to proceed to the corridor on the east end of the house, which looked to be a match of the one he had just come down, or descend. Taking a few tentative steps down the stairs, he judged the sounds to be growing louder and hurried on.

The piece being played grew bolder, harsher. Increased emotion built into a medley of light frolics offset with low undertones. Under the guidance of the magnificent piece, a vision unfolded in his mind, of a child playing alone, serving tea to her dolls on a clean, sweet lawn, while a slavering beast lurked just on the edges of the forest. And every so often a moment of disquiet entered the child's consciousness as she became increasingly aware that she was being watched by a predator.

As he moved stealthily down the corridor, Adam marveled at the vivid picture in his mind. Never having been a man given to great contortions of imagination, he blamed the music. It was incredibly moving, incredibly passionate.

He paused, cursing himself for a clodpoll. Of course—the music room. The problem was he wasn't certain where it was located. His wanderings that day had taken him all over the house, and he couldn't rightly place it.

Trying a door, he winced at the long, agonizing protest of the hinges. The sound was like a wail of pain. The pianoforte music ceased.

In the darkness, he called, "Hello? Who is there?"

There was a silence, then a soft scrape and the light brush of footsteps retreating quickly.

Cocking his head, he tried to gauge their direction, but the vaulted ceiling and polished floors created a cavernous chamber where the untraceable sound echoed, then died.

It had to be her, of course. Helena. He couldn't imagine the servants were used to making free with the musical instruments, and only one who had been subject to careful—and expensive—instruction could play with that combination of skill and passion. And yet it seemed impossible that thin, wasted waif who had scowled and screeched at him had so much within her.

But if there was one thing he was learning, and learning quickly, it was that Lady Helena Rathford was rarely what one would expect.

Helena spent the morning in the drawing room she often used, sewing with Kimberly. Their project was to alter the contents of her wardrobe, trying to transform the outmoded gowns into some semblance of current style. Inspecting their efforts, Helena held up a green silk. She could not say she was pleased. Not particularly talented with the needle and unskilled in working the delicate fabric, she had drawn the material into unsightly puckers as she stitched.

"I think I have no choice but to go to Strathmere and visit the seamstress," Helena said, bundling up another botched effort and tossing it on the floor.

"If yer vanity must be appeased, so be it," Kimberly replied darkly, not looking up from her own sewing.

"If I do not wish to go about with my bosom exposed, I must."

Kimberly looked up. Helena stared back at the watery blue eyes. There passed between them a moment of shared astonishment. Helena did not speak this way to Kimberly. She simply didn't.

Drawing in a nervous breath, she proceeded more calmly. "It is not conceit to wish to be dressed properly. I am, after all, a noblewoman, even if we've all forgotten that fact."

Kimberly's great irritation, which was clearly apparent on her freckled face, did not frighten Helena. Well, perhaps a little bit, but her mind was already made up. She simply would *not* allow Adam Mannion to see her in these rags.

"Are ye, now?" Kimberly purred. She placed the dress she'd been working on down and rose to her full height, which came to just under Helena's chin. Of course, Helena was taller than most, but this only made Kimberly's small stature all the more noticeable. "I'd o' thought ye'd be beyond that kind of conceit. After all, ye're not so high and mighty as ye once were, when your mama was alive and ye thought ye were the toast of the land. Ye know what 'appened then, eh, missy?"

"Yes," Helena said, fighting the tremor of reaction at the mention of the accident. "I know what happened then, Kimberly. And if I ever forget, no doubt you will hasten to remind me. Nevertheless, I am to be married. I cannot disgrace my husband. And I would think you'd wish me to make a better impression, as he is my *destiny*."

"That he is. But why impress him? Who is 'e—a commoner, not a nobleman. An' 'e's come for yer money. What difference does it make 'ow ye look, my pretty bird? Yer destiny is not to be a pleasured pet. Ye best remember that, eh?''

Whirling away, Helena headed for the door. "I think you've said enough. I—" She broke off, staring at Adam, who was standing just outside the room.

"Hello." He cocked his eyebrows and flashed her one of those half grins he favored. She supposed the tarts he was used to dealing with found the expression absolutely adorable. "I was just about to knock."

"What are you doing?" she demanded.

"Why looking for you. You weren't at breakfast. Naturally, I wondered where you had gotten to."

"I cannot see why my whereabouts would be of such interest."

He shrugged, another gesture of appealing nonchalance. "There is little enough diversion for a man up here in the wilderness."

"It is not the wilderness." Gad, she sounded like a harridan, even to her own ears. With an effort, Helena softened her posture and modulated her voice. "It is a perfectly respectable part of the country and we are quite civilized."

"Compared to London, it is positively primitive. Why weren't you at breakfast?"

She was disconcerted. As it was not the family's custom to take meals together in the dining room, it hadn't even occurred to her to go there this morning. However, her father had no doubt given orders that they were to institute this ritual for the sake of their guest. She was simply forgotten. She said, "I rose late today."

"Slept in because you were up all night, did you? Do you always play like that when you can't sleep? No use denying it. I heard you at the pianoforte last night. Excellent performance, if a bit odd in timing.''

Kimberly made to leave, glaring at Adam as she brushed past him. Swiveling his head to follow her path down the hall, he muttered, "I'm afraid she doesn't like me."

Nothing else he might have said could have melted Helena more readily. She fought back a smile. "It would seem not."

He turned back to her. "I would like it if you would play for me sometime."

"That is impossible. I do not play for anyone but myself," she answered honestly.

"Really? We shall see, then."

Whenever he and Helena were sparring, his eyes had a habit of sparkling, as if they danced in delight at some amusing secret he held from the rest of the world. She got the strongest feeling that if there was a joke there, it was most certainly on her.

"Sewing today, are you?" he said.

Helena bristled. She hardly wished him to be made aware of the fact that she had spent the morning frantically attempting to refashion her wardrobe in order to make a more pleasing presentation—for him! Her response was reflexive. "No, no, not at all. Why do you say that?"

That debonair grin deepened, showing a single dimple. His hand came up and she flinched, catching herself and flushing with embarrassment at the instinctive response. She didn't like being touched, as a rule.

He didn't hesitate, however. Long, tapered fingers plucked a snippet of embroidered silk from her hair. They moved down to her shoulder, where a tendril of thread stuck to her bodice.

Faced with this evidence and nearly undone for his forwardness, she stared at him. "Oh, *sewing*. Yes, well, we were doing our usual mending. A few hours here and there. I am so used to it, I barely notice it anymore.'' She ended with a nervous laugh that fell flat.

His smirk told her he guessed the truth. Her humiliation knew no bounds.

''I could take you into the village if you need... supplies.'' A heartbeat later, he added, ''For your mending.''

''I don't need...'' What was she saying? It was no use denying that her wardrobe was a shambles. ''Actually,'' she began, ''I saw today that my mending has rather taken its toll on my old dresses. Of course, I normally couldn't be bothered with such things, since no one ever comes here. However, given the state of things, I was considering purchasing a few new items. Gowns, I mean. Just because the other ones are beyond repair, you understand.''

He was tactful enough not to let the quivering of his lips blossom into a true smile. ''Every bride should have a trousseau.''

''I am hardly an ordinary bride,'' she stated smartly.

He ignored her show of vinegar. ''All the more reason for the ordinary rituals to stay locked in place, yes?''

She didn't know why he was being so kind. He could very easily expose her, or even cock one of those sharply arched brows, and she would be totally humiliated.

''Does tomorrow suit you? Or did you have other plans?''

''No, no plans.'' She said haughtily, as if there were some possibility of her having plans. Which was ridiculous. She'd be devoured by flesh-eating maggots before she'd admit that to him, though. ''Tomorrow should suit me.''

''After breakfast, then?''

''I'll meet you in the dining room for the meal, and we can go immediately afterward.''

"Good." He folded his arms across his chest and regarded her with a pleased expression. "Then I can make certain you eat something."

She saw him go off to the stables some time later. Less than three-quarters of an hour after that, he went galloping across the meadow and into the woods.

It was a relief not to have him about, not to have the possibility of him chancing upon her at any moment. Her days were usually spent either in the kitchens or together with Mrs. Kent, undertaking some house chore. There was an endless supply of them, what with the shortage of staff. It was Helena's fault, that was, and she felt obligated to help. She might be a lady of noble birth, but she was not one of leisure. She toiled alongside the lowest-paid servant, and didn't mind a bit. For one thing, it kept her busy and helped her fall exhausted into bed most nights. For another, it meant she could keep the amount of strangers in her house to a minimum.

Since the accident, she couldn't tolerate intruders.

Therefore, this planned jaunt into Strathmere tomorrow threw her into a fit of anxiety. Of course, going anywhere with Adam would be bothersome. They were likely to quarrel the entire way.

But more than that, she would be seen. She hated being seen. She hated the whispers and the looks.

She almost changed her mind. Just imagining what it would be like turned her legs to water. But she simply could not be a faded frump any longer. When he left to return to London, she'd get her precious solitude back, but until then she would have to contend with his presence. His *intrusion*.

And she would simply have to get some new clothes. What a bother he was!

Yet she found herself watching all afternoon for his return.

Chapter Six

Besides being cold most of the time, Adam very quickly learned, the Northumberland shire was very troublesome in its terrain. His horse didn't like it at all, the spoiled beast. No doubt longing for the civilized streets of the city, the gelding snorted and generally made known his displeasure at having to traverse the crude paths. When they came to a fallen tree, he balked at the jump. At the edge of a stream, he rolled his eyes testily and refused to take one step into the water.

In no mood to have a difference of opinion with the ornery beast, Adam sighed and resigned himself to following the bank for a while. He let his mind wander.

There were plans to be made, tasks to be seen to. He had to post several letters tomorrow, which he had written early this morning. One to his friends to inform them of his staying on in Northumberland for a period of two months, and of the impending nuptials. He grinned, imagining their response. There had been no small amount of coin wagered on his success in this venture, and he wished he could be there to see the naysayers who had put their money against him pay up.

Two other letters were to solicitors. Mr. Fenton was his

father's old solicitor. It would be he who would receive the bulk of the five thousand to settle Adam's father's debts, compounded by his own ill-fated attempts to cope with them through wagering.

Mr. Darby was a new fellow whom Adam had contacted just before setting out. On the chance he was successful in getting his hands on the Rathford money, Adam had arranged for Darby to handle all future transfers of funds. The clean break with Fenton was needed. This would signal the end of a chapter in Adam's life, an unpleasant one. He was now a wealthy man and the troubles of the past were behind him.

There was a fourth letter, written to a Trina Bentford, advising her that their association was to be terminated due to the occasion of his marriage. It was something that had been coming for a long time. As a friend, Trina was exuberant and deliciously wicked. She never ceased to make him laugh and always was ready for whatever wild scheme anyone could come up with. As a mistress, she was exhausting. Not in bed. In fact, her interest in that department was negligible. Of course, she understood how it went and did her best to keep him pleasured, but she was hardly inventive or particularly stirring in the sensual way. No, her talent lay in craving attention, and her appetite for that had been far too voracious for him.

It was a good time for a break here, too. She would be miffed, naturally, since marriage was not necessarily an occasion for ending a liaison, but by the time Adam was set to return to London she would have cooled off enough to forgo the usual tedious scenes.

Thinking of tedious scenes put him in mind of his future wife. He smiled as he kicked his horse up the sloped embankment and cantered home, although why thinking of Helena Rathford should bring on a stupid grin was beyond his comprehension. She was a bothersome piece, completely incomprehensible and constantly contradicting reason. A study in contrasts at every turn—cool as ice one moment, then wild as any untamed virago the next. And all the while shrouded in that cursed air of mystery that was beginning to wear on his nerves.

But damn, her eyes could look straight through a man and touch something in him. Adam scoffed at himself. Lust was what it was, if one could be besieged by that affliction for such a slip of a girl. He mentally compared her to the voluptuous Trina, then dismissed his former mistress, to linger only on Helena's attributes.

She had incredible grace. Her neck was like a swan's, giving her the most elegant aspect. Her air of reserve seemed to taunt him unmercifully, driving him to distraction with wanting to strip it away and find out what passions it hid.

Because there was passion in her. He had heard it in the incredible music she had produced. Absolutely tantalizing.

He was still thinking about her when the house came into view. It was past luncheon, nearly teatime. He wondered if she'd eaten. Good God, he was becoming her nursemaid, worrying over her. He told himself it was because he didn't want to bed a skeleton. By their wedding night, at which time he had promised to do his best to keep his end of the wretched bargain he had struck with Rathford, Adam wanted a more fleshy version of the woman to warm his bed.

He wanted the Helena in the portrait.

"Hello, sir," the groom called, coming to take the horse. "Have a nice ride?"

"The damned beast almost broke a leg on those rocks."

"Gotta stay off of them rocks," the man agreed. "Gotta

go south to get to the good hunting grounds. That's where the master goes.''

"Hunts, does he?" Adam was interested. "Where exactly does he go?"

"The woods that stretch from here to Strathmere, then all the way to the castle." Seeing from his expression that Adam didn't know about the castle, the man explained, "Where the duke lives. You'll see it when you get near. It's a huge old place, sits way up high on a big hill. The woods whip around it and go all the way up to the cliffs, and there's lots of game in those woods. The duke don't like you hunting the deer, though. Got a cousin what comes up once in a while, and he and the master have a rout, getting the foxes off the farmers' lands and rabbit hunting.''

"Keep me informed when the fellow arrives, if I'm about. I fancy a good fox chase. What's your name, fellow?"

"Kepper, sir."

"Glad to know you, Kepper," Adam said amicably. He noticed the man's surprise at his familiarity. There were certainly many things that had changed about him in the years since he was himself touching his forelock to members of the aristocracy, but he'd be dead and rotted through before he'd neglect a courtesy because of his newfound status. "Thanks for the tip. I'll need a carriage or curricle to go into the village tomorrow. I'll be taking Lady Helena with me, so something not too rough, man.''

"Lady...? Lady Helena, you say? She's going into the village?"

"That's what I said." Adam's good-natured smile sagged at the man's apoplectic expression. "Is there something wrong with that, Kepper?"

"She don't see nobody, sir. Don't go out none, either."

"Why not?"

He shrugged his wide, bony shoulders. He had the wiry build of a man whose frame held a deceptive amount of strength. There was an air of competence about Kepper, as if he'd seen a lot in his life and knew how to keep it locked up tight behind closed lips. "Don't want to, I guess."

"Yes." Adam knew Kepper wasn't going to gossip, so he took his leave and mulled over the latest titillating bit of strangeness about his betrothed.

He was losing count of them.

One of the few advantages Rathford Manor could boast was its good cook. Her name was Maddie, and last night's herbed roast beef had been perfection, complemented with a delicate sauce and mashed turnips. Mashed turnips had hardly been chief on Adam's list of favorite delicacies, but this dish was incredible, as was the delicious cake soaked in rum served for dessert, with steaming hot coffee strong enough to make the roots of his teeth ache. Just how he liked it.

He feared he would grow quite fat and lazy here at Rathford Manor. As he sat down this evening and surveyed the dressed fowl and glazed carrots on the sideboard, ready to be served, he considered this a definite possibility. That thought reminded him of the necessity of daily exercise, which in turn put him in mind of the possibility of hunting with Lord Rathford.

"I was told you are fond of the hunt, sir," Adam said.

Lord Rathford was seated at his customary seat. He cocked his eyebrows. "Indeed I am, sir."

"I fancy a good run in the woods myself. I was told you sometimes go out with a fellow from a nearby castle."

"Yes, when he is visiting his cousin, the duke. The, ah, Duke of Strathmere is an old family friend." The glance he cast Helena was nothing short of conspiratorial.

Adam frowned. What was this, *another* secret?

"Do you keep hounds, Lord Rathford?"

"Used to have a fine pack, but I don't get out as much as I used to and they turned bad, most of them. Lost the scent, or ran off." He waved his hand in the air.

Adam was now truly perplexed. A good hound was as valuable in hunting circles as an excellent mount. One did not simply neglect them, or allow them to "run off."

"I don't understand." Leaning on his elbow, Adam took up his wineglass, which had just been filled. "How do you hunt without the hounds?"

"There's a bitch in the stables that's still good, and a dog or two who'll be up for a romp occasionally, but they're too lazy to run for long."

"They need training, that is all. And steady exercise to build up their endurance." Looking to Helena, who had maintained a decorous quiet during this entire exchange, he asked, "Do you hunt, my lady?"

Her lowered lashes lifted lazily. "No, Mr. Mannion, I do not have the slightest interest in chasing poor, defenseless animals. There seems to me to be no good reason for this exercise other than to experience a rush of pleasure at having demonstrated superiority over a hare."

"You put it so cheerfully," he countered as a servant came to proffer a plate loaded with pheasant, "that it makes me absolutely champ at the bit to get out there and track the wretched beasts. I believe it my most profound duty to drive them down into the ground, where they belong."

She tried to appear cool, but her lips twitched before she lowered her gaze back to her plate. When the servant came to her, Helena selected a few morsels.

"Excuse me…Bissel, is it?" Adam asked. "Ah, then, Bissel, if you would place a few more slices of the fowl on your mistress's plate, it would please me."

"Excuse me," Helena interrupted archly. "You are not presuming to select my food for me, are you?"

"Indeed, I am. I am concerned about your health, Helena. You skip meals and eat sparingly whenever you do take a meal."

"Let me guess." Her smirk was childish, but it actually looked good on her. She was angry, and the emotion gave color to her cheeks and made those blue-green eyes sparkle radiantly in the candlelight. "You prefer your women plump."

"I enjoy many things in a woman, not the least of which is a pleasant disposition, but I am not aiming to please myself. I simply thought that since you were to be fitted for some new dresses, you might want to see to filling them out a bit."

She reacted as if he had slapped her. "How dare you make reference to my garments and their...fit."

"I was merely observing that it must get damned tiresome being so scrawny."

The look in her eyes was murderous. "Did you hear that, Father?"

"Yes," Rathford agreed mildly, not at all offended on his daughter's behalf. "The man has appalling manners, I agree, my dear. Nevertheless, he is correct. You look like an urchin. It's about time someone told you so."

"Father!" She sprang to her feet, clearly devastated. "I cannot believe you would take sides against me."

Leveling a serious look at her, Rathford said solemnly, "Never, Daughter. That I'd not do. And if you listen closely, you'll not hear a disparaging word in what I said. It is merely the unfortunate truth."

"Sit down, Helena," Adam interjected. "I am getting tired of you running out of a room every time you realize you cannot win an argument."

She waited a long time before she did anything. Adam was half-afraid she'd dismiss his taunt and run, anyway.

"Will it help if I ask nicely?" he said, wanting to offer something in return when she slowly sank back down in her seat. "*Please* eat your pheasant. There. And have the carrots, too."

"I will eat what I wish, and you can be damned."

Adam merely smiled back at her. "Did you hear that, Lord Rathford?"

"Indeed, and I agree with her. Now shut up and eat before I resort to paddling the pair of you and sending you off to bed without dessert."

Adam addressed the contents of his plate with gusto, pretending not to notice how Helena ate. He would not have put it past her to deny herself out of defiance against him. But she didn't. She consumed a healthy portion at dinner and had a slice of iced sweetroll for dessert. He even detected her stirring more cream into her coffee than he had seen her use last night.

He couldn't keep from crowing to himself at his victory. This marriage might just be fine, after all. All he had to do is refer to his wife as "scrawny" and she'd do his will.

God, that thought—of Helena doing his will—brought up images no man should have about a woman while sitting in the presence of her father.

Chapter Seven

Some days were too winsome to bear. Everything about them was perfection, from the soft yellow of the sunshine, and the sweet smelling breeze, to the call of birdsong, sounding so brave and promising in the wood.

There wouldn't be many of these days left in the summer. Already the foliage was beginning to wilt and brown, and the promise of cooler times ahead made the mild weather all that much more precious.

It was a day such as this when Helena and Adam left the manor and headed in a stylish curricle down to the village. Kepper must have been hard at work to get the vehicle in order. The smell of fresh paint was detectable, as was the lemon oil used to rub the hide seats clean and supple. In no way was it a luxurious conveyance such as Adam's friends in London utilized, but it was a damned sight better than he had expected. As was Helena. She appeared bedecked in a scarlet cloak and wearing an air of indifference that was as thin as the gossamer tucker folded into the neckline of her dress.

Climbing into the open carriage, she didn't say a word.

Adam took the reins and pulled out.

After a broad silence, he said, ''The banns will be read

Sunday." He kept his eyes trained on the road ahead. "It is useful that we are going together on this outing. It is helpful for us to be seen together. It won't come as so much of a shock to your friends, then, when the news comes."

"There is no one I call friend." She said it without any hint of sadness or regret.

He was startled. "How odd. Are you such a misanthrope?"

"I am simply a private person." He heard the rustle of her dress as she twisted in her seat. It was an anxious motion. "Which no doubt meets with your disapproval. Everything I do seems to meet with your disapproval."

"Not entirely. I like your hair that way, for instance. Your rudeness to me, however, that is an entirely different matter."

"Oh, really? And how am I supposed to act toward the man who has so gallantly ridden all the way from London to *claim a purse*. Oh, and take a bride in the process, a rather minimal consideration."

"I do not think it so unusual. Most girls of your illustrious acquaintance no doubt never met their husbands before their papas picked them for them. I always thought it an odd custom of the aristocracy to treat their children like cattle, to be matched and bred for the good of the estate. Don't tell me you don't know this."

"I am no sapskull. I am rather better versed on the 'odd customs' of the aristocracy than you, I should think."

"Touché. I am, after all, a lowly commoner. Completely unworthy of your exaltedness."

Her voice was full of accusation. "You sound bitter, Mr. Mannion."

"Come to think of it, how is it you escaped the net of marriage? Did your father never find a suitable man who was willing to brave your harpy tongue?" Adam looked over at her, his gaze taking in her stiff profile, her face turned resolutely ahead. "Or were you waiting for love, Helena?"

"For your information, I was engaged once."

"Pray tell what happened."

"He preferred someone else."

The news was a jolt to Adam, wiping the smile from his face as soundly as if he'd been slapped.

Good God, what a sod-head he was! He had taunted her horribly when she had been nursing a broken heart all along.

"I'm sorry," he said gruffly. "I didn't know."

"I'm surprised at that. People hereabouts love to talk."

"Actually, I have found the one person whose conversation I enjoyed damned reluctant to give me any facts aside from where the best hunting grounds could be found."

She looked over at him then, and those large blue-green eyes softened. "Who was that?"

"Kepper."

"He's a good man. He's very loyal to my father."

Adam allowed a silence to lapse while he berated himself for his thoughtless jibes. He wondered if this were the reason for her seclusion—the oldest reason in the world. Had she retired from society to pine for the unrequited love lost years ago?

The idea of it disturbed him. He had been disturbed, however, since the moment he laid eyes on her, so he should be getting used to it by now.

Nevertheless, he was surprised to realize that he was more than a bit curious. And perhaps a tad jealous.

"I'd like to ask you more, but I know you won't answer. I have quite a lot of questions, Helena. I wonder why there are so few servants in so large a house. Why do you live alone without seeing anyone? I haven't asked a one of these, and I'm not asking now. I just want you to know those questions are there.''

He didn't know what he wanted her to say. He didn't even know why he had uttered such an inane statement—as if she would rush to explain herself if she knew of his interest.

No, it wasn't merely interest. It was becoming an obsession. He wanted her to know he would listen if she ever wished to tell him the strange secrets that governed her hermetic existence, that he wouldn't judge or mock, and he wouldn't betray her confidence. He wondered if she knew that, if he had expressed it properly in his awkward little speech just now.

It was a moot point. She said nothing.

As they crossed Darby Creek, Helena became aware of a growing terror arising in her breast.

They topped a hill and she could see the large cluster of buildings in the distance. Passing a farmhouse, she noted an old woman wrapped in a shawl staring at them. Adam raised his hand in a greeting. The old woman didn't respond. Helena wondered if she were imagining the antagonism in the wrinkled face.

Swallowing painfully against her dry throat, she clutched her reticule tightly in her fist. She had been mad to come. Why hadn't she thought to simply summon the dressmaker to the manor? Because of Adam Mannion, that was why. She could never think properly when he was around.

On the outskirts of the village, a prosperous community that had grown by leaps and bounds in recent years, the presence of the population became more noticeable. A cart crossed the road ahead of them. While they waited, Helena scanned the faces of the children playing in a nearby field, wondering if they would recognize her. And if they did, would they flee in fear?

"Helena?" Adam's voice was full of concern. "Are you feeling ill?"

He couldn't know—he mustn't know. She shouldn't have come this far. She could have made some excuse and had him turn back the moment she felt the first twinges of fear. But now she was fixed.

A tremulous smile quivered on her lips. "Not at all. Just a bit nervous. I—I don't enjoy going away from the house very much."

He stared at her for a long moment. She could feel the touch of his eyes and it made her skin prickle. "Another question that wants answering."

Jerking her head about to face him, she snapped, "There is no exotic mystery, just sordid truth, and you're better off not knowing. And when you do find out, don't say I didn't warn you."

He leaned in closer, inclining his head so that he was staring at her through those lashes that were ridiculously long and thick for a man. "Since you say you want to be rid of me so badly, why not tell me all of these dastardly horrors you keep hidden? Maybe I'll just run like a madman all the way home to London, pulling my hair out all the way as I think of how close I had come to unmitigated disaster."

He made a face of such exaggerated dread that she burst out laughing before she could help it. Sobering quickly, she ducked her head and plucked nervously at her dress. "Joking will not cure a thing, Mr. Mannion. And I suppose you will find out what you wish to know soon enough. As for myself telling you a single thing, you can dispel that notion immediately. I'll never explain myself to a reprobate and wastrel and admitted *fortune hunter.*"

"Ouch!" He grinned and sat back. "I believe my pride has been pummeled quite soundly."

He didn't look as if his pride had been pummeled. He looked, in fact, as if he were inordinately pleased with himself for having goaded her.

She settled back into her seat. Her fears returned as they drove into the village square.

"Where is the modiste?" he asked.

She made a sound alarmingly like a snort. "There is no modiste, Mr. Mannion. You confuse us with posh London. There is a dressmaker."

Helena saw a woman walking on the side of the road stop in her tracks and gape at the passing carriage. Jaw slack, eyes wide, she dropped the basket of baked bread she was carrying. The golden brown loaves rolled in the dust. The woman she had been walking with noticed Helena at about the same time. Her reaction was just as dramatic. She stumbled and stared without any care for manners.

Helena wished she could look away with a haughty lift of her chin, but she couldn't seem to tear her eyes from them. Miserably, she watched helplessly as the two women ducked their heads together and commenced whispering vigorously.

"Ah, I see the sign," Adam said, oblivious to the little dramas taking place all around them.

Across the street, the butcher had rushed out of his shop. The thin, fussy tobacconist hurried over to confer with him. Their gazes seemed to blaze clear into Helena's forehead.

Adam continued, "I'll bring you inside, but I won't wait. Can't stand that sort of thing. Can barely manage to keep my own wardrobe up. What do you say we meet at the tea shop at…oh, say, twelve? We'll lunch there. If you are too busy and can't make it, send word and I'll go ahead without you…Helena?''

She sat motionless. Adam took her hands, his own warm and strong. She fought a sudden desire to fling herself into the protection of his arms.

What would make her have such a thought? Her terror had her too confused to think properly.

''Something is wrong.'' Adam's voice was demanding. ''Don't play the martyr now, for God's sake. Tell me.''

''The people…'' She couldn't bring herself to meet his eye. ''They are looking at me, talking about me. They frighten me.''

''Nonsense. They are merely looking at you because you are so lovely today.'' She did glance up then, incredulous and painfully suspicious that he was mocking her.

There was kindness in his eyes. True kindness, not a false show or, worse, pity. His well-formed mouth was slightly curved in a smile that was soft and seemed to be genuine.

Her hands felt warmer already. ''This is why I never come out,'' she said in an emotion-roughened voice. ''The gossip. The dreadful staring. I cannot stand it.''

''Well, you see, that's the trouble.'' His tone was low and reasonable, yet without a trace of patronization. ''They never see you, and since you live so close, they no doubt find this odd. Now that you appear, they understandably take notice. It is a temporary condition. It will surely pass as soon as they become used to you being about. Come now. Let us go into the dressmaker's—which, thank you for correcting my error, is not to be confused with a modiste.''

He leaped down and put the box up against the side. With a flourish, he handed her down. Once her feet touched the floor, he held her a moment longer—long enough to bestow a quick kiss on the gloved knuckles. He raised his head and said, "If it's gossip they desire, that morsel should do nicely to keep them busy for a while."

She wanted to weep with gratitude. She might have if she weren't still so afraid. But, somehow, he made it easy for her to ignore curious faces as they walked down the street to the dressmaker's shop.

The word had apparently spread. Shopkeepers were coming out of their shops, mothers rushing outside with squalling babies, tradesmen pausing—all to stare at her. She could feel their gazes crawl over her like a swarm of slugs.

"Did you arrange to make an appointment?" Adam said. She latched on to his voice, so sensible among the madness growing inside her. She wanted more than anything to flee. It took all her concentration to put one foot in front of the other. *Keep your eyes fixed straight ahead. Steady on.*

At the door of the dressmaker's, he paused. "If you don't have an appointment, then I will wait to see if she will see you. You don't mind if I do? I know I said I have an aversion to dressmakers and such, but in this instance I shall make an exception, as I'd hate to see you lose the morning to waiting." They entered, setting the little bell tied over the door tinkling furiously. "I come by it honestly. My aversion, I mean. You see, my mother used to drag me about as a boy when she did her shopping. It was horrible torture for a rambunctious lad."

His voice was like a touchstone. Helena forced herself to listen, to concentrate on what he was saying. She suspected he was talking to distract her from the churning apprehensions burning in her belly.

How odd that he should come to her rescue. He had been her enemy from the moment he had stepped foot on the doorstep of her house. Now he was her unexpected ally.

A pang of guilt grabbed her. He didn't even know why

it was she feared the village folk, or going out among them. He didn't know the answers to any of her secrets—all those questions he had admitted plagued him. And still he had been kind to her.

If he knew, it would change things. It would change everything. He would no longer be solicitous, and he surely wouldn't be cajoling her so effectively out of her terror.

No. One was never kind to a murderess.

Chapter Eight

Adam stayed at the dressmaker's shop the entire time Helena was being fitted. Lounging in one of the chairs Mrs. Stiles, the proprietor, had dragged in for his use, he accepted tea and selected sweets from an array of biscuits. Helena smothered a smile as she watched him so suavely handle the fuss and bother being made over him with only the vaguest suggestion of how uncomfortable all of this must make him.

Mrs. Stiles and her assistants, Betty and Hannah, were efficient and possessed an astonishing degree of skill. Helena had entered the shop with the intentions of purchasing only a few gowns. When she saw the many sketches and materials to be had, she found she was overcome by a rush of frivolous pleasure that had her ordering far more than she ever intended.

There was luscious silks embroidered with sweet florets, one in a fabulous royal blue that would bring out the color of her eyes vividly. Soft muslins in buttercup yellow, lime and the most extraordinary shade of shimmering peach were perfect for everyday dresses. She had never been allowed to select her own garments, and most of what she had was done up in stuffs and styles not to her taste. She indulged herself in a fabulous binge.

Whether motivated by the heavy amount of Helena's spending or true kindness, Mrs. Stiles pulled out all the stops and showered Helena with her attention, turning away at least three persons who came in while Helena was there. And she did it all cheerfully, trotting out drawings and quickly sketching up the alterations that Hannah, who seemed to have an impeccable eye for what Helena liked, would suggest.

"This one would look wonderful on you, my lady," Mrs. Stiles pointed out. "With your height, you would carry off the straight lines most elegantly."

"In that pale pink crepe!" declared Hannah with a flash of her dark eyes. "No, no. It is too light, too ethereal for such a powdery shade. Try this. See how the weave leaves it loose, so it will drape softly. And the deep rose color would be superb."

"Yes, I like that," Helena agreed.

A dour-faced Betty frowned. "Dark burgundy ribbon. Just a touch. You can't do too much, you'll ruin the lines. You're long and need classical styling." She spoke it without an ounce of inflection. Rather than take it as a sign of her disapproval, Helena gathered that this stoic countenance was Betty's usual fare. "And no ridiculous bonnets, which are the fashion for reasons I cannot understand. A cap, there, just on the crown. I'll get the milliner to put a feather in it if you like, but that is all."

The haberdasher was called in as a favor to Mrs. Stiles, and Helena selected undergarments right from the dressmaker's shop. Then there were accessories to be ordered. Gloves, reticules and every other manner of feminine decoration were paraded before her. She made her selections sparingly, feeling guilty about the expense, although she knew it to be much less than when her mother would order her wardrobe under the auspices of a French designer named Monsieur Tangrimonde. To Helena's mind, the man had possessed atrocious taste and been exorbitantly over-priced. And she'd had the most sneaking suspicion that he hadn't been French at all.

When they were through and the orders had all been written up, she went out to the front of the shop. Adam rose. She felt badly for him having to wait about, especially when he had told her it was such a nuisance to him, but he didn't look at all annoyed. In fact, he was smiling quite warmly at her, one of those smiles of his that took over every muscle in his face.

Flushed already with the exhilaration of her purchases, she felt the glow inside her burn brighter under this affec-tionate regard. "Did you enjoy yourself?" he asked as she fitted her hands into her old gloves.

"I did, but I'm afraid you didn't. It must have been hor-ribly boring sitting about all morning."

He shrugged. "It was not the most excitement I've ever enjoyed, but it was nowhere near the most boring. One of my friends was invited to see Brummel make his toilette, and insisted I go along. I swear, it took ponderous hours, and we were supposed to act as if each glimpse of his fine cravat-tying was a deep and abiding honor. I almost grabbed the man's jeweled razor and put it to my wrists, just for some blessed relief from the dullness."

She laughed and they exited the shop onto the street. Immediately, her good humor wilted. She had almost for-gotten where she was. Furtively, she slid her gaze left to right, scanning for onlookers.

Helena went stiff as she walked alongside him, her hand on his arm nearly clawing until she remembered to relax it. He pretended not to notice, but she knew little escaped him.

He said, "I am as stuffed as a Christmas goose from all that they fed me, but you must be hungry."

"No. I'm too nervous to eat." A group of women was standing on the corner, trying to appear casual and failing miserably as they sneaked glances at the two of them.

"Nonsense." Adam noticed nothing. "We'll stop for luncheon."

"Really, I couldn't eat, I—"

"Don't let's have a row in public, Helena. You will feel much better with something in your stomach."

If she couldn't win this argument with him in the privacy of her own home, she wasn't even going to attempt it on the streets of Strathmere. Pressing her lips together, she allowed him to take her across the street to a pretty inn with a white door.

They sat at a table by the window. Adam chose it, and she could guess why. If everyone wanted a look at her, they would get their chance. He wouldn't allow her to cower in front of their rude curiosity.

With him seated beside her, making easy conversation, she found she was actually able to relax. And to her surprise, she did feel better once she had eaten. He ordered for her—a hearty lunch she never would have selected and she ate a good portion of the cold sliced roast beef and potatoes. His appetite returned and he ordered the same platter as she. It was served and devoured by the time it took for her to push her plate away, pronouncing herself able to eat no more.

He picked up his fork and sampled what she had left while they chatted aimlessly. The proprietor served them coffee. Adam ordered a tart for his dessert.

Helena regarded him with a blend of amazement and

amusement. Dimly aware that he had done it again—made her forget her self-consciousness, her fear—she smoothed the napkin lying on her lap. "I see why you are always after me to eat. I have never seen one person consume so much food."

"A compliment if I ever heard one." He grinned. "It is my curse. I have a great fondness for food. And a great capacity for it."

"It's a wonder you are not fat." She immediately flushed, noting that indeed his lean, athletic build showed no signs of overindulgence.

"To the distress of my tutor and the exasperation of my father, I seem to be imbued with a great deal of energy. It tends to wear one thin if one doesn't eat properly."

She raised her eyebrows at his term "properly." She laughed. "Excessively, you mean."

"Food is one of the great joys to be had in life. One you should experience."

"Because I am so *scrawny?*"

He looked embarrassed. "I didn't mean that at all. You...you are *not* scrawny." He paused meaningfully, and she felt heat steal over her once again. It was a wonder she didn't combust one of these days under those intense perusals he was apt to give. "It is just that you are so serious all the time. Don't you ever just let go and experience pleasure for its own sake?"

It was a bold statement, and she was required to be indignant. "Really, Mr. Mannion!"

"What about your music?" He popped the last morsel of the tart in his mouth. "Food is like music. One can allow oneself to get swept up in the experience, be it a tour de force of taste or sound, and barrage the senses with stimulation meant to elevate experience to a higher ground. Therein, one achieves the status of...well, a god, quite frankly, bounding upon the Olympian plains with all the joy and sublime sustenance of any muse-driven ecstasy.''

He was joking, of course. He even waggled his eyebrows at her to see if she was impressed. She bit the insides of her cheeks. ''A bit of a reach in the metaphor, don't you think?''

He shrugged and took a sip of his coffee, but the corners of his mouth kept their impish curl.

She fixed her own coffee with sugar and cream, stirring as she thought over what he had said. She was seeing a side to him she hadn't expected. Was it treason to admit she liked it?

She didn't laugh often, yet today she had done so frequently. She never forgot the cloud under which she lived—how often had she wished, prayed even, for a half hour's respite from the past?—and today she had lost herself not once, not twice, but three times in the pleasures of diverting conversation and the purely feminine joy of shopping, of all things!

Had Adam Mannion made so great a difference in so short a while? He was unlike anyone she had ever met. Being well acquainted with the severe reserve of the most blue-blooded of English aristocrats, she found Adam's unbridled zest astonishing.

He was not a peer, not of the aristocracy in which she had been born and within which she had moved with confidence. The fact of his less than blue blood was abundantly clear in nearly everything about him—the purposeful way he moved, the easy smile and the way his eyes crinkled at the corners. When she spoke, she had found, he didn't feign indifference or maintain a cool detachment, but tended to lean forward intently, as if she were speaking the most important words he had ever heard. His mobile features reacted to everything. And yet, although not of the stifling noble bearing, he was as far from common as Helena could imagine. He was vital and vibrant and full of many interesting differences that seemed to her to hold him above the other men she had known.

The door opened just as Helena and Adam were rising. Helena's heart plummeted all the way to her stomach when she heard a lilting, French-accented voice say, "Helena? Is that you? *Oui!* Lady Helena Rathford, my goodness, it is!"

Sinking into a curtsy, Helena replied, "Your grace."

Chloe Hunt, the Duchess of Strathmere, rushed forward, arms outstretched and an expression on her face that bespoke utter joy. "It is wonderful to see you, and in the village, no less! It is a great surprise. I was planning on coming by next week to visit."

The accent and the exotic quality of her movements elevated this rather ordinarily pretty young woman into one from whom it was difficult to remove one's gaze. Rather tepidly, Helena returned her embrace, saying, "I am sorry, but we were just leaving. We've finished our lunch, you see. I...we...I was purchasing some new dresses and—"

"How fun! Oh, but I am so disappointed that I cannot hear all about it. What a pity, I would enjoy it so very much." The woman sighed and glanced artfully at Adam, who had finished his business and was watching them with interest. The gesture begged an introduction.

Helena made the presentation, biting back her reluctance and trying to appear as pleasant as she could.

Chloe was as delightful as always. Helena always had liked her and bore no ill will from the fact that she had married Jareth Hunt, the Duke of Strathmere less than two months after Helena herself had accepted the man's proposal of marriage. And to her credit, the duchess traveled to Rathford Manor at least every season in tireless overtures of friendship, which was more than a woman of her social standing should have to do, especially given that her overtures were not reciprocated. Helena simply couldn't bring herself to accept them, as much as she wished she could.

Every time she saw Chloe, Helena remembered that day at the inn, in that room at the top of the stairs. And the blood. When she saw Chloe, she remembered the rancid smell of the blood.

As if he sensed her tension, Adam intervened with a polite excuse. Chloe bade them goodbye with a promise to come to visit as soon as the dresses were delivered so that she could admire them.

As Adam and Helena strode to the cobblers, he said, "She is not at all what one would think of when one sees a duchess."

"Oh, yes, Chloe certainly is an unusual woman."

"Chloe?"

"I still address her by her given name." Helena's breathing was returning to normal. She heard the note of fondness in her voice as she spoke of the Duchess of Strathmere. "She insists on it. Once she scolded me soundly when, in private, I addressed her as 'your grace.' In a public place, she understands the necessity of such formality, but she'll not tolerate it between friends."

He was pensive. "Then she is your friend? By the way you reacted in there, I thought there was some kind of strain between the two of you."

Helena took a careful breath, thinking how best to express this. "There was. It was..." Her courage deserted her. "It was a long time ago. A misunderstanding. There are no hard feelings, I'm sure, but it makes me feel awkward sometimes. Today has been a strain, in any event. I suppose my mood is poor."

That was a bold-faced lie, and she knew it. Murder was hardly a misunderstanding.

She ignored the pull of her conscience. It was none of his business, anyway. What was he but a London dandy come hunting for a fat purse to bring back to his tarts and his gaming halls and his drunk, lascivious friends? He might be an amusing rake, but he was a rake nevertheless, and she'd be a fool to think differently.

Only a lack-wit would think his gentlemanly show today was anything more than him making the best of the situation. After all, he was a self-confessed opportunist. All the rest, even his passing curiosity at her many "secrets," were just a momentary diversion until he could get back to London and his true interests. With her money!

She wondered if he had a mistress there.

The thought stiffened her spine, and her chin came up reflexively as she mentally retreated behind her icy exterior. At their stop at the cobblers, she dispatched her business with a no-nonsense air. Several pairs of slippers in kid and soft brushed leather were selected without much prevarication. The shoemaker promised he would confer with Mrs. Stiles to get the colors right for the dresses ordered. At Adam's insistence, Helena purchased a pair of riding boots as well.

Out in the street, people were still milling about in a bad imitation of having some business for being there. They continued to stare openly when she and Adam emerged from the shop.

She was suddenly weary, although—surprisingly—not afraid any longer. She told Adam this and asked him to fetch the old coach to take them home. Upon pulling up the drive, she noticed that the sight of her home did not bring welcome relief as it had done in the past.

No. It gave her the strangest, most distinct feeling…as if she were returning to a prison.

Chapter Nine

Adam was sick of the questions. There were no answers anywhere, just questions that kept multiplying like proverbial rabbits. The afternoon spent with Helena a few days ago had left his head aching.

To ease his mind, he spent his days in the barn. Kepper was excellent companionship—no mysteries here—and happy for the help with the horses. It was just him out in the stables and carriage house, and Adam knew he worked hard.

Adam didn't bother to ask why Kepper was alone with such a large stable. The head—and sole—groom was likely to shrug off any inquiries with which he wasn't comfortable.

After his morning ride one day, Adam brushed down the chestnut mare he had taken out. She had proved to have a good spirit and a sensitive mouth. He had enjoyed himself a great deal and he now rewarded her with a slice of sugarloaf pilfered from the breakfast table, and a compliment whispered in her twitching ear.

"She's a fine filly, she is," Kepper said in admiration as Adam led the horse out to the paddock for a trot. "Got manners."

Adam gave the horse an affectionate stroke on her muscled neck. "She's a good girl." He grinned at the stableman. "That is *if* she likes you. When I approached her too fast the first time, she let me know I was to keep my distance until we were better acquainted."

Kepper returned the grin. "All the horses in this stables likes *me,* 'cuz I'm the one what brings 'em their suppers."

A movement caught Adam's eye. Kepper looked down, too, and grumbled when he saw what Adam did—a mongrel dog. He was a mottled shorthair, with huge ears that bespoke of hound in his undistinguished heritage, and soulful brown eyes. His tongue was hanging out the side of his panting mouth and his tail was wagging furiously.

"Damned bother!" Kepper groused. He stomped his foot. "Get! Get I say."

Adam put a hand out to stop the man. "Whose dog is it?"

"Nobody's that I know of. Just showed up one day and made himself at home. *Very* at home, especially with the master's prime bitch. She don't need a bellyful of worthless pups what's just like 'im."

The dog sat down, his ears cocked and the strangest expression on his face, as if he were perfectly aware he was being maligned. This he tolerated with fatalistic resignation.

Hunkering down, Adam stretched out his hand. "Hey, boy," he whispered. The mutt rose, walked three steps and sat again—within reach, so as to allow himself to be petted.

His coat was coarse to the touch. He certainly wasn't the most beautiful of dogs. But his eyes twinkled with intelligence. Liking the treatment he was getting, he lowered himself in small steps, his tail thumping a few times.

"He's not the least bit wild," Adam noted. "Must have been someone's pet. Maybe someone in the village. Look how friendly he is."

"Don't encourage him. I almost got the master's flint-lock and put a ball in him more times than I can count, but then he looks at me with them eyes, all trusting and hope-ful, and even an old curmudgeon like myself can't do what needs to be done."

"Let him alone," Adam said, deeply disturbed. "Don't think of harming him."

Kepper looked at Adam. "Those dogs and bitches were some of the finest hunting hounds in these parts. But I guess there isn't much harm this one can do, now. They've run off, some of 'em, and the rest left untended, all gone soft and lost their noses, anyhow."

"Shame," Adam agreed. He hated to hear it. Straight-ening, he looked to the horse he'd been tending. "Mind finishing up with my sweetheart, here?"

"Sure thing, sir." Taking the reins, Kepper led the mare out of the barn and into the paddock.

Adam regarded the dog. "Are you hungry?" He laughed when the dog got immediately to his feet and looked ex-pectantly at him, as if he understood perfectly. "You *are* a clever fellow. Come on then, I'll see what I can coax out of Cook for you."

He headed toward the house, the dog close on his heels. It gave Adam a ridiculous swell of pleasure to have it so, almost as if they were companions. He liked the idea of having a canine companion.

After giving the mutt instructions not to move from the garden door, he went into the kitchens.

The baking room was empty. In the pantry, Maddie was snoozing by the window in a big old rocking chair. The scullery girls were not about.

He walked into the large, vaulted preparation area. This was where he had found the sausages before, so he thought he might have some luck. Instead he found Helena seated at the scrubbed oak table, with her maid, Kimberly, hovering over her.

Something about the scene made him stop. Helena had her head bent. Kimberly was talking, saying something he couldn't hear, but it was clear she was speaking vehemently. As he moved forward, their voices became audible.

"...fripperies and such nonsense," the maid was saying.

"Please," he heard Helena say softly, and it sounded suspiciously like a plea. Adam's curiosity was piqued and his anger as well. He didn't like the helpless sound in Helena's voice.

Kimberly bore down on her. "What do ye think ye can do with a new dress and curls in yer hair? People will laugh at ye. They will always remember, ye know."

Adam reached them and wasted no time in grabbing the servant's arm, yanking her away from Helena. Ordinarily, he wouldn't manhandle a woman, but every rule had exceptions. "What are you doing?" he demanded, glaring into the ruddy face.

After a brief flash of surprise, Kimberly donned a sneer. "I'm talking to Mistress Helena. Like I've always done. Her mother depends on me."

What the devil was this? "You were being disrespectful. I heard you. You had better never speak to her in such a manner again or I will have you dismissed."

The malevolent look Kimberly leveled at him was undiluted. "Ye think so, do ye, my fine stallion?"

"Do not address me like that," he commanded, although he was feeling very much out of his element. He was not, as the saying went, to the manner born, and the open defiance of this impudent woman had him disconcerted.

"Ye've much to learn here. But I'll not take offense at yer ignorance. I'm sure yer new wife'll set ye straight, and right soon after ye tie the knot. Then ye'll take care when ye speak to old Kimberly, won't ye?''

"Get out of here. Go on now. *Now*.''

Kimberly's eyes moved to Helena. "Ye tell him, girl. I'll hold my temper this time, but not another.'' She exited.

"You should not have done that.'' Helena's voice sounded small.

Adam turned. Helena wore a stricken expression—eyes wide, cheeks pale, bloodless lips tense and tight. He frowned in confusion. "Why in the world would you tolerate such insolence and disrespect? Helena? What is the matter with you?''

"Now she will be angry. You shouldn't have scolded her.''

"Of course I should have. The woman was bloody threatening you.''

"She speaks for my mother.''

Helena seemed to be in some kind of shock. Adam leaned in closer, asking, "Is that why you let her treat you this way?''

"She was her…confidante. Her consultant.'' She made a harsh, humorless sound. "In the Far East, sultans have viziers to advise them. Kimberly was like my mother's vizier.''

"I still don't understand why that gives her permission to browbeat you.'' He pushed his fingers into his thick hair, puzzled. It was probable that since she missed her mother, Helena allowed this servant these liberties because of her close ties to the dead Lady Rathford. His gaze dropped to her plate, which was half-empty. "She disturbed your meal.''

"I…'' She seemed surprised to find the food in front of her. "I suppose I was hungry….''

Adam took her hands. "It would be too much to hope

that you are still hungry.'' Helena shook her head. ''Well, then, we have no choice but to work up an appetite. I was just about to take a mare out for a run.'' It was a lie, of course. He had just come in. ''Why don't you take her, and I'll get a chance to exercise my stallion as well.''

She tried to pull away. ''No. I don't feel up to it.''

''You do ride, don't you?''

''I used to.'' She hesitated. ''I hardly know the first thing to do if I found myself back upon a horse.''

''It will come back to you. Come now, it will be a great help to me. I shall not need to tend both horses, and they need the exercise badly.'' At her hesitation, he added, ''You do not wish to see fine horseflesh growing fat and lazy, do you?''

''Very well,'' she agreed with a degree of uncertainty. ''I think one of my new dresses should do as a riding habit.''

''They've arrived, have they?''

''Some.'' She was still hesitating. He grabbed her hand and pulled her to her feet. ''Good, you'll enjoy wearing something new and pretty. And bring a cloak. There is a chill in the air.''

Despite her initial misgivings, Helena thoroughly enjoyed the outing. Dressed in a crisp black skirt trimmed with camel ruching and a white blouson complemented by a light-brown redingote with a stand-up collar and voluminous folds, she felt smartly turned out and confident.

They didn't converse much. When she had joined Adam in the stables, she had found him feeding biscuits to a wiry looking dog. The friendly creature had come snuffling about Helena's skirts.

''No, Cain,'' Adam scolded.

Helena looked at him. Defensively, he said, ''Well, he

had to have a name. He looks like an unfavored sort, doesn't he?''

"Cain...killed his brother. Why would you give him the name of such a wicked man?''

Adam helped her mount, then sauntered to his horse. "I always thought he was a sad sort of case. I mean, God never was pleased with anything he did. That's the reason he killed Abel, because Abel was always the one to get the approval from God, and Cain never could." Adam paused thoughtfully. "He didn't use a weapon, remember, but the jawbone of an ass. That means it was a sudden thing, as if he was overcome by the hell of the situation all of a sudden. A crime of passion. Maybe he was even driven to it.''

Her look was incredulous. "That is a very unique way to look at it.''

"Mitigating circumstances do change the way one views things that, at first glance, seem wrong. Anyway, when I saw this pathetic thing, I thought he might know how Cain had felt. See, he's a mongrel, so that means no matter how good he is at anything, he's worthless to his master. He may have a superior nose, or a great canine intelligence, but the worst purebred still has a higher value.''

The air was crisp, with that overripe tang of early autumn. Helena gnawed on her bottom lip. "Hmm. I do understand, but did it occur to you that with your name being Adam, you are carrying a biblical theme to rather an extreme?''

He laughed, astonished, as he swung astride. "I didn't think of that. Damn. That will never do. Oh, well, boy, we'll have to come up with something else for you.''

He tried out new names as they rode. The eager dog kept pace with them, wagging his tail at every suggestion. Apparently he had no preference, but Adam pronounced it useless. He was set on Cain, and no other name would suit.

For herself, Helena was taken with what Adam had said about circumstances changing the right and wrong of a situation.

Not many people recognized the fine shadings of gray in a matter, but dealt in black-and-white. Right and wrong. And murder, of course, was wrong. Always.

Adam had voiced a much different opinion. Was taking a life to save a life mitigating enough to redeem one of having murdered one's own mother?

The thought brought on the unrest it usually did, so Helena pushed it aside. If she were too pensive, Adam would notice, and she didn't want to draw his curiosity. Her sense of disquiet thinned without her being aware of it, and soon she relaxed in the saddle and took in the scenery around her.

Filling her lungs with moist, cool air, she smiled. The bracken that surrounded them on the wooded paths was gnarled and already browning. The trees were still cloaked in leaves, but they were dry and some had begun to fall off. The grass, when they came to a clearing, was a grayish green.

Nature was ready to sleep, and yet she felt in curious opposition to the world around her. In her heart it was spring, and she was waking after the long winter, like Sleeping Beauty after true love's first kiss.

A silly, frivolous thought from a woman who didn't have many of those, but it made her smile just the same.

The parson and his wife came to dinner a few nights later in order to discuss the wedding. Lord Rathford had extended the invitation without Helena's knowledge, informing her after it was done that they were to have guests and that she should be dressed and ready to receive them by half past six o'clock.

It was useless to protest his high-handedness. Her father was quite set on this marriage taking place as planned. He was also set, it seemed, on the dreary isolation of the past five years being revoked, and moving toward some semblance of a normal life.

Her solitary existence was being ripped from her without her having much say about it. Changes were taking place at an alarming rate. She didn't even have time to resent it. It didn't occur to her that she might not resent it, after all.

Several of the dresses she had ordered had already been delivered, mostly the simple styles that had been made up in a hurry to tide her over. She chose one that she thought rather elegant, taking great care with her toilette. She had to do it herself. The services of a ladies' maid hadn't been needed for a very long time. She wasn't bad at it, however, even if her arms ached from the long brushing she gave her hair, but she didn't stop until she saw traces of its previous luster. She piled it in large coils atop her head and heated the curling tongs. Carefully, she twisted spiral curls along her cheeks, forehead and down the back of her neck. She succeeded with the simple style without a single burn. Turning this way and that, she studied the results in the pier glass.

Not as well as her maid would have done, but not bad, either.

The dress she chose was a deep, dusky rose silk complemented by a single row of ecru lace and a wide satin ribbon under her breasts. She found a pair of old gloves that were almost the same off-white and put them on. Digging furiously among her belongings, she found a strand of pearls for her hair. It would have been better if she had a ribbon to match the one on her dress, but at least the creamy color was the same. An almost new pair of kid mules from the back of her wardrobe proved a perfect fit and complemented the ensemble.

Surveying the finished effect, she was pleased. Her lips were curved in a half smile without her being aware of it. Spots of color staining her high cheekbones made her eyes sparkle.

Straining closer, she almost thought she recognized something in her reflection. The Helena of old had never looked this excited or...or happy. But there was a similarity. She was filling out, she noticed, and looking decidedly less wan.

Less *scrawny*.

The curve of her lips deepened. She was looking forward to seeing Adam's face when she appeared downstairs. She expected he would most definitely notice her transformation. It was a scene she savored as she finished her preparations and descended the steps.

Adam detested formal wear. The cravat, which he tended to wear loosely tied for day, was positively strangling him. It was all he could do to keep from sticking his finger into the knot and loosening it.

One look at the parson, a Mr. Gerret, and his wife, Genevieve Gerret, told him no such informality would be tolerated. Pleasant and eager to please, they offered instant avowals of friendship within mere seconds of their having been introduced. They were given drinks and settled into seats, and Lord Rathford, in an astonishing show of hosting finesse, steered them into conversation. It didn't take much to wind their spring. They immediately began a thorough rousting of each and every inhabitant of the "neighborhood," and Rathford, having done his part to get them going, settled back to nurse his whiskey.

Adam took his drink with him to a seat. He watched

them, amused at the smooth synchronicity of their dual conversation. One would speak, then the other would effortlessly pick up the conversation, finishing the sentence or anticipating flawlessly the direction of the next comment.

"Well, Beth's too fond of her wine," Mrs. Gerret said of one poor victim.

"And has a tendency to belch," Mr. Gerret added.

"Quite loudly. But—"

"She is a dear." Mr. Gerret patted his wife's hand. "Indeed it is so."

"Her husband is a saint."

"Right-o. Robbie worked for their grace, up at the big house. Loved her grace, he did."

"The new duchess, not the old one."

"Oh, heavens me, not the old one. He detested the old one, the present duke's mother. You never met her." Mr. Gerret wrinkled his face. "Wretched woman."

They shivered in unison.

"But her grace is a divine creature. Robbie always adored her. Even when she was the governess to those two poor mites and fighting all the time with his grace, Robbie stuck by her."

Adam's head ached already, trying to keep track of so many persons. None of whom he had the slightest interest in, although he did perk up when he finally deciphered that the beloved "her grace" to whom they referred was the charming Chloe, whom he had met in the village.

"Tell us about you, Mr. Mannion," Mrs. Gerret asked suddenly.

He had expected their curiosity and was prepared. Launching into a harmless yarn about his past, he amused them until they were disturbed by a rustle of silk at the door.

All eyes glanced up—and stuck. His included. Every jaw in the room dropped to gape. His included.

Helena had arrived. At least, he thought it was Helena. Or a ghost. It was as if the portrait in the unused parlor had come to life.

Chapter Ten

Helena had...changed. She was beautiful. Radiating beauty and confidence, she immediately dominated the room with her presence, and Adam found he had completely lost track of the lies he'd been telling.

"Hello, Parson. Hello, Mrs. Gerret." She sailed into the room with breathtaking grace, hands extended to grasp those of the guests. Then she went to her father and reached up on tiptoe to give the old bear a peck on the cheek. Adam thought he saw a tear in the old man's eye as his gaze followed his daughter.

Adam surmised it had been a long time since Lord Rathford had seen Helena look so well.

She came to his side, looking for all the world like a woman eager to be with her betrothed. Then he remembered he was supposed to breathe, so he did, and that seemed to snap him out of shock.

Helena knew exactly what effect she had had on everyone, he could tell right off. Giving him a smile beguiling enough to melt the stockings off his feet, she slipped an arm through his and cocked her head in such an incredibly coquettish fashion that a thin sweat broke out upon his upper lip.

"I was just telling the Gerrets how we met," he managed to say. Thank God he didn't sound as stupid as he felt.

Her eyes widened.

"Hunting. You were walking and I came across you and we talked. I remember it as if it were yesterday." Turning back to the Gerrets, he chuckled and patted Helena's hand. "She hates for anyone to know about that. You see, she was wearing men's breeches and riding astride, so she feels rather embarrassed to have me tell anyone."

"Mr. Mannion!" Helena was appalled at his embellishment, and it gave him great satisfaction to have gained the upper hand.

He merely shrugged at Mr. Gerret. "See how she is when I tell the story? Then, of course, being that she fell into the stream and I had to fetch her out, it was indeed a wretched beginning."

"Adam." Helena tried again, more softly. Her voice held a pulse of tension that carried over her stiff smile. "I think you are going a bit far—"

"Do you? Oh, I'm dreadfully sorry. Then I shouldn't tell them about the bear routing you out of the bushes where you had gone to hide, while I was hanging your clothes up to dry for you?"

"Adam!"

"Mannion!" Lord Rathford roared. His glare would have put a stop to a demon.

Adam only hiked his brows up innocently and sipped his sherry. "Oh, dear. I've always had a wretchedly big mouth. I suppose those particular circumstances should remain… private." He gazed innocently at the Gerrets. "I can trust your discretion, can't I?"

Mrs. Gerret, who was wide-eyed and mute, nodded vigorously.

"In any event, I was madly in love right then and there,

and I followed her home.'' His dancing eyes lit on a smoldering Helena. "She was rather reluctant to receive me at first, but Lord Rathford was kind enough to invite me inside and soon, as our acquaintance grew, Lady Helena and I knew we simply must be together forever.''

There was a silence, then a loud sigh. Adam glanced over to see Mrs. Gerret's hands clasped in front of her huge bosom. Mr. Gerret cleared his throat. "Well, that sounds like quite an adventure.''

"Love, my dear vicar, is always an adventure.'' With a flourish, Adam took up Helena's gloved hand and brushed the knuckles with his lips.

She snatched it back, flushing profusely. Her look was murderous.

The footman came in to call them to dinner.

"Tell me more about yourself, Mr. Mannion,'' Mrs. Gerret purred, sidling up beside him as they proceeded into the dining room.

"Gladly, Mrs. Gerret.''

He resumed his tales, quite enjoying himself as his yarn took on fantastical proportions. As for the looks he was getting from Helena, he simply ignored them and addressed himself to the meal. Maddie had outdone herself in honor of their company, and he was more than pleased to reap the benefits.

After dinner, the ladies went to retire. Helena was still glaring spikes at him, as she had been doing all during dinner, when she led Mrs. Gerret out of the room. Impishly, he lifted his wineglass as if in salute. Her blue eyes glinted like chips of ice, and then she whisked through the door and was gone.

He felt a surprising and unanticipated rush of guilt. Not rude as a rule, he had felt compelled to it when she had walked through the parlor door and taken his breath away, as well as his composure. The sight of her, the effect of that deliberate beauty, had been like an attack. No...not precisely. Perhaps more of a challenge. The gauntlet thrown down.

Lord Rathford immediately fell into a doze. Adam would have liked to conk the old bear on the head. Gerret was a bore and Adam was tired of spinning outrageous tales just to keep from yawning himself silly.

Then the spindly old man gave his host a surreptitious glance and leaned forward. "I say, the change in Lady Helena is remarkable. Love certainly does agree with her, eh? My goodness, she's a different person. Almost back to what she was."

Of course, Adam thought, how stupid of him not to have realized that the vicar would have known her all her life. The man might be able to provide some clues to what the hell had happened to Helena.

Elbows braced on the armrests, Adam peered at the curate over his laced fingers. "It was such a horrible thing, all that business."

The lead worked. The old vicar blanched and rushed to say, "Indeed it was. The poor girl. There was so much talk. It drove her to terrible solitude. But you seem to have cured all that, and in so short a time!"

"Still," Adam said, pulling the conversation back to the past, "it was a great deal to have gotten over. The talk still bothers her, you know. She doesn't even know if they are saying the truth anymore or if the tale has gotten so completely out of hand that she's now implicated in the Guy Fawkes Rebellion."

"Poor Helena. It was all cleared up, you know, and not a shred of any evidence to cast even the smallest doubts, but you can't stop folks from wondering. It is true that a great deal of false rumor has circulated, but rest assured

Mrs. Gerret and myself put it to rights whenever we hear of it."

"Yes. Yet sometimes those rumors can be so damaging, no matter that they are later proved false."

"Ah, well, it is in the past."

Damn the man. Without knowing it, he was being more evasive than if he had set his mind to it on purpose.

In the silence of Adam's uncertainty on how to proceed, the parson sighed and mused, "Seeing her tonight brings it all back. The parties, the balls. I remember when she was young. Ah, beauty like that can make you think you're seeing angels, I tell you. We all loved her. Her mother, well...God rest her soul, she was a bit hard on her, but Helena always had that something, you know?"

"Did she have many suitors? Helena is so modest, but I always tease her that she picked me after so many men throwing themselves at her feet."

"She could have, of course, but the only one allowed near her was the duke. Her mother was very particular, you see. She had the duke in mind from the first, I think. No, there was no one else for Helena, although not for lack of them trying. Althea saw to it she was kept from anyone else's influence."

Adam was disturbed. "You make it sound like some sort of...prison or something."

"Or something. But we shouldn't speak ill of the dead. Not that I'm criticizing, mind you. It's just the way it was."

"So what happened at the cotillions or dinner parties? Wasn't Helena allowed to speak to admirers?"

"Goodness, no. You must understand how different Helena was from the woman you met in the woods. Helena was an ideal. She only spoke when spoken to, her accomplishments were astounding, her beauty and grace and perfect deportment were a heady combination. She had this quality, like she was above anyone else. She never was arrogant about it. We all recognized it. And, yes, she had many admirers, but they all kept their place.''

''Which was quite a distance away.''

''Exactly. I suppose her mother wasn't taking any chances of an unplanned circumstance ruining her scheme.''

''The duke. But the duke married Chloe...ah, the current duchess.''

''Yes.'' The vicar's expression grew dark and he pressed his lips into a line, as if sealing them. ''I think it's time we joined the ladies, don't you?''

Adam didn't. Adam wanted to know more, but he could hardly bully the man.

Rising, he gave away none of the impatience that gnawed at his gut. ''Of course. Should we wake Lord Rathford?''

The vicar was alarmed. ''Have you ever seen George Rathford when he first rouses?''

And then it was Adam's turn to listen to an incredible account of how Rathford once sent a man through a window when awakened from a nap, without ever knowing he was doing it. Adam frowned, considering this news about his father-in-law's capacity for violence.

Strange family.

Chapter Eleven

The Gerrets took their leave at half past ten. They were no sooner out of the house when Helena whirled on Adam.

He held up his hands as if to ward her off. "I know, I know. You probably want to kill me."

Her thunderous expression exploded into something... like panic. She recovered, sputtering in a broken voice, "Kill you? Wh-why would you say a thing like that?"

He certainly couldn't blame her if she did. "I know I took some liberties to embellish matters—"

"Some? You were outrageous, Adam. You utterly humiliated me. Your lies had me running naked through the woods within moments of meeting you."

It hit him immediately that she had called him by his given name. Why did that make him all warm inside?

"For a good reason," he corrected. "And think of all the delicious gossip that will come of it."

"That is exactly what I am thinking of!"

"And if they are talking about your running about in a state of undress..." he paused as she flung up her arms and whirled about, unable to bear the mention of it "...then they are not supposing and surmising and casting their evil little minds about for the real reason we are being married.''

She froze. Slowly, she turned to look at him, her face thoughtful.

''Aha. You see how clever I am?''

''You want me to believe you've lied so baldly...*to protect me?*''

''Well, I didn't think you'd want it put out that your father is forcing you into this, and that I had never laid eyes on you before I showed up on your doorstep.''

Her eyes narrowed. ''And maybe you don't like people knowing you are marrying a total stranger for the benefit of money.''

Tightly, he replied, ''Maybe. We both have good reason to keep our private motivations just that—private. So the outrageous tale will keep them happily churning the gossip mill and they will have no need to look for anything further to say.''

She smiled. ''You could have told me what you planned.''

''Planned? I didn't plan it. It simply...came to me.''

''How fortunate for me that you can be clever so spontaneously.''

Adam took a step toward her. She was getting over her anger even though she didn't want to. He was fairly good at reading her by now, and he knew when her jaw set just so that she was fighting a smile. ''I have a great many talents, or haven't you noticed?''

''I really know very little about you,'' she answered. Her eyes caught the candlelight, sparkling at him. He smiled and sidled closer to her.

''For example,'' she continued, ''I very much doubt your parents took you to Africa where you were raised by an aborigine tribe after they were lost for two years in the jungle.''

Grimacing, he said, ''A bit too much?''

''And the four year expedition to the Far East under the protection of the high rajah—whatever that is…I found that highly doubtful.''

He held up his finger to stop her. ''Every word of that was absolutely true.''

Her lips twitched. ''I don't believe you.''

''Well, it didn't happen to me, exactly, but a fellow I once met in a tavern swore it happened to him.''

''Um-hum.''

He was close enough that he could smell the womanly scent coming off her. He liked it. It was mysterious, as she was. Somewhat exotic, somewhat sweet, somewhat…just fresh, clean. Female.

''I like your dress.''

She ducked her head.

''And your hair. It's nice.''

Her lashes rose and she peered at him cannily. ''I would be flattered if it weren't so obvious you are changing the subject.''

She was a clever girl. Her scent filled his head, making his brain feel sluggish.

''We were discussing your past.'' She paused. ''Where did you really come from, Adam Mannion?''

''London.''

''Please.'' She wasn't sparring with him any longer. Her tone was serious. ''I want to know. I think I deserve better than Zanzibar and wild Vikings carrying you off.''

''But that is so much more exciting than the facts. Plain dull truth of it is my father was a tobacconist who had a fondness for horses—betting them, not riding them. He was a good man, but not a lucky one.''

"You like horses, too. And you are no better at it than he."

"Not true. I am fond of cards and dice as well."

"Hardly commendable. Tell me about your mother."

"She left a long time ago. She took my sister. I haven't seen them since they left. I think there was a man. After my father's death, I found there had been a bill of divorcement granted. He had never spoken of it."

"Oh." Helena felt at a loss. The mention of his mother had obviously touched something vulnerable inside of him. His entire manner had changed. Gone was his light, teasing tone and the way his dark, liquid eyes squinted when he was amused, showing the crinkles at their corners. He was a man who had a great capacity to enjoy life, and it was etched on his face. But now he was too serious, and she was sorry for having ruined the mood.

She realized she had been having fun with him up until then.

"I think I see why you invented the Vikings and the aborigines."

One corner of his mouth hiked up. "I didn't even get to my story about being captured by Red Indians in the Americas."

"Well, we don't want to give Mrs. Gerret *too* much to tell everyone. Save something for the next visit."

"I believe the vicar said the next time we'd be seeing them was at our wedding."

Helena stopped.

He was very close. His gaze was lowered, fastened on her lips, which felt suddenly dry. So dry she had to lick them, which she did. And saw her mistake.

It was hard to say what changed, precisely. There was just something in his look that…deepened. She knew that look. She had once known the look of desire on a man's face—on many men's faces. They were as frequent as the admiring glances and ready smiles that had welcomed her whenever she was at a party or mixing with her mother's friends. But none of them had ever affected her like this.

Deep inside, some nether region of her innards rattled. That was what it felt like—rattling. Humming, vibrating, rattling—she couldn't tell which. It felt wonderful, as if silver threads of pleasure were woven throughout her body, and were being plucked by some unseen hand, like an angel expertly playing a harp.

She felt a bit dizzy of a sudden. Her eyelids felt heavy.

"It is less than a fortnight until our wedding," Adam said thickly. He kept looking at her mouth, intensely studying it. Without seeming to move an inch, he somehow was closer. "Not long…"

"No. Soon."

Her brain reacted to these inanities, but she kept perfectly still. She hardly dared to breathe for fear of doing something to break the spell.

He seemed to be moving closer. His head lowered by degrees. He was going to kiss her, and she could do nothing but stand there, frozen on the spot, and wait for the touch of his mouth.

Slowly at first, his mouth moved over hers, coaxing gently until she responded. She didn't want to, didn't mean to, but the heat that touch evoked stole up from some secret part of her and set flame to every nerve ending in her body. Timidly, she tilted her head, afraid of the fire and afraid of what he might do next if this—this brush of his mouth to hers—could leave her so devastated and raw.

She had good reason to fear, she soon learned, for when he slipped his arms around her and held her tightly against him, his kiss deepened, rougher now and demanding something that touched a primitive part of her she had not known before. His tongue ran along the seam of her lips, coaxing them open to the rough play of his tongue. It was utterly shocking, but she didn't stop it. She let him open her mouth. She let him taste her.

She grasped his shoulders as a tidal wave of reaction poured through her body. Molten pleasure rippled like the surface of a glassy lake after a disturbance, only it didn't dissipate but grew in intensity, leaving her breathless and clinging to him with clawed fingers.

When he stopped, he pulled back only inches, just enough to look into her eyes. His seemed bottomless, dark as pitch and just as inscrutable. He hesitated, as if undecided for a moment, and then he straightened.

A hot sense of loss scalded her. She was so bemused by what had just happened, she couldn't think straight.

He stepped away from her, as if craving distance. And all she wanted to do was fling herself back into his arms. Getting hold of herself, she breathed against the ache in her and swallowed back the ragged, hitching sounds that trembled in her throat.

He said, "It's late. You're probably tired." He wouldn't look at her.

"I...yes, it is late. I'm an early riser, so I should go...to bed." It was strangely embarrassing to be saying those words, as if that kiss had heightened her awareness of all things sexual.

Belonging to Adam... It wasn't as bad a thought as she had once imagined.

That kiss...

"Good night, then."

She blushed hotly. He was dismissing her.

"Good night, Mr. Mannion."

His head snapped around. "What happened to Adam?" At her questioning look, he said, "You called me Adam a few moments ago. It was very nice. It made us...well, if not precisely friends, then less each other's adversary.''

''Oh.'' She hesitated. ''Very well. Good night. Adam.''

He grinned and those little crinkles appeared at the corners of his eyes again. ''Good night, Helena.''

Chapter Twelve

Adam stared at Helena's portrait.

The wedding was ten days away and he was *nervous,* of all things.

Nervous of what? he asked himself more than once. It was exactly what he wanted, what he'd come here for. He should be elated. All the arrangements were made to receive the money, and he'd already had his solicitor send a portfolio of prospective investments. When his first quarter's stipend arrived, he'd be ready to funnel it into worthy venues.

So what was there to make his heart pound and palms sweat every time he thought of actually marrying Helena?

Pensively, he stared at the portrait some more.

Curiosity burned white-hot within him. He wanted to *know.* And yet he didn't. Was he afraid?

Yes, he was afraid. Afraid of what he might find out about Helena. Afraid that it was something dreadful and irrevocable. How would he feel then? He knew damned well how he'd feel—it would kill him to think she was never going to look at the world again like she did in the painting, with that slight haughtiness. It wasn't at all contemptuous, he decided after staring at her expression for a good long time—just as the parson had said. Rather, she looked as if she silently communicated her softness, her mystery even while she posed in daughterly duty for the portrait her mother had commissioned.

The fact that this was Althea's Helena poised for posterity was about all he knew of that "dark time" that was part of the shroud that hung over this place. He had gotten that much out of the servants, at least. Mrs. Kent, who had taken a liking to him, had related a few sparse facts until she remembered herself, and that was the end of that.

And yet Adam could see *his* Helena looking out at him from that perfectly composed face.

His Helena? Since when had she become his Helena?

The entrance of the footman rescued him from having to ponder that disturbing notion too long.

"Someone to see you, Mr. Mannion," the head footman said.

"In the front parlor, Jack."

It was the habit of all wealthy families to refer to their servants by the impersonal address of "John Footman" no matter what their Christian names. Adam refused to do this, but as the head footman's name *was* John, he had christened him "Jack" to differentiate from the aristocratic tradition. Jack seemed to like this affectation and always smiled broadly when addressed by his new name.

Adam went around the back way to the fancy parlor— there was a door cut out of the paneling that the servants used—arriving just before his visitor was shown in.

"Hello, Adam," she said, amusement dancing in her eyes at his shocked reaction.

The appearance of his mistress—his *former* mistress— was enough to steal his faculties for a good long time, during which Trina Bentford smirked triumphantly and waited for him to recover. Finally, he was able to say, "You cannot think this is in any way appropriate."

"What?" she cooed, gliding across the room with an airy wave of her hand. "Aren't you pleased to see me? Is your new wife so wretched she doesn't allow you to entertain old friends?" She paused, tapping a well-manicured nail against her cheek. "Oh, but she isn't your wife...yet. Is she?"

"This isn't a game. You should leave."

"Money is well and good, Adam, and I gather you are getting a lot of it to be putting up with all of this," she stated, her outstretched arms indicating the gloomy old house around them. "But, honestly, you cannot allow it to control you. I never thought I'd live to see the day when Adam Mannion was a puppet to a wife whose purse strings doubled as a marionette's wires."

His teeth clenched. He knew he was a bastard, he knew he was marrying Helena for her money and using her mercilessly, but he hated like the devil to have anyone say a thing about it. "What do you want, Trina?"

"Just to talk. That's all." She was coy. That *wasn't* all, and she was letting him know it in that sly, indirect way opportunistic people had. She was just going to play cat and mouse for a bit longer.

She was punishing him, he realized. The hair on the back of his neck stood on end and he pulled himself up stiffly.

"I'll call Jack to take you to the front door." He moved to the portal in the paneling. "It was nice of you to come to see me."

"Don't you dare!" she shrieked with a stamp of her foot.

He paused, donning a bored look as he waited. Getting Trina's goat had always been ridiculously easy.

"You...you...you were beastly! How dare you write to cast me off, as if I were no better than a street-walking doxy you'd picked up on the docks? I am good and mad at you, Adam Mannion, and I think you owe me an apology.''

"I wrote you a very courteous letter," Adam said patiently, "in which I explained that I felt it best to inform you immediately of my plans to marry so you would not waste time waiting for my return."

She tried a brazen smile, eyelashes fluttering. "But you are being so silly. I mean, I know you are worried about my feelings." He stayed stock-still as she pranced up to him, trying to look sullen. "But I don't care," she went on. "It wasn't like I ever pressured you to marry me. We just had fun together. There's no reason why it can't continue."

He grabbed her wrist when she reached up for him. He didn't want to be cruel, but he was acutely aware of where they were. This was Helena's house, with Helena's servants and Helena's father and *Helena,* and he would be hanged for a fool if he would allow himself to be caught coddling his former mistress in the parlor a week before the nuptials.

"Trina," he said, making his voice soft, "I don't think you understand. It wasn't Lady Helena's request that had me send you that letter. I did it because I wanted to."

"Oh, I don't believe that. We were always so good together."

"No, we actually were not very good together."

"I never refused you when you…when you wanted to…*you know.*"

He smiled. That put the problem quite succinctly. "You can't even say it—when I wanted to make love? No, Trina, you were quite docile, and very generous in allowing me to make love to you when I wished. But I never got the idea that you liked it very much."

"Adam! Why, you are a most virile man and quite generous...in...in that...in that regard."

It wasn't his virility he had ever questioned. "And you are a gorgeous woman with a great deal to offer a man. I wish you well."

"Well, it's not fair. I could have had other men. Richer men than you, Adam Mannion. I stuck by you when you had nothing."

He was stung. "You never complained before."

"I love you, that's why." He doubted that, but he wasn't going to get into a useless argument with her. She stuck her hands on her hips. "And I don't see any reason why our *arrangement* has to end just because you are getting married. You'll have a wealthy wife now, and plenty of money to spend. Think of all the fun we could have. What fine figures we will cut this coming season. And how jealous they will all be at our fall of fortune."

His head came up as the truth hit him. She was after her share of the Rathford money!

The idea of spending Helena's money on another woman made him feel vaguely sick. He wondered why. This sort of thing was done all the time.

It was that thought, and only that thought, that kept him from throwing Trina out without another word. Controlling his temper, he said, "I'm sorry you came all the way up here for nothing, Trina. Our affair is over. You'd best find another protector."

Then he reached for the doorknob. When he felt Trina's clawlike hand on his shoulder, he sighed. He didn't want for this to get ugly. Turning around with reluctance, he stopped as his gaze caught the figure poised uncertainly in the doorway.

Helena stood there, her face inscrutable.

He didn't even look at Trina. "Please go. You will understand if I do not make the proper introductions."

Trina—whatever she had been about to say now forgotten—had seen Helena as well. Trina looked about her a bit desperately for a moment, and he could almost hear the gears clicking in that scheming brain of hers, calculating her options. She was not without intelligence and must have soon deduced that those options didn't exist, for she departed without a word of protest, cutting a wide swath around her rival. Helena watched her, held her head high as the other woman gave her a sneering perusal from head to toe and made a face to say she pronounced her weak competition.

The silence in the wake of this inauspicious exit was as thick as aspic. Then Helena said, "The next time you want to avail yourself of a whore, make arrangements to see her in the village. I don't want them defiling my home."

She turned on her heel and was about to walk out the door when he dashed forward to cut her off. "Don't. I can explain."

"I am not interested."

There were tears in her eyes, he was surprised to see. He felt a flush creep up to singe the tips of his ears. My God. He was actually embarrassed.

He said, "It's not what you think. She's not...well, she was...an old friend."

Helena cocked her fists on those slender hips and jutted out her chin. "She never shared your bed?"

Damn. "She did," he answered honestly. "She was my mistress."

Her face congealed in a mask of bitterness. "How dare you."

"I didn't invite her here. I didn't—" He broke off, appalled at himself for the blundering apology. No, it was more like groveling. "Helena," he said more steadily, "if you would care for an explanation, I would be happy to provide one for you. However, despite how it looks, I have done nothing dishonest or in bad faith."

"If my father knew what a liar you were, I wonder if he would be so keen on this marriage?" She turned her face away, but didn't move otherwise. "I don't want to ever see that trollop or any other of your…*old friends* again. It is disrespectful to me. I can hardly tell you what to do, since ours is not a conventional marriage by any means. But I will not abide such flagrant indiscretion."

It was strange, the cold disappointment that settled in his chest, almost as if her dismissal of his offer to explain actually hurt him. She was right. There was no reason why she should trust him.

Helena continued, "I cannot tell you how to spend your money. If you weren't a wastrel and a ne'er-do-well, you wouldn't be so desperate to marry a withered and *scrawny* wife like myself."

That hurt. Even so, he was aware that she was hurting as well. He reached out for her. "Helena—"

The moment he touched her, she spurred into action, whirling out of his grasp so that his fingertips barely brushed her shoulder before she rushed out of the room.

He felt a keen sense of loss, and wondered at it. He tried to tell himself it was just a misunderstanding, that was all.

But it didn't seem to him a small thing. It seemed like something had been broken between them.

Chapter Thirteen

It didn't mend, not that day or any of the next. Therefore, it was with stiff formality and icy reserve that Adam and Helena exchanged wedding vows in the small cathedral in Strathmere.

Helena had wanted to hold the ceremony at the house chapel, but her father wouldn't hear of it. Nor would he heed her argument that this marriage was a dreadful mistake and he ought never to have forced her into it. She cited her fears that Adam would make a laughingstock of her by openly parading his birds of paradise. Lord Rathford listened patiently, his old, rheumy eyes taking in the sparkle that lit her face—even if it was from rage—and the animation that moved her once gaunt body in bold, telling gestures. He seemed to waver for a moment, weighing her feelings carefully against whatever it was he found meritorious in this ridiculous union. In the end, however, he had stood firm.

She wondered why she didn't just defy her father and send Adam packing herself. There was no answer, except perhaps that she had been obedient for so long under her mother's dominion that it didn't seem as if she had any other choice but to do as her father wished.

At the reception, held in grand style at Rathford Manor, Adam showed himself to be in no better a mood than she. He handed her a plate heaped with canapés. When she placed it on a table, untouched, he accused her of having lost weight again and frowned at the ill fit of her gown.

He couldn't have wounded her more deeply than if he had said outright he found her wanting. No doubt he pined after that bloated cow who used to warm his bed.

Looking down, Helena felt suddenly dowdy. This morning, when she had dressed in the mint colored silk dress, she had felt like a princess. Mrs. Stiles had done an impeccable job with it. The fault lay with Helena's still too thin form.

His disapproval made her cross and she found herself snapping waspishly at him for the rest of the afternoon. From the looks on the faces of the few guests, she was behaving badly.

One of those who frowned deepest was the tall, elegant Duke of Strathmere. Jareth found her by the refreshment table and with a few clever maneuvers got her by herself down by the end.

His dark eyes regarded her with intense scrutiny. "Helena, I've never seen you like this. It is supposed to be a happy day."

She realized her error in indulging her temper, a new luxury but a troublesome one, it seemed. She hadn't intended to attract this kind of attention. "It is," she said blithely, but her smile refused to stay put on her lips.

"Did you and Mannion quarrel?"

"We...we had a disagreement, yes." Her eyes scanned the room nervously.

"Surely you can put it behind you, today of all days."

She sighed. She could trust this man, after all they'd been through. "Jareth, I thank you for your concern, but I don't think Adam and I will ever be able to put our differences behind us.''

Her impending confession was prevented by Adam's appearance. He bowed to Jareth, his broad shoulders insinuating themselves between herself and the duke with the gesture. ''Your grace, you are monopolizing the bride.'' He slipped one of his big hands around Helena's waist. She could feel the heat of it through the material of her dress and had the sensation that he was making some kind of territorial gesture, as if staking his claim to her—his wife, now.

Jareth's glance was full of the aristocratic arrogance he usually avoided. The duke had chosen a wayward governess as his wife, defying all custom and duty, because of love. He was truly an egalitarian, but one would have thought him the purest snob for the look he aimed down his finely pointed nose.

''You seem to be doing a damn poor job of keeping her content, Mannion. She looked like she needed some cheering up. She appeared to me to be quite troubled today, which is not a sight one sees on a bride's wedding day very often.''

Adam looked neither agitated nor cowed by Jareth's setdown. His smile remained in place and he didn't even blink. ''If the bride needs cheering, I believe it is my job to see to it. With all due respect, your grace.'' That last was said without a trace of sarcasm, and yet it throbbed with challenge.

''Not if you are the cause of her poor spirit,'' countered Jareth.

''If I am or am not, I don't see how that is any of your concern.''

Desperate, Helena leaped when she saw Chloe approaching. ''Here is your wife, your grace!'' she announced anxiously, hoping the diversion would serve to stop these two from snarling at each other like mongrels lusting after the same bone.

"*Mon amie,* you look absolutely divine." The brunette linked her arm through her husband's and beamed at them all. Chloe had an infectious smile, and the sheer power of it brought down the tension a bit. "Doesn't she look fabulous, Jareth?"

The duke's eyes were still cold and still fastened on Adam, but his voice was soft and so full of his abiding fondness for his wife it made Helena want to weep with envy. "Of course she does, darling. Helena looks wonderful, as she always does."

Chloe looked at him approvingly, and that was when Helena understood that the duchess knew exactly what was going on between her husband and the bridegroom. Not for the first time, Helena felt a swell of affection for the woman, but it wasn't, for once, followed by the sting of traumatic memory. The two of them exchanged knowing smiles, and Chloe led her husband away with some excuse.

Helena was left staring at hers.

Adam showed his annoyance now. It didn't detract from how handsome he was today. Their wedding day, a day so bittersweet her throat ached from the tightness in it.

God, she had better not bawl like an ill-bred chit!

"I'm getting fatigued," Adam said. "I think it is time we retire."

"Go ahead," she said, making to walk past him.

He grabbed her arm, halting her. "Together."

Helena's eyes shot wide-open. "T-together?"

He inclined his head in a short nod. She swallowed.

He couldn't mean... Surely he didn't want to...he wasn't planning on *bedding* her. Was he?

''Take your leave of the guests and your father. I'll wait for you on the stairs.''

She did take her leave, then fled to her room. This was too much—it was impossible!

She hadn't thought this would be part of it all. He only wanted money. He had his whores for amusement. Why would he want to do this?

Did he think *she* wished it?

The idea brought a scathing flush from the roots of her hair to the tips of her curled toes. Good God—the kiss! Had he thought she was a wanton because of how she had given herself in the kiss?

The fact that she had responded so enthusiastically had shaken her until she had realized that it was only shock that had caused her to go limp in his arms and allow him those unspeakable liberties. Any lady of breeding would have reacted so.

She mustn't forget Adam was common.

If he had kissed her like that, what would it be like to have his big hands touch her, his hard, lean body over her…entering her….

She made a short, high sound of panic and buried her face in her hands. She knew what to expect from a husband in that regard. Her mother had told her, preparing her from a very early age.

A wicked husband may tempt you to give in to the baser urges a woman of higher social class trains herself to avoid.

Oh, yes, she could well imagine Adam Mannion tempting her.

There will be excruciating pain. You must bear it bravely and resist any attempts on his part to ease this suffering.

It is a mark of breeding to hold the act of lovemaking in contempt.

She couldn't let Adam touch her.

Her flesh shivered; darting spasms of excitement rippled through her. Pleasure. She imagined Adam's bird of paradise found great pleasure in that chiseled mouth, those long fingers, that tall, broad-shouldered form....

A soft knock ripped a startled yelp from her. She faced the paneled door, her hands clasped in front of her mouth as her brain flew over one insane plan after another. The only thing she could think of was to leap to the door and shoot the bolt home.

Too late. The knob turned and the door opened slowly.

"Helena?"

His voice was soft. So appealing, that raspy baritone.

All of a sudden she was in motion. She was across the room in a flash, flinging herself against the door. Because he wasn't expecting it, he was knocked back.

The door shut and she slid the bolt.

Panting, she waited in the silence.

"Helena?"

The softness was gone. Anger made his tone sharp. "Open this door, Helena."

"Go away."

"Don't make me do something we'll both regret."

"You can't break it. It's solid maple and as thick as the length of my hand."

"I can make a racket to bring whoever is left downstairs flying up here to see what is the matter. I know how you hate gossip, so I'm giving you plenty of warning before I commence."

"Go ahead. I doubt it will do your reputation much good to have it around that you were reduced to pounding on your bridal chamber door."

There was a short silence, then, ''Damn you. Open this door this minute or I'll—''

''You'll what?'' When she heard the strength in her words, she realized she was gloating a little. She gave a quick laugh. ''Huff and puff and blow the door in?''

''Fine. Have it your way.''

She folded her arms across her chest, and even though he couldn't see her, she struck a defiant stance. ''I intend to.''

''You are behaving like a spoiled brat.''

''Then you will have no trouble imagining me sticking my tongue out at you. Now go away.''

''Maybe I'll just do that. I've had enough of this mulish behavior. I ought to go to the library. I might spend my time more fruitfully perusing Shakespeare's *The Taming of the Shrew* to pick up a few bits of advice about handling a recalcitrant wife.''

Her mouth pursed tight at the insult. ''Oh, really? I only wish *I* had a book to read. I fancy I would rather enjoy a comedy. Perhaps *A Midsummer Night's Dream*. I think the tale of that presumptuous braggart, Bottom, transformed to an ass would amuse me tonight.''

She could imagine Adam gnashing his teeth. ''After *The Taming of the Shrew* I will probably go directly on to *Othello*. I have no doubt the tale of man driven to strangling his wife would give me ease.''

She nibbled her bottom lip frantically. Her forte was classical music, not classic literature. She had read Shakespeare, Milton, Spenser, Ovid and Homer, but she didn't have a great facility with remembering them well enough to find ready fodder for a rejoinder.

''Helena?'' he said at her long pause. His tone had lost its edgy sharpness.

''What?''

His sigh carried all the way through the maple door, which was indeed as thick as the length of her hand. ''Very well. Take the time you need tonight. I'll see you in the morning, when we shall discuss this like grown-ups.''

She hadn't expected this. Forgiveness? A flash of anger died before it was fully born. *Why should he forgive her?*

What a ridiculous question. There was no doubt that locking herself away from him was the right thing to do for her sanity, but no one would argue it was the correct thing for a wife to do.

Not on a wedding night. Wedding nights were made for consummation.

Just the word fluttering through her mind drained her legs of strength.

She laid her cheek against the cool wood. ''Good night.''

But he was already gone.

Chapter Fourteen

Adam did not go to the library and consult the brash Petruchio for advice on how to tame a wife. He didn't read *Othello* to vicariously purge himself of the need to throttle Helena. He went to bed, climbed in, then tossed and turned and cursed and groused until the watery dawn trickled through the windows.

He dozed, woke to a pounding headache, rose and washed. He had to hurry, because he didn't want to miss Helena at breakfast.

Although he was admittedly worried she wouldn't appear, he had a feeling she would be loath to admit her cowardice by hiding today. As it happened, he was correct. She came into the dining room a half hour after his arrival.

He was on his third cup of coffee and finding the thick brew Maddie made for his iron stomach not especially helpful today.

"Just a chocolate," Helena said to the footman.

"Not eating?" Adam inquired.

"I am not hungry."

She was wan and frail looking this morning. It annoyed him. "Right. We wouldn't want anyone to think you too healthy. It would ruin that beautiful martyr look you so arduously cultivate.''

"I would ask what you mean by that, but as I don't care, I shan't waste my breath.''

Her hot chocolate arrived, and Adam smoldered while she blew on it as she stirred.

His rage was growing. "Is this some perverse punishment you have planned? You are going to starve yourself right in front of my very eyes just to drive me insane. You know it drives me insane, don't you, to see you wasting away? What I don't understand, exactly, is what the devil I've done to be punished for.''

"As difficult as it may be for you to grasp, my every thought and action is not geared toward you, favorably or unfavorably.'' She looked up at him and he saw the gray cast to her skin. So she hadn't slept any more than he had. "What you do is utterly your concern and none of mine. You married me for my fortune, and it is my understanding that you now have what you want. I do not understand why you are complaining.''

Now he understood. That comment about what he did not being her concern jogged his memory. It wasn't too difficult to figure out from there what was bothering her. "I didn't ask her here, you know.''

The jerk of Helena's head as she glanced away confirmed his suspicion.

He threw his napkin down on the table and rose. "I told her to leave before you came in.''

"That must have been wretched for her. I heard her professing her tender feelings for you and the wonderful plans she had to make use of your fortunate windfall of funds.''

"You can't believe I'd do that.''

Helena gave him an obstinate look. "Why? Because

your sterling character speaks for itself in matters of moral fortitude?''

He stopped and blinked.

A flash of something passed across her face. She seemed to realize she had gone too far.

She *had*.

He tried to find something to say, but his throat was locked up tight and he doubted he could have managed to say anything without it coming out like sandpaper on stones.

So, that was what she thought of him.

Without making a retort, he spun on his heel and went out, stopping only for his redingote before heading to the stables.

Helena wrestled with a sour feeling until she called John Footman to fetch her some cooked oats or porridge. Despite her resolve not to pay a whit of attention to anything he said, Adam's snarling about martyrs and her unhealthy looks had bruised her pride. Again.

Adam had a problem. He had to find a way to make love to Helena.

Under the terms of the contract he had signed with Lord Rathford he had to bed the girl before he was allowed to leave. His first two months of ''duty'' would be up the following week, and he'd be free to return to London.

Just the thought of normal people without shrouds of secrets weighing them down, and houses full of light and free of cobwebs, made him feel better. He wanted away from this place, and away from the mysterious, maddening Helena Rathford.

Helena Mannion. His wife. Once he bedded her.

That was the trick. *But how?*

Cain found him out by the paddock, where Adam was

getting a pretty mare with a white star on her forehead ready to be taken through her paces. He hadn't found Kepper about and was feeling fairly lonely until the hound showed up.

"I'm not used to this," he explained to Cain after giving him a thorough rub behind the ears. The dog liked that so much, he flopped on his side and rolled over, all the better to provide access to his belly.

"I need people. No offense, but conversation needs to be reciprocated."

Uncannily, the dog barked.

Adam smiled. "That doesn't count."

The dog barked again and leaped to all fours. He was alerting him, Adam realized, and turned to see who was coming.

"Hello," a gentleman said with an easy smile.

Adam straightened and gave the man a narrow look. He was leading in a horse, a good-quality one. Dressed in a well-cut suit, he was tall and narrow with a high brow from which an M-shaped hairline sprouted mouse-brown hair that was caught straight back into a queue. "Hello." Adam's voice held no welcome. In fact, it was nearly challenging.

"Is Helena or Lord Rathford about?"

"Inside."

The man tossed Adam the reins of his horse. A shiny copper piece followed. "Rub him down for me, and water and oats, too. That's a good man."

With a jaunty gate, the man began to saunter up to the house.

Adam frowned at the coin he had caught. "Hey!" he called.

The man turned and Adam shot the copper back at him.

Ducking, the man didn't even try to catch it. As a result it hit him in the arm.

Rubbing it as if it stung, he looked cross. "Blast and confound you! How dare you accost me in this fashion? If you want more, you'll not get it now."

"If you want your horse tended, you had better do it yourself. Cain and I don't have time."

"What is your name!" the man demanded.

"Adam Mannion. What is yours?"

"I, sir, am Howard Balfourt, Baronet, and you have just insulted a peer of the realm." His arrogant delivery stalled and he looked a bit stricken all of a sudden. "Wait a jolt. Did you say Mannion? Are you...? Drat it, man, you're the one she's married, ain't you?"

"And who might you be?"

"Her cousin." The man was disconcerted, obviously trying hard to figure out what he was supposed to do now— be apologetic or continue to act insulted. Adam decided to take pity on him. He certainly didn't need to fight another front today.

"You weren't at the wedding. We've never met."

"Yes, well, couldn't get away." Apparently, he'd made up his mind, for he smoothed his hair and said, "Bloody bad form, eh, chap? Too bad to be starting out this way. Didn't know who you were." He gathered his redingote more closely around him. "Blast, it's deuced cold up here."

He hadn't exactly apologized, a fact Adam noted but didn't take exception to. "I must be used to it. I hardly notice it anymore."

"London's awash with rain. Dreadful," he groused. "Will you take me to your new wife, then? I am looking forward to seeing Helena. Imagine her *getting married.*"

"She's inside," Adam said tightly, jerking his head toward the house.

"Right. I'll, ah, I'll just leave my horse here. When the stableman comes back, can you tell him to, ah..." He was hinting to Adam, hoping he'd offer to take care of the horse.

"I'll tell him," Adam said curtly. Howard made his way into the house. Cain barked after him, one sharp, tight yip.

Adam stared hard at the man's expensively clad back. "Right. I don't like him, either."

Chapter Fifteen

Dinner that night was an exercise in the absurd.

Howard stared at Adam, then stared at Helena, then stared back at Adam again. Helena stared at her plate. Lord Rathford drank so much he was snoring by the second course. Adam, disgusted with the lot of them, attacked his food.

In between the intermittent and feeble attempts at conversation, the tinkling of their silverware was the only sound in the room.

Howard tried one more time to lighten the dour atmosphere. "Oh, listen to this one. This chap I know sallied off down to Bath just to see old Prinny, and when he got there, he realized it is *Brighton Beach* where the Regent goes!"

Chortles and laughter hit the paneled walls and fell dead.

Helena smiled. "He must have been quite vexed," she said mildly.

Disappointed, Howard cleared his throat and took up his fork. With careful precision, he placed a delicate bite into his mouth without his lips ever touching the tines. After mincing the morsel with rapid movements of his jaw, he paused. "I daresay he nearly strangled his post chaise driver. Deuced funny, though."

Adam raised his eyebrows and shoved a forkful of the braised hare into his mouth. He knew Howard's type. Howard was the kind of man who slept, ate and breathed society. Gossip was as much a part of everyday routine as dressing. Strict observance was made to every detail of others' appearance and deportment—of course, more substantive qualities like strength of character or kindness were irrelevant—and flaws were relentlessly criticized. To avoid being the object of ridicule oneself, behaving like a snide, overconfident snob was required.

Nothing personal, of course, but Adam happened to despise this particular type.

"So, coz," Howard said, rolling his large eyes toward Helena, "the house looks dreadful."

Helena stiffened. "It is difficult to find servants."

Adam knew this for a fact to be untrue.

"You should come stay with me. London's the place, then out to Greenwich for a jaunt."

Helena stiffened. "I couldn't leave Father. He loves the country life. You know that."

"Hmm." Howard cast a look at Lord Rathford. "Seems like he does nothing but drink and sleep, which he can do much more comfortably in London, I daresay. But I suppose he'd miss his hunting. He still loves his horses, I assume. Does he ride, or is he…you know. *Unable*." To illustrate the reason for his doubt, Howard pantomimed tippling motions.

There was an awkward silence. Adam considered the swell of protective anger that welled up inside him. When he glanced at Helena, she was giving him a look meant to quell any retribution he might wish to dole out on her behalf. He wondered how she could have known his strange reaction when he never would have guessed it himself.

Adam leaned back in his chair as his plate was cleared away and asked, "Are you interested in horses, Howard?"

"No, my good man. Filthy creatures. Beasts of burden, that's all there is to it, and anyone who aggrandizes them as more is a twit."

Without missing a beat, Adam replied, "Love them, myself. They are like poetry in motion. Beautiful and powerful and full of personality—each one as unique as you or I. Ah, when one is astride a swift mount, racing over the meadow, dashing into the copse…it is incredibly invigorating." He took up his fork again and attacked the slice of pie that had been placed in front of him. "At least to us twits."

"Dessert, Howard?" Helena interjected.

The man shook his head, having gone a shade paler.

The sound of cutlery stirring coffee and clinking against pie plates dominated once again.

Howard was settled in a guest suite. Mercifully, he retired early, as did Helena. Adam was irritated at not having a chance today to speak to her alone.

They had to settle this thing. He had to persuade her to consummate their marriage.

London was waiting. He felt as if he were putrefying here in the countryside.

Now, of all times, to be kept away when he finally had the means to walk among them as an equal… No. Perhaps not an equal. He'd never be that. His father had been a tobacconist, a gambler and a drunk—not that most of Adam's friends couldn't complain of the latter two in their own patronage. But his father was a common man.

What money Adam had came to him from his mother's

side, wrapped up tightly in a trust that had been protected from his father. It had ensured Adam an excellent education. He had attended Oxford, guiltless and unaware of his father's plunging fortunes, and while the tobacco shop was being sold for debt collection, he was enjoying himself among the English aristocracy and foreign royalty without the slightest idea of how dire things had gotten. He blamed himself for that later. He should have known, but youth is impetuous and rash, and he was having a grand time.

He was the kind of man other men liked having around, both for the fact that women liked him—and therefore were attracted in droves—and that he excelled at their masculine interests of boxing and cards. His friends, therefore, didn't mind his poverty. They cheerfully included him in their follies and never made mention of his lack of coin. It was an equitable arrangement—he spared none of his charms to win the favor of women they sought to impress, and his friends spared no amount of coin in their entertainment of those women, and him as well.

Adam hated that he required their good graces to get along. He resented every time they absently tossed a handful of coins on a tavern table to cover their night's carousing. It gnawed at him when they'd order a flurry of new coats, or make a whimsical wager they were sure to lose, or when they'd dash off to this place or that with no thought to expense. Oh, he was always included. But he never *belonged*.

But luck finally visited him. It came in the form of an idle conversation one evening at White's when, sitting around the tables in front of the bow window after a depressing night of bad cards, someone had made mention of the Sleeping Beauty of Northumberland. Adam had lit on it like a bee to nectar. A rich, reclusive beauty of noble blood without a betrothal?

Surely luck—so lacking in all these years—could not be so generous as to provide so succinct a solution. But it had and he'd wedded her. *He had married an heiress*—been elevated both by her money and her family's position so that he was one of them now. No more the poor mouse lagging after the generosities of his "betters."

He'd be damned if he were going to rot away at Rathford Manor as Helena seemed content to do. But how to bed a reluctant wife?

She was hotter than a forge about Trina. Whatever intimacies he'd been able to coax from Helena before were gone now. She was not going to allow him within a stone's throw of her, he knew that for sure.

He came up with no ideas on how to get past her reluctance as he undressed. Forgoing a nightshirt, he stripped down to his drawers and sprawled across the bed, one bare foot still on the floor. He fell asleep like that, vowing that in the morning he'd once again apply himself to solving the conundrum.

Music woke him.

Chapter Sixteen

Adam sat up, rubbing his hand briskly over his face as the strains reached his ears. It was lively, almost manic, and played with effusive joy. He climbed out of bed, his bare toes curling against the cold floor. Wrapping his arms around himself against the night chill, he didn't waste time searching for a shirt but quickly lit the lantern and went directly to the door.

Helena's playing was magnificent, once again.

He knew where she was. He had searched out the music room after the last incident of midnight music and made a mental note so that he could find it easily. He went there straightaway, but was puzzled to find the melody grow fainter as he neared.

It dawned on him that Helena had the pianoforte moved after the last time. He had mentioned he had heard her, and she must have wanted to avoid discovery. Damn.

He stood in the darkened hallway in just the loose-fitting drawers he had slept in. Making a quick decision, he went back upstairs and turned down the corridor where Helena's rooms lay.

The music grew louder.

He slipped inside her bedchamber, but she was not in

there. Coming out again, he went to the end of the corridor, to find a winding staircase leading upward through a turret of sorts. Yes, here she was. The music was coming from up there.

Clever girl. She must have thought it would be too far away for anyone to hear. Adam climbed the stairs, treading silently on the wooden boards. The small tower opened onto a large room. He was now on the third floor, directly above her rooms.

By the light of the lantern in his hand, Adam made his way carefully, inspecting his surroundings. There were several desks lined up, one large and a few smaller ones. A blackboard was smeared with dust and old chalk. A large map of the world was tacked up on a wall. Its edges were yellowed and curling.

He supposed this was a schoolroom, or a nursery. He turned about, inspecting the place. A globe, a low shelf stacked with books... There was a door beyond this, with a thin crack of light showing along the floor.

The light from his lantern caught on a sea of faces, and he hissed sharply in shock, stumbling back. The lantern jostled, casting revolting images helter-skelter around the room. He blinked and swallowed against a tight throat. Before him were placid, blank faces. Dolls. Only dolls. Many of them, lined up and staring like sentinals. The light caught their glass eyes, making them glitter with flat malevolence.

Unmindful of his encroachment, Helena played on, the music louder and stronger now, with flat chords tolling softly. The sound of her voice greeted him as well, soft and plaintive. She keened a song of mourning to match her playing.

Adam moved to the far end of the room. He pushed open the door. She was dressed in a white night rail and seated at the pianoforte. Her hands danced swiftly over the keys; her head was bent, her eyes closed.

As if welded to the spot, he watched her. She sang of longing, and it was so sweet he felt a lump come up in his throat.

Opening the door further, he winced as a hinge protested. The tiny squeak was loud enough to bring Helena to a sudden halt. Hands poised, body utterly stiff, she whipped her head around.

Adam stepped into the room. "Don't stop," he said.

She stood. The bench she had been sitting upon screeched as she knocked it backward in her haste, and her hip brushed up against the instrument, almost sending the candelabra toppling over.

"What's wrong?" Adam said, advancing. My God, she looked terrified.

"Why did you come up here?" she demanded. "How dare you! Leave." Her face crumpled, furrowing. "Please."

"I heard you playing." He held his hand out to her. There was something terribly fragile about her right now. Her whole body was tense. "Come and play some more. Play something for me."

Helena couldn't move. She couldn't speak, she couldn't think.

He was naked.

He wore only a pair of drawers drawn loosely about his hips, but everything else was completely revealed. Had he no shame?

His chest was bathed in the light of the three candles set upon the pianoforte—broad, hard, sculpted with strong shoulders and deep grooves where muscle met muscle. She couldn't keep her eyes from it. His arms flexed in a smooth contraction of sinew as he held out his hand to her, indicating the bench.

"Please? It was beautiful." His voice was soft, like the brush of velvet on warm, dry skin.

Beautiful. He was beautiful, possessed of the masculine sort that stole her voice and thickened her blood so that she could actually feel its clumsy spurts through her veins.

"I c-can't," she stammered at last. "I cannot sing for anyone anymore."

"I am your husband, not just anyone."

Her husband. *Her husband.*

"I cannot."

He took a step closer and she had to draw upon every shred of courage she had in her not to flinch. His gaze flickered downward, taking in the thin cotton of her night rail, and she was suddenly aware of the flimsy barrier.

He didn't lay one finger on her, but her breasts began to tingle in the most shocking manner as his dark eyes lingered there before moving back up to her face. She crossed her arms over her chest defensively, and the pebbled hardness of her nipples brushed against the back of her hands.

"You have a beautiful voice," he said, "and your talent at the pianoforte is extraordinary. I don't understand why you hide it."

"I...I can't explain."

He angled his head at her. "Another secret? Does it not get tiring, Helena, having so many?"

He stepped closer. She could smell him now. Her nostrils flared and a tight string in the pit of her belly suddenly spasmed with pleasure.

"Would you kindly back away?" She refused to look at him. All that naked flesh directly in front of her... "I can barely breathe."

He chuckled. She didn't know if it was her imagination

that made it sound diabolical. "My being near you makes it difficult to breathe?"

"You are too close," she countered, putting her hands up to push him away. Too late, she realized what she had done. Her palms splayed flat onto his wide chest.

Before she could retract her hands, he captured her wrists and held them where they were. "Helena," he murmured. "Such a formal name. It doesn't suit you."

"I never liked it," she said.

"Shall I give you another? A pet name?"

She had to giggle. It was a vaguely hysterical sound, fed by the feverish rush stealing over her. "I fear you will call me Eve. You are rather bad at names."

"I suppose that means you'll have to choose the names for our children, then."

She hissed in a breath and her heart exploded at once into an ache.

Children?

The idea melted her insides, bringing her temperature up. Children. Babies of her own, to love, to cherish and nurture—and she would be a good mother! Not like her own.

She'd not be so alone if she had a child.

Children.

He leaned forward, bending her hands back at the wrists. On his mouth, a dangerous smile quivered, and his eyes danced darkly. She tried to remind herself of all the reasons she must resist him. Bemused, she wondered what was happening to her, why wasn't she stomping her foot and putting him in his place. She felt paralyzed, caught as surely as the proverbial fly.

A husband of nobility would be disgusted by her curiosity, but Adam—Adam was a man of a different sort. He was not disposed to delicate sensibilities or starched reserve. He attacked life with vigor. He laughed loudly; he ate voraciously. How, then, would he approach the marriage act?

The flesh under her hands seemed unbearably hot.

"I believe I'm going to kiss you. Would you object too much?" Adam asked. She stiffened, but with anticipation, not displeasure, and waited. Wanting surged up and held her still and breathless, and for a miserable moment, when he didn't do it right away, she recalled the laughter in his voice and thought perhaps he were merely joking. Her eyes searched his and she saw that he *was* joking. But he was still going to kiss her. His bent head lowered and his mouth touched hers, brushing lightly at first.

She heard him sigh, as if he were releasing a great amount of pent-up tension, and then he gathered her tighter. She found herself pulled fully against all of that splendid naked flesh as his lips pressed firmly against hers, taking her up and away and into heaven.

The erotic spark he'd been kindling exploded. His hands cupped the back of her head, holding her as he opened her mouth and dipped his tongue inside the sweet recesses of her mouth.

The taste of him was like a drug, sending her whirling helplessly out of control.

She reached around and felt the wonder of the muscled back, shamelessly touching the warm skin. The feel of him was incredible—hard under the smooth skin, shifting muscle as he slid his hands over the sides of her hips in a caress that was exquisitely possessive.

A loud bang, like the sound of something toppling over, crashed through the silence. A male voice muttered a curse. Howard's voice. "Blast it, I can't see a thing. Helena? Are you in there?"

Helena reacted violently, jerking herself out of the kiss with a cry of alarm. Her eyes locked with Adam's, wide and startled as her own must be, before she whirled toward the door, her hands clutching at the modest neckline of her night rail.

"What is going on here?" Howard, holding a single candle in one hand and rubbing his shin in another, peered in through the door. He frowned at them from under his pointed nightcap. "I heard noises. Music."

Helena backed away, waving vaguely at the pianoforte. Her other hand came up to cover her swollen lips. "The…I was playing." After a short pause, she declared, "The pianoforte, I mean!"

"Good God, Helena. What is that thing doing in the nursery?" As he entered, she saw he was dressed in his nightclothes, with his bandy legs showing from under his nightshirt, his feet stuffed into slippers with curled-up toes like the silly footwear one associated with a jester. With a flowing silk wrapper overtop, he looked like a refugee sheik.

"I had it moved here, so I wouldn't disturb anyone. I play at night. When I can't sleep."

"Madness!" he declared. "This place has gone to rot since Auntie's death." He squinted at them, finally registering their state of undress. "Dear God, I hope you weren't…that is to say, I trust I didn't interrupt."

Breaking out of her shock, Helena shot forward, almost knocking Adam over as she brushed past Howard to get to the steps. "You did. You both did. I shall play no more."

The shadows swallowed her whole. Howard frowned, staring after her before turning back to Adam.

"I knew it. She's gone completely and utterly out of her mind. A veritable loon," he pronounced, shaking his head. Then he disappeared as well.

Chapter Seventeen

Kimberly came in while Helena was fixing her hair the following morning.

"Yer cousin is preparing to leave this afternoon, as soon as he concludes his business with yer father." Her small, watery blue eyes shifted briefly to the bed. Helena noticed how she covertly inspected the neatly folded counterpane and barely creased linens, then gave Helena a narrow look.

"I am sure they will be busy all morning." Helena gazed at the woman through the pier glass, keeping her poise with an effort. "Is Adam...is Mr. Mannion in meeting with them?"

Kimberly's freckled forehead creased. "What would yer husband have to do with the running of the estates? He didn't come here lookin' to make money, girl, but to get some to spend."

The sour reminder sat like lead in Helena's stomach. She set about pulling on her stockings. "He'll have plenty to spend, I should think. Father was uncommonly generous with him. No doubt our London solicitors will have an apoplexy when Howard hands them the papers."

Howard was her father's protégé in the running of the Rathford holdings, which was only proper, as he would eventually inherit the title. The son of George's cousin, he was the only male relative eligible to receive the few entailed estates, most of which still yielded a modest income, as well as the right to the heraldic arms. This house, however, was not the family seat. It had been built by Helena's parents early in their marriage from the funds her father had furnished through some excellent business investments in India. Therefore, Helena knew that, by provision of her father's will, it would always be her home.

"Aye, he's got a fine fortune now. I wonder what he'll do with it, do ye think?"

"No doubt," Helena said bitterly as she slid her leg into a stocking and secured the garter, "my husband is eager to spend it on his various pleasures and his plump and pretty birds of paradise." She jerked so hard she tore a small hole in one stocking and had to toss it in the dustbin and fetch another.

Her eyes stung. Damn the man. He had kissed her like…like she was a trollop. He had no right to do that. He was nothing but an unprincipled opportunist, a mercenary, a cad—even if he was her husband!

And she would be a fool if she forgot for one moment, one fragile, lost moment spent in the arms of an amorous handsome man, that he was only seducing her to seal the devil's bargain he had made. It didn't take too much imagination to realize the reason he wanted to bed her.

The lump in her throat swelled to painful proportions. He wanted to bed her only to ensure the marriage could not be annulled in the future, causing him to lose his wondrous boon.

But…but Adam, for all his numerous faults, had never been anything less than honest. Painfully so, at times. He had called her scrawny. He had admitted his loathsome motivations.

Would he lie with his mouth, with his kiss, to lure her to him and peel away her defenses? Had he meant that kiss? Did he truly want her?

The tears that had filled her eyes splashed, fat and heavy, onto her lap. Self-consciously, she swiped them away and angled a look at Kimberly, hoping she hadn't seen. The servant's eyes were closed, her head slightly tilted back. Her mouth was slack, her body utterly still.

Helena knew that stance very well. She froze, and all thought drained out of her.

When Kimberly opened her eyes, she leveled an intense and direct gaze at Helena. "Yer mother is pleased."

The shoes Helena had been holding dropped to the floor with a thud.

"She won't allow me into her bedroom," Adam stated.

"That is your problem, my boy." George Rathford glared at his son-in-law. "The deal is done. You don't expect me to alter it now."

"I expect you to be reasonable. I have to return to London, sir. Short of forcing your daughter to comply, I cannot get her to allow me to…to fulfill my end of our bargain."

Rathford cocked a bushy eyebrow at Adam. "Then you'd best find a way, because you are not going anywhere unless she's properly made your wife, and if I hear tell you've hurt one hair on her head I'll skin you and gut you like a jackrabbit."

The ferocious snarl on the man's bearlike face left no doubt that he meant what he said.

Adam blew out a disgusted breath and turned away.

Howard stuck his head in the room. "I'm nearly ready, Uncle."

"Everything in order?"

"I seem to have managed. My horse is being brought

round. Did you have those accounts I asked you to look over?''

"Damn. I took them to my room last night. I'd better go get them.''

"La! Call the servants to fetch them.''

"Don't trust the blasted servants. They've got looser tongues than a gaggle of matrons. Be right back.''

As soon as Lord Rathford was out of earshot, Howard rolled his eyes. "Lot of good his advice is going to be.'' To Adam, he said, "The man used to be brilliant. Made a fortune when he saw the future of trade with India. Spices are worth more than gold, man. But he's no good now. Drink's ruined him. Depends on me for everything.''

Circling the room, he strutted importantly while Adam followed him with his eyes. "Yes, indeed. All of this rests on me, while he drinks himself stupid.''

Adam tried to resist but was unable. He crossed his arms over his chest. "How so?''

"You don't think Helena's going to take care of any of it. Not that she isn't bright enough, and I'm not one of those that thinks a woman can't be as good as a man. My own mother—God rest her—kept my father's books and doubled the family's worth in the ten years since he was gone. But Helena? My good fellow, *that* woman is positively ghoulish. I swear, Aunt Althea may have been a bitch, but at least she had them all marching to her tune when she was here. This place was something then. Now look at it. It's a disgrace, that's what it is.''

Adam felt an unreasonable irritation at his observations about Helena. They were, after all, quite accurate. Still he felt the need to defend her. "Helena is a private person. Who are you to judge? She's had terrible times.''

"She's no more traumatized than me. Guilt-ridden more likely.''

"What are you talking about?"

"The murder." He looked again at Adam's frown of incomprehension. "The murder, man!"

Adam felt his hands involuntarily curl into fists. "What murder?"

"Oh, blast! I can't believe this! They didn't tell you— no one told you? How the devil did they manage that?" Howard stuck out his chest and crowed. "Oh, Mr. Mannion, I think they've been keeping a terrible secret from you. You see, my good man, *Helena is a murderess.*"

"No." He was lying. Adam knew his type; they loved to spread their bile. They got joy from other people's miseries. He had thought Howard the harmless sort of dandy, but now he saw his mistake in not taking the poncey fool seriously.

"Oh, yes. Ask your father-in-law. Why, ask Helena herself. She won't lie to you outright, although they've both deceived you plenty. A direct falsehood is much different from a lie of omission."

He was too smug, too righteous, to be lying. Adam's heart twisted. "Who? Who was it she…she murdered?"

Gleefully, Howard rubbed his hands together. "Can't you guess? Dear Aunt Althea."

The roar of blood in Adam's ears nearly overrode the snide words Howard crooned with delicious precision. "Her mother."

Helena kept thinking of children.

She wanted very badly to have a child; she had for a long time. Being far beyond the years where most women marry, and having no likely husband in sight, she had thought that dream lost to her. When Adam had come into her life, it hadn't occurred to her that their "marriage" would in any way include a life beyond his pockets being filled. She had never thought he would want her to have his children.

But now...now there was a possibility that she could be a mother. Just thinking of it uncoiled a longing in her chest. And, unable to help herself, she began to plan.

She liked the name Isabella for a girl. For a boy, she had always admired Stephen.

Thinking of a child to brighten this gloomy house brought on smiles, and visions of sunlight dappling through the huge leaded windows. Laughter would ring in these hollow halls, and music....

She would play for her child. And sing. To Isabella. Or Stephen.

Drawing in a ragged breath, she made a decision. Tonight, she would invite Adam to her bed.

"She is not a murderess." Lord Rathford fumbled clumsily for the decanter. Adam thought he would shatter it as he clanked it against his glass, pouring himself his third drink in less than a half hour. "The inquest cleared her of all wrongdoing. Of course, the devils around here like to speculate. I am surprised at Howard for being so foolish, but he was always a slave to gossip. It is unfounded rumor, nothing more."

"Her mother was shot. I found that out, at least, and Helena told them she had done it."

"No. That was a misunderstanding. The duke and duchess were there—they saw everything. The duke confessed to shooting Althea in self-defense. After all, she'd shot him. The duchess backed him, and Helena admitted she had...eh, been confused. The shock of it all, you see. They all agreed. Helena was completely cleared." Rathford drew in a long breath and continued in a softer tone, "She was just upset, that was all. It was always like her to take responsibility for things she wasn't guilty of. She'd apologize for a storm that wrecked my hunting, or 'make it up to me' when Althea grew cross.''

Adam rubbed his chin thoughtfully. "Then why does she hate people, hide away as she does? It makes no sense that there would be something like this to drive her into hiding.''

"It's the gossip, that's all, the same as what's got you all up in arms. Look, Mannion, her past isn't your concern.'' The old man shifted in his chair, an expression of pain crossing his fleshy face for a moment. "It's her future I want you to do something about.''

Adam noticed Rathford's hand was shaking. To cover it, the man put his glass down quickly. Adam felt a twinge of concern, then dismissed it. Sitting forward, he demanded, "I want the truth, Rathford. You owe me the truth. The whole story now. Why the devil did your wife shoot the duke?''

"Althea had gone after the duke because he'd broken the engagement to Helena so he could marry Chloe.''

This news hit Adam hard. Helena had been engaged to Jareth Hunt, the Duke of Strathmere, before he had wed Chloe. "Did Helena want Jareth?''

"Helena was happy to let Jareth go to Chloe, but Althea...she wanted that title for Helena. All that wretched bitch ever wanted was for Helena to be the duchess. Althea went there that day to murder the two of them. She had it all figured out, you see. Gerald, the cousin, the one I hunt with—he would inherit. He liked Helena well enough and...well, my wife...she was evil. I didn't know it, though. Should have. Yes. I should have.''

His brow creased and his face crumpled.

"But Althea didn't murder Jareth.''

"Oh, she tried. Althea shot him, wounding him. She had

brought two firearms, however—one for Chloe and one for Jareth. The duke managed to wrestle the other flintlock from her after he was shot, and it went off. It was an accident. That was the ruling.''

It was an incredible story. Adam took a moment to find his voice. "Then why, if it is all so simple, is there still rumor?"

"Helena was beautiful, accomplished, impeccable. She was perfect. Perfect. When her mother died, she crumbled. You know what happened to her, how she stopped caring about herself. Stopped living. People said it was guilt. They said Jareth took the blame because he felt he owed her something." Rathford pondered some spot in the middle distance. "The rumor you heard I have heard, too. They say she killed her mother out of a fit of pique at what she saw as her mother's failure to secure her the title of duchess. Now, you know Helena well enough to know she never cared a whit about that. She wasn't sorry to lose Jareth. She didn't kill her mother."

Adam thought this over. There was truth enough in some of what Rathford was saying. Having witnessed for himself that Helena certainly bore the noble couple no ill will, he was inclined to believe the story. In fact, he had noticed a sort of steady fondness among the three, as if there were in truth some bond they had shared that forever forged them together. But it didn't explain everything. For example, if Helena never wanted the marriage to Jareth, why she was so traumatized by the event? Was seeing her mother killed enough to explain her utter collapse into the dismal existence in which Adam had found her?

And then there was Lord Rathford's behavior. Although Adam wasn't inclined to believe Howard, his father-in-law seemed to be uncommonly nervous. There was sweat trickling down his brow now and he'd already untied his cravat.

He went for another drink.

Adam said, "If you're lying to me, Rathford, I'll make you pay. Our bargain will be off and I'll still have Helena's money."

"What does it matter? The past is done. Bed the girl and you'll get a bonus." Rathford's look was bitter. "Three thousand pounds. And you can go back to London the very next day."

Adam stared at the man, dumfounded. What was he to make of this? Would a man with nothing to hide offer so much? Yet, Adam had to wonder why a man as clever as Lord Rathford had to give so obvious a diversion.

But he was a desperate man, George Rathford was. Adam saw it in his bleary eyes. And, to his embarrassment, the multiple chins quivered as Rathford said in a watery voice, "Give her a life, man. Give her something to live for. Whatever her reason for this hell she's locked in, it doesn't matter. You can break her out of it."

Adam exhaled loudly and went to pour a glass of whiskey for himself. "Like damned, bloody Sleeping Beauty, right?"

What the hell? He'd never figure out these insane secrets. Besides, it all came down to the fact that he wanted to do it. He wanted to make love to Helena. Yes. He burned for her, and it was easy to dismiss all the rest when the chance to have her was all he really cared about.

Last night. And that kiss...

Just the memory of her bare hands on his skin set his groin aching. And that diaphanous gown, rendered so by the strategic lighting behind her, so that her womanly form was completely silhouetted... He had seen for himself that her severe slenderness did nothing to take away from her very unique, very attractive gamine femininity.

All through the afternoon and on into the evening he

pondered on exactly how to seduce his wife. They all endured an excruciating dinner fraught with enough tension to cause a person to choke on the coq au vin.

Helena was particularly skittish. She refused to look at Adam, and spoke less than a half-dozen times, and then only when queried directly.

It didn't take a genius to understand why she was so withdrawn. She was thinking about the kiss, too, but apparently she had a much different response. No doubt she despised him even more than she ever had. And that was saying something.

Fabulous. He had really loused up his chance by barging into her private moment nearly naked and pawing at her like some randy schoolboy.

He saw no way to break through her ironclad resistance to him and was prepared to give up any hope of returning to London when she came up to him timidly after they had dined and uttered five words in a small voice.

He nearly keeled backward onto the Aubusson carpet.

She said, "You may visit me tonight."

Chapter Eighteen

How did one make love to a wife?

That was the question that tortured Adam's poor brain as he divested himself of his clothing and donned a dressing gown. He'd made love to many women, and although some of them had been wives, none had ever been *his* wife.

Wives were different. One couldn't toss them on their backs and smother their bodies with hot, sultry kisses until the need was intense and urgent. One couldn't drive deep within them and lose one's self to ecstasy.

That was what he wanted to do. She'd been driving him mad from the moment she had slammed the door on his foot.

No, he cautioned himself. There could not be passion. Women of breeding didn't expect or want that sordid sort of thing from their husbands. The lusty ones took lovers after their childbearing duties were done, and the cold ones shriveled into disapproving old hens.

Certainly Helena would not delight in knowing the wild, erotic things he wanted to do to her.

Pulling himself up straight, he cinched the dressing gown around his waist. He always hated these things. They were for fops, as far as he was concerned, but he couldn't risk offending her by bursting in in his loose, drawstring drawers. Again. He had to strictly observe decency. It would be difficult enough for Helena to succumb to the proceedings she would no doubt find disgusting.

Besides, it reminded him that he wasn't visiting a lover. He was visiting a *wife*.

A soft knock and Adam entered.

The moment Helena saw him, her mouth went utterly dry. He looked completely ridiculous in that dressing gown. It was far too elegant for the primitive masculinity he wore so easily. She much preferred the bare-chested, barefooted apparition that had visited her last night.

The thought shocked her, but she didn't bother to feel guilty. The memory was too tantalizing to resist mulling over for a moment or two.

For herself, she was wrapped up tight in a silk robe with her thickest cotton night rail underneath, buttoned all the way up to her ears.

"Good evening," Adam said. He wore a pleasant smile.

Gone was that diamond-hard glint in his eye that had kept her helpless last night.

"Good evening, Adam."

He crossed the room. Nervously, without anything to do, her hands fluttered. Finally, they found each other and clasped in a white-knuckled grip under her breasts.

"Thank you for coming."

He smirked, as if she'd said something funny. She frowned. They stared at each other awkwardly for a moment.

"Maybe you'd be more comfortable over here," he suggested. To her horror, he indicated the bed.

"Oh." Of course. They shouldn't waste time. Get this horrible embarrassment over as quickly as possible.

On wooden legs, she moved in obeyance of the hand at the small of her back. Toward the bed.

She gulped back an eruption of panic.

He undid the sash of her wrapper. "I think you'll be more comfortable without this."

"The lights!"

"I'll douse them." His tone was reassuring. Placing his hands on her shoulders, he pushed her gently onto the bed. She sat first, then, stiff as a corpse, lay on her back, feet still on the floor.

"Relax," he said, and went to extinguish the lamp.

Helena didn't move.

He left one single candle burning, which he brought to the bedside table.

Helena didn't move.

He climbed into the bed. She kept her eyes pinned to the ceiling, feeling the bed sag under his weight. The heat coming off his body registered all along her left side.

Helena didn't move.

Long fingers touched her chin, turning her face toward his. "You are a virgin?"

"Of course I am!" she snapped. "How can you ask that!" She sat bolt upright in one jerky movement. "That's it! I knew this was a mistake."

His big hand caught her squarely in the middle of her chest and sent her sprawling onto her back.

"Helena," he said patiently, "I didn't mean to insult you. Think about it from my perspective. There are all these unanswered questions about your past. Many things in this house are not what they seem. It was no comment on your character, but a simple question so that I know what to do. It makes no difference what the answer is, except now I realize you do not know what to expect."

"I know what to expect. My mother told me. I...I am prepared to submit. You know what to do, right?"

He bit the inside of his cheeks. The lighting was poor, but God spare his hide if that smile blossomed to the full. "I have a general idea."

She let out a long breath. "Then go ahead."

She didn't move.

Adam didn't, either.

"Maybe it would help matters along if we rid you of this." He touched his fingers to the collar of her gown. "Generally, the preamble to the act helps the woman ready herself to take the man."

She wanted to melt into the mattress and never draw breath again. "My mother said I shouldn't. Just...just lift the h-h-hem."

"Ah, hell," he muttered. He seemed uncertain and, to her horror, utterly disgusted. She understood men generally enjoyed the act. When they found the woman desirable, that is.

That last thought was crushing.

His hand grabbed a fistful of her night rail and began drawing it up. The moment her legs were exposed, she gave a small cry and yanked it back down.

"No. I'm not ready yet."

"This is ridiculous," Adam muttered, and flopped onto his back.

There was a long silence.

"I'm sorry." Helena's voice sounded so childlike to her own ears that she winced. "You can try again now. I'm all right."

"Helena, I can't do this. Not like this." He rolled over and propped himself up on his elbow. "It isn't fair to you, I know, but I've got to kiss you."

Her heart lurched. "You do?"

''If you'll permit it.''

She shouldn't like the idea, but she did. And if it was what he needed to get the act accomplished... For the child they were to have, and that sake alone, perhaps it would be all right to participate just this little bit.

She gave a little nod of acquiescence, figuring that he might or might not see it in the stingy light, so in a way she was leaving the decision to break proper form up to chance.

Fate decreed a kiss. He leaned over her and brushed his lips against hers.

The reaction that shot through her body was immediate, intense, galvanizing her from head to toe. Her fingers dug into the mattress and she stiffened, but otherwise didn't move.

He brushed again, as if testing her readiness. The third time, she could wait no more and she lifted her chin to join her mouth fully with his.

She kept her hands at her sides, a concession to the propriety she'd been taught. There would be no wanton groping tonight. She knew precisely what it was she was to do—lie still and let him do what he must.

Think of the child, she told herself.

Think of the...oh, God, the feel of his mouth was so very delicious. Soft, yet firm, and now he was demanding more from her. She heard small noises, like gentle whimpers, and realized they came from her. Then he touched his tongue to her lips and she groaned before she could stop herself.

Misreading the noise, he jerked back. ''I'm sorry, I'm sorry. I didn't mean to...''

She wanted to scream. Her hands came up off the mattress and began to reach for him, but she stopped herself just in time. Fists hovered, wanting to touch and not daring.

"Helena, please." The sound of his voice heavy with passion drove the last vestiges of thought from her mind. "Let me touch you." His arms went around her, one behind, one across the front of her, holding her loosely as he gazed down with heavy-lidded eyes. "I've got to...I need to hold you."

"All right," she said faintly, her head swimming. She waited, proud that she didn't shout "Yes!" Her heart beat so violently, she feared it would tear a hole in her chest. He pulled her up tight against him and she felt the steely hardness of him all along her body.

He swallowed hard and his lips tried a smile. "There. That feels...so good. You feel good."

Her insides clenched and her palms itched to touch him. She wanted to feel, too.

Running his tongue over his lips, he seemed to be out of breath. His broad chest rose and fell as his eyes burned her. "I want...to..."

She found she was panting, as well, her breathing quick and ragged, catching sharply when his head lowered and he took up playing his mouth against hers again. This time she couldn't keep her arms from circling his neck, nor her back from arching to press herself into him.

The noise he made, the way his hands splayed across her back, tightening, digging into her flesh, tilted her world into wild abandon. She ran her fingers along the hairline at the nape of his neck, feeling the silky curls that twined there. Venturing down his back, she felt the firmness of muscle as it shifted under her questing hands. The robe whispered tauntingly, the exotic feel of silk crisp and smooth beneath her fingertips.

His hand moved, sliding up her side, and before she could utter a protest, cupped her breast. The air rushed into her lungs, then out in stuttering degrees as he squeezed slightly, the pressure stealing any thoughts of protest at this unthinkable liberty. It wasn't at all necessary for him to touch her there, but it felt wonderful and she couldn't think of a reason why she should object. His thumb began a rhythmic stroking over the sensitive peak, sending her body into a complete convulsion of shock, of pleasure that rapidly transformed into yearning. Straining against the caress, she reveled in the mounting delight as his hot mouth took possession of hers, this time quite differently. Hungry and demanding and...oh, and wonderful.

She was dying, she thought, dying a death so sweet she had no care of it. He moved to the other breast, shifting himself to touch the quivering flesh. That nipple was already hard beneath the demure night rail, throbbing, aching with need. He pulled on it gently, and darts of exquisite pleasure shot from his fingers to the farthest points of her body. Their kiss deepened, and when his tongue again invaded her mouth, she eagerly opened to allow it. He thrust boldly, a titillating promise of what was to come, before he ripped his mouth away.

He removed his hand from her breast. "Can I take this off?"

She could barely speak for lack of breath. "My nightgown? You want to take it *completely* off?"

"It will get all bunched up between us. It may be uncomfortable."

Naked? Lie naked together. Suddenly, doubts assaulted her. "I don't know if I'm supposed to do that." To lie with him, nude and fully exposed. It was appalling. Wasn't it? Yes, definitely horrifying in the extreme, and absolutely exciting, as well.

"Sweet Helena—" He cut off his gruff epithet and drew in a heavy breath. "Okay, then. I'll just lift the hem."

"No. No, I suppose we could try."

His fingers moved to the buttons at her neck, his darkly handsome face intense. Her body quivered at the light brush of his agile fingers. In no time, he had three of them undone, and Helena lost her courage.

Pushing aside his hands, she did up the buttons again. "I think we shouldn't."

"You must be joking." He undid them again.

"It's not proper. It's not done this way."

"Blast how it's done. I'm not embalmed. I'm a man and I can't make love to a woman I desire without feeling her against me. If that makes me a cretin, then so be it. I tried, Helena, I did. I'm sorry if this offends you, but I can't just shove your gown up and hump you like a dog on a bitch. This is the cruelest madness I've ever known!" He rolled onto his back again and covered his eyes with the back of his hand.

Chapter Nineteen

Helena waited, her brain sluggishly registering what he had said.

He desired her. Adam desired *her*.

But she had ruined it now. He wasn't going to touch her or do *it* to her. He wasn't going to give her a child—

He *desired* her?

He thought she was scrawny. He had his plump mistress with the burgeoning bosom and fleshy curves. How could he actually feel desire for *her?*

Slowly, Helena looked over and saw him, face covered and lying flat on his back. The dressing gown had come undone and there was absolutely nothing hidden in the faint candle glow.

She had seen his chest before and had been mesmerized by the complex weave of muscle and sinew, and had glimpsed the flat, hard abdomen. She could look her fill now. He wasn't watching. Her gaze lingered, long enough for her to feel a little whirl of something edgy inside her. In the low-riding drawers he had worn last night, she had glimpsed the lean hips. Now she could see them fully exposed. And his manhood was nestled in a bed of dark curls right at the apex of his legs. It looked...hard, like a bone. How did he fit it in his trousers?

The sight of it was shocking, and still a tight band of excitement gripped her. She forced her gaze to move on. His legs were long, fitted with muscle and finely shaped. His feet were broad and strong looking, like the rest of him.

Her gaze returned to his sex and she swallowed hard.

She was not going to let this night go by without him putting...that into her. She knew enough to understand that it was that part of him that held the child.

But there was more than just the desire to conceive that spurred her on. She wanted to feel that part. A ripple of pleasure ravaged her as she considered doing a very unladylike thing. She knew he wanted to touch her. Kiss her. See her and feel her against him, he has said.

The thought of it left her weak and tingling.

Sitting up, she said, "Adam, please don't be upset."

He slid his hand down and looked at her.

With shaking hands, she undid all the buttons of her night rail and slipped it off her shoulders.

Naked to the waist, she closed her eyes and waited. She fervently hoped he would take over from here, because it had taken everything in her to push herself this far. To disgrace herself, most probably.

It was for the sake of her child, she told herself, but she wasn't thinking too much about babies just now. She was thinking of the way he had touched her breasts and that they were now naked, exposed and tight and ready for him to take into his hands again.

He did nothing. Appalled, she opened her eyes.

He lay immobile, gazing at her. She began to wonder if she'd made a terrible mistake. Perhaps she'd misunderstood. Perhaps she should pull her nightgown back up—

"Oh. Helena," he said, then he reared up and took her

in his arms in one smooth motion, his mouth claiming hers in a kiss that sent her whirling into delirious delight.

He wanted her and she wanted him, and every other consideration vanished.

He shrugged out of the silk garment and stripped her quickly of her gown. He ran his hands up her legs, his palms skimming over the exposed flesh hungrily. She moaned when his kisses trailed a path to her breasts, convulsed when he suckled and tongued her nipples. When he slipped his hands down to the juncture of her legs to part her and test the moist heat hidden there, she whimpered. Clamping her legs shut, she tried to pull him away, until he gently explained that he had to ready her. Then he muttered an expletive and groaned, saying something about how she was already hot and wet.

Blushing furiously, she turned her face into the pillow. His mouth teased her earlobe, coaxing her to relax. His fingers entered her, slipping inside easily. "You're tight," he said, and her heart soared because he said it in a low, guttural voice that seemed heavy with pleasure.

He withdrew his fingers, then stroked outside her opening, brushing against something incredibly sensitive, teasing maddeningly with the lightest of touches until she moaned again. Clutching his shoulders, she found herself muttering incoherent pleas. Her hips surged, rising against the teasing of his fingertips, and he continued, driving her higher, pleasuring her, taunting her, fulfilling her until she exploded in a wicked shattering ecstasy.

Floating, falling, traveling through leagues of blissful sensation, she heard his voice. He murmured comforting words to ease her, to tell her what he would do next. There was a bolt of joy that went through her, for she understood this was the mating. Unable to move, she let him part her legs and lean over her.

His shaft was hard and hot against the tender flesh he had just caressed. In a flash, she was afraid again, remembering about the pain. Her mother had warned her about the horrible pain.

She braced herself, the lassitude gone. He sank into her, slowly. It…it felt good. He eased his hips down, kissing her all the while. The long, careful stroke built quickly into the pain she was expecting. She froze, steeling herself. She knew it was the most horrible agony to be born; she'd been told.

He said something, but the blood was roaring in her ears and she couldn't hear. He moved deeper. She felt her body rip as he pressed himself fully into her, and she tried to push him off in a moment of panic because she knew the torment would only get worse.

To her surprise, he stayed very still. All sense of pleasure gone, she lay under him, trembling and immobile. He pressed sweet kisses along her jaw, across the swell of her cheekbone and the bridge of her nose. His strong teeth nibbled at her ear, sending a ripple of reaction through her. His breath fanned across prickled skin and she shivered with pleasure.

As he moved out of her slowly, she was aware of a sharp pain that dimmed rapidly after his next stroke. An ache replaced it when he entered her again. Then his hands set to work touching her all over, and when he came into her the next time, she began to like the feeling.

He moved harder, quicker, his breath tearing out of him, and with it came broken words as he tried to tell her it was all right and how beautiful she was and how sorry he was he had hurt her but he was so glad she was his.

Love words that would mean nothing later, but were wonderful to hear now. She could let them take her up and away on their wings, but she couldn't let herself believe them.

Well. She would let herself believe them for a little while.

He rode her, hard and sweet, until his body jerked and surged against hers. His manhood stretched her, filled her so wondrously that she cried out with joy. The sound that came from her blended with his, a groan that was a virile growl of pleasure. Slick with sweat, he braced himself over her as his hips moved, and he arched, head back, teeth clenched, and she knew he had found release.

He relaxed, still moving but slower now. His mouth descended, claiming hers, and his kisses, too, grew gentler as his body ceased its motion. Rolling onto his side, he kept his legs twined with hers and wrapped her up in his arms, tucking her head under his chin.

They didn't say anything. She couldn't think, yet her mind seemed filled with so much—thoughts, feelings, bits of recollection of what had just transpired.

Contentment lulled them to sleep.

Adam awakened her when he crept out of her room just before dawn. He didn't know she had felt his lingering kiss, his smooth caress on her supersensitive skin, or heard the reluctance in his voice as he wished her good-night. She fell back asleep, content and peaceful, to wake with the blissful knowledge that she would be a mother.

With naivete that came from misinformation, she was under the impression that the wonderful act was a fail-safe method of impregnating a woman. It didn't occur to her that conception might take more than one occurrence. She had been taught that the act was for procreation. They had done the act. Now she would procreate.

The knowledge that a new life would begin to grow inside her intensified her pleasure. She could hardly wait until the child was born and weened so that Adam and she could set out to make another one.

The thrill of that thought raised gooseflesh on her naked arms as she pulled on her wrapper and sat at her dressing table.

A slight sound brought her out of her reverie. Kimberly stood in the doorway.

"I am dressing," Helena said, meaning for the Irishwoman to shut the door.

"He is leaving."

"Who?"

The corner of her mouth quirked up. "Yer husband, Helena."

"Leaving?"

"His duty's been done. He was tellin' yer father of it. I heard him meself. He wants to go back to his home. London. Where he belongs, he says."

Pain blossomed crisply. It coursed through Helena, soaking her in an instant. "Of course he is going home," she said, trying desperately to hide her crushing disappointment. She would not for the world let Kimberly see that she hadn't known of Adam's plans.

"Ye knew?"

"I know exactly what my place in my husband's life is, and what this marriage means to both of us."

That was so wrong Helena thought for certain the sly old servant would see through it. Kimberly narrowed her eyes and nodded. "That's good, ye see, because ye can't be thinkin' it's more than it is. He's here to purge ye of yer sin, ye know that. Ye must focus on yer redemption, my lady, an' not be lookin' for somethin' ye have no right to."

Like happiness.

The thought jarred her, and she had to look away. Sometimes Helena thought the old witch had the ability to read her mind. She had used her knowledge of the map of Helena's soul to manipulate and control for five years.

"Leave me," Helena said.

"Yer mother wants ye to know she's watching ye." Helena's head came up sharply. Kimberly gave a sage nod. "Oh, yes, girl. She sees into yer heart. She knows that ye want to forget her."

Helena shivered. "I'll never forget her," she said sotto voce. "Now go. Please."

She was surprised when Kimberly obeyed, and intensely relieved. Helena was sick to death of her cryptic "messages" from beyond the grave. She didn't believe for a moment that her mother haunted her. It was Kimberly tormenting her, with her crafty skills at plucking a tormented conscience.

Yet today the disturbance within Helena died down quickly. She had a far more important dilemma to consider. Adam was leaving.

She admonished herself for not having anticipated it. He loved London, having come here only to finance that city way of life. He would return in a few months for his obligatory visit, just as the contract stipulated. Her father had told her this much of the arrangement. She found it humiliating knowing Rathford was forcing her husband to visit her.

It was a good thing she didn't know about the other stipulations of the agreement, or the new bonus her father had tacked on, which Adam was collecting at that very moment.

Tucking the banknotes in his inside coat pocket with a terrible sense of guilt, Adam executed the slightest of bows and left Rathford, going out to the stables. He sat with Cain, trying to explain to the soulful-eyed hound why he had to leave.

"I'll be back," he promised, but the expression on the dog's face called the promise into doubt. "I swear it."

God, he was an idiot. But he wasn't stupid. He knew himself well enough to recognize the slithery feeling in the pit of his belly as old-fashioned—and well-deserved—shame.

He went back into the house. He had a life to get back to, and a fortune to make. In fact, he had lingered here too long already. Opportunities were slipping by every day, and they weren't going to come to Northumberland. No. If he were going to make his stake in the world, he had to go to London. There was nothing he could do to change that.

The Royal Exchange—that was where he needed to be. His luck at the tables and at the track had betrayed him in the end, but those endeavors relied too heavily on the fickle whims of Lady Fortune and not enough on the power of one's ability to comprehend, filter and analyze information about the complex world of trade and the burgeoning industries just now venturing out of cottages and into factories. This was his time, long in coming, and he was supposed to be delighted to be leaving this ghoulish old pile of stones and finally seeing his plans through.

"Sir," Mrs. Kent said, "your valise has been loaded onto the carriage. Was it just the one piece?"

"Yes, thank you."

He supposed he should find Helena and say his farewells.

A searing heat ripped a straight line from his throat to his gut. Last night, he had won his freedom by making love to her. But he had this feeling he had lost something, too.

He didn't feel quite himself this morning.

Ignoring the niggling pangs of conscience, he went upstairs to find his wife. He came across her in the hall, looking staggeringly lovely in a violet dress embroidered with pink and yellow sprigs. Her hair was fixed in a very simple, very elegant sweep. Last night, he had sampled how soft it was as it twined around them. His groin tightened and he steered his thoughts to tamer subjects.

"I understand you are leaving," she said. She sounded very prim, very flat.

"I have to. I have business in London."

"I see." Cool, aloof, nearly regal—this was the Helena of the painting in the parlor. She was hurt. The tilt of her head, the clipped words were as easy to read as a newspaper headline. She had a right to be. Suddenly, he was overwhelmed with an absolute conviction that he was the lowliest of worms.

"I've been away for so long," he explained. "I need to talk with my solicitor. You see, he's my investment advisor as well, and we have to meet about our strategy."

"I understand."

"Why don't you come?" he blurted.

She stared at him, those blue ice-chip eyes of hers thawing. "What?"

Why hadn't he thought of that before? "Come with me. My apartments are abominable, but I daresay you aren't so used to better that you'd find it a hardship. Still, they are in a good area of town and my friends would enjoy meeting you, although…" He trailed off when he saw her face.

"I cannot. You know I do not leave this house."

"Yes. Right." He looked down, embarrassed by his impulsive enthusiasm. He'd been practically pleading. "It was a foolish idea. Well. I suppose I shall have to content myself to write to you."

"I should not wish you to trouble yourself."

He wanted to kiss her, but Mrs. Kent came in just then with a basket covered with a linen napkin. She smiled maternally as she handed it to Adam. "Maddie insisted. She swore you were likely to starve to death in between stops if you didn't have provisions."

He peeked under the napkin at the assortment of baked goods nested in the basket. "Thank you, Mrs. Kent. And tell Maddie thank you as well. I'm going to save at least one of each of these to share with my London mates just to drive them wild with jealousy."

The housekeeper beamed at him. "Very well, sir. Safe journey. Don't be away long." She slid a quick glance at her mistress and moved on.

"Carriage ready, sir," Jack the footman called from the front door.

Helena started, and for a moment her face showed a flash of naked anxiety. She covered it quickly. "Yes, safe journey, Adam."

"Thank you."

She lowered her head. How badly he wanted to touch her.

It was ridiculously difficult to move his feet toward the door. Climbing into the carriage, he was keenly afflicted with this strange, most urgent desire to sweep that frail, willowy body into his arms and carry her up to her bedroom and make love to her in the middle of the blazing afternoon.

He would take his time, stroking her, stirring her....

The images this brought on nearly drove him over the brink of madness all the way to the inn where he was to meet the first post.

Chapter Twenty

The dog, Cain, was a bloody nuisance.

Helena squinted at him, her arms crossed, as she decided what was to be done with the mangy looking thing. Not that she would harm him, but he had to be taught to keep away from the house. Adam had spoiled him, feeding him right from the kitchen door that led to the vegetable garden. Now that dog was out there every day, barking like an Irish banshee.

Maddie never complained about him, and Helena suspected she kept the mutt well supplied. But then, she'd feed a band of demons if she thought it would please her beloved Mr. Adam.

Heaving a sigh, Helena decided to use logic to counteract this annoyance. If Adam had trained the dog to come to the kitchen door for food, she would train him otherwise. Gathering a large bowl of scraps from Maddie, she set off to the stables with Cain yapping at her heels.

"You'll get them, boy. You just have to learn you'll be fed out here, in the barn."

She passed Kepper, who grinned broadly at her. "He's a mite impatient," he said, indicating the dog.

"Enthusiastic, too." She glanced down at Cain's leaping

and bounding and other antics spurred by his delirious excitement. "You would think he'd never eaten before. He is as fond of food as his master."

She placed the bowl down near the barn door, and Cain dipped his head in, snatched a beef bone with scrap meat still clinging to it, and ran off.

"Probably gone to bury it," Kepper grunted. "Strangest thing, that. Why they want to put the thing in the ground to rot, I'll never know."

Then Cain was back.

"That was quick." Helena watched him take out another item from the bowl, this time a hunk of crust. Without eating it, he ran into the barn. "Odd dog. I suppose he wants privacy."

"I wonder..." Kepper started out after the dog. Helena followed.

Cain popped out of one of the empty stalls in the back and raced past them, back to the bowl.

"I'll be damned," Kepper said, then gruffly apologized for his rough language.

Helena waved away his explanations as she drew alongside him and stared into the stall. A lovely sad-eyed bitch was lying in a heap of straw. Cain's offerings were scattered around her.

She was either too finicky for such coarse gifts or just plain not hungry.

Helena stepped inside. "Is she sick? See the way she's panting? Her tongue is kind of lolling. Kepper, is she in pain?"

"Aye, she's hurting, all right. Come out of there, my lady. The bitch is getting ready to birth. See her belly? And her teats are all swollen. She's ready to go."

Cain came back in with another offering and plopped it down with the others. Noticing that his efforts were not being appreciated by the object of his devotion, he barked at her. It sounded astonishingly like a reprimand.

Helena bit back an unexpected giggle. Adam was always after her to eat, too.

Kepper tsked. "And there is the father of the brood, no doubt. Shame. Makes the litter worthless. Makes the bitch worthless once a mongrel gets to her like that. She was one of the last purebreds we have left. Mr. Mannion talked about breeding her to get the pack back up again."

"Look. Cain's worried about her." Helena was amazed. "He's bringing her food to cheer her up."

"She's not going to eat. She's got some work to do."

"Well, you better get him out of here. She hardly needs him about while she's trying to get those pups out. Kepper, do you know anything about helping a bitch along with her pups?"

The man was so flabbergasted he couldn't manage to get his mouth closed. "Miss, the bitch will be all right. We should go. It's not a pretty sight, and—"

"Oh, I'm not leaving her. Get me hot water and clean linens." At his look, Helena threw up her arms. "I feel like I should help."

The stable master seemed about to object, but then he broke out in a grin so broad it looked like it might split his weatherbeaten face. "Yes, my lady."

"And get this anxious father out of here."

She hunkered down next to the panting bitch and reached out a tentative hand. Her pat seemed to soothe.

"There, girl. It will be all right soon. Do you have a name, huh? I'll have to ask Kepper when he gets back. You're one of my father's old pack, aren't you? You stuck around when the others ran off." Settling more comfortably, Helena stroked the canine, and the dog looked up at her worshipfully. "That's right, I'm going to help you. If

Adam were here, he'd know what to do. But we're just going to get along without him. You know, I'm going to have a baby soon, too.''

Kepper arrived with the water and linens, complaining bitterly about Cain, who was evading him quite skillfully and refusing to go. In the end, Helena permitted him to stay as long as he didn't interfere. Again demonstrating that uncanny ability to understand, Cain stayed by the door, watching everything but never stirring once to make a nuisance of himself.

Five hours and four pups later, Helena stood and dried her hands as she surveyed the wriggling arrivals. "That's it, then," she announced.

"That last one was a problem," Kepper said, straightening. "I was a bit worried."

"The tiny thing was just twisted, that's all." Helena gazed fondly down at the four squirming pups, clambering over one another looking for a teat to suckle. Their mother was cleaning them, looking tired and serene as she presided over her new brood. "She'd eventually have worked it out. I only helped."

"Look at that one," Kepper said with a chuckle, indicating Cain. "Proud as any papa you'd care to meet."

"He is an extraordinary dog," Helena agreed. Drawn by their talk, Cain looked over at them and gave a single bark.

"He's thanking you!" Kepper declared.

Helena laughed and gathered up the soiled linens and put them into the empty bucket. "I'm sure everything will be fine now, and I fancy a good soak and a nap."

On the way to her room, she passed Kimberly. Helena ignored her look of astonishment, never considering the sight she must present. Thrusting the bucket heaped with dirty linens at her, Helena said, "Ask Mrs. Kent to have water boiled for my bath. And have the tub brought to my room.''

The Irishwoman sputtered, her tiny eyes flared wide with rage. ''What would yer mother say to see ye right now? Jes because yer married to trash doesn't mean ye should be actin' like it.''

''You've used my mother to make me afraid of you. Well, I'm not afraid of you anymore, Kimberly. My mother is…is dead, and I am your mistress now.''

Her heart beat wildly. It wasn't true that she was no longer afraid of her. She wanted it to be true, but she waited with trembling anticipation for what the belligerent servant would do next.

''Ye'll be sorry ye spoke to old Kimberly like ye did.'' She paused, an evil smile lighting her ugly, flat face.

Helena turned away, losing her nerve. The happiness of the pups' birth evaporated and she found herself wishing Adam were here. She had come to rely heavily on his strength. It was something of a shock to realize just how much.

''My business dealings are going much more satisfactorily than I had anticipated,'' Lord Rathford read, ''and I am thinking of traveling north for the Christmas holiday.''

The old man looked up from the bold, scrawling script. Adam Mannion's hand was as brash and unapologetic as was the man himself.

There was a quickening in his heart as he read over that last part to see if he had understood correctly. Yes. The devil take it—the man was coming for Christmas. Reading further, Rathford found his hope swelling.

''I am thinking often of Helena and wondering after her health. Mrs. Kent should watch for signs of her appetite weakening. She also might suggest daily exercise as this, I have found, has remarkable restorative powers.''

He was *worried* about Helena.

''I promised her I would write, but as she did not seem receptive to this, I have not done so. Perhaps you would be good enough to convey my regards to her.''

The palsy gripped him, shaking the page so violently Rathford could read no more. He put it down and reached for his glass.

The pain was increasing. The drink wasn't dulling much any longer.

Slowly he drew in a shaky breath and wondered if it were just the delirium of an old, dying man or if what he suspected could possibly be true. It was what he had hoped for but not dared to believe could happen. Could Mannion have developed true caring for his daughter?

The feeling that seized Rathford rivaled the pain, though it filled him with taut joy instead of the racking aches that sent him seeking bottle after bottle to provide relief. The doctor had given him laudanum, but the tincture tasted vile and made him feel ill. Lately, however, he had begun to think he might use it anyway. He was afraid. Afraid of the pain and of leaving his beautiful daughter without another soul to care for her.

He wasn't a gambling man, but he had gambled mightily on Adam Mannion. With his own death staring him squarely in the eyes, he'd grasped wildly at the one chance he had seen to provide her with the protection she would need when he himself was gone. And Mannion was a good man.

He winced, remembering the lies he had told. Despite his motivations, Adam had been scrupulously honest, and therefore had deserved no less than honesty in return, but Rathford just hadn't been able to take that chance. For his beloved Helena, he'd lie to the devil himself and trade his soul in the bargain to bring her back to the beautiful, vibrant woman she once was.

Helena had killed Althea, but she, too, had died that day at the inn. Althea's curse—still controlling her daughter even from the grave.

Not if he could help it. Before he died, he would see Helena happy. He'd see her laughing and ripe with child, and full of blissful, fulfilling life.

Adam Mannion could give all that to her. Mannion would. *He cared about her.*

Laying his head back, Rathford concentrated on that instead of the pain that was slowly, slowly leaving his consciousness as he drifted into drink-induced oblivion.

Adam Mannion cared about Helena, and everything was going to be all right.

"Tell us about her," demanded Delrich.

"Is she truly beautiful?" Urland inquired, leaning across the table.

Adam glanced around at the other patrons at White's, the premier gentleman's club in St. James. "Keep it down, fellows. I'll be strung up before I'll bandy my marriage about like so much gossip."

More softly, Urland urged, "Well, is she?"

"She's very beautiful," Adam admitted.

"And very rich?" Quinlan asked.

He ground his teeth together. "The reports of the Rathford fortune were not exaggerated."

"La! My good man, you are to be envied. Tell us how you won her."

"Well, after she tried to slam the door on my foot, I knocked her on her arse and demanded we be wed. Naturally, no sentient woman could resist such tactics, and we were bound together in holy matrimony as soon as the banns were read."

All four of them gaped at him.

Simpson said, "Really?"

Quinlan was irate. "Of course not, you dolt. No doubt Adam doesn't want it revealed how he cajoled and romanced the poor girl. God knows no woman can resist his charms once he turns them on to full capacity."

"Actually," Adam mused with a half smile, "the woman proved remarkably stalwart."

"She gave you a hard time, did she?" Delrich exclaimed, his face alight with his love for juicy details.

"Well, she isn't an idiot, Del," Adam snapped. He was irritated with the lot of them. Their routine of mischief and various and sundry pointless activities seemed suddenly arduous and completely devoid of attraction. "It wasn't difficult for her to grasp the fact that it was her fat purse that had me hieing off to the north country and proposing marriage to a complete stranger."

"Ah, God save you. An intelligent woman, eh? She sounds like a shrew."

He was genuinely offended. "Indeed not, although if that is the manner in which you define a girl who spots a fortune hunter when she sees one and lets him know she's got his game, than I cannot argue the charge."

"I can't believe you actually went through with it. It was such a wild idea. Only you, Mannion, could make it work, by Jove. Blast you, but you have a way with the women!"

Urland narrowed his eyes. "What exactly happened? You were up there a good long time, after all. I mean, did you seduce her, force her to compromise herself? Is that how you got her? What, Mannion? Give over."

"Nothing so tawdry." Not to say the thought hadn't occurred to him, Adam had to admit with a pang of shame.

"I spoke with her father, and he was amenable. She...she needed a bit more convincing."

The men chuckled knowingly. He scowled, shooting murderous looks to each one in turn.

"I don't know why you're so annoyed." Urland, the worst tempered one of the bunch, bristled. "We are merely curious. I mean, who cares, after all? It's not like you'll be having to see her again."

There was a tense pause before Adam said, "Actually, I am returning for Christmas."

Urland was indignant. "I thought you were coming to holiday at Heathgrange."

"She's...she's delicate. I'm concerned about her. She never eats any damn thing. There is this wretched nurse that is always hovering about her...." He trailed off, taking in their incredulous expressions. "What? What is it?"

The four exchanged stunned looks.

"Nothing," Urland said.

Delrich grinned. "Not a thing."

Quinlan chimed in, "Deal, Mannion. You have all of that lovely money and you owe it to us to give us a chance to take it from you."

Helena woke up, blinking away sleep to focus on the familiar shapes of her room. She was comfortable in her own bed. Sighing, she rolled over and fluffed her pillow.

The softest of hisses brought her eyes open again.

It sounded like a whisper.

She waited, hardly daring to breathe... There! There it was again.

She sat up and cocked her head, straining her ears. Her eyes scanned the darkness. Reaching for the bedside table for a faggot to light her candle, she knocked over her cup. She was fond of chocolate before bed and had one, liberally laced with nutmeg, in bed each night while she read a novel.

The heavy piece of crockery hit the floor with a thud. The sound, coming as it did in the stillness of the night, was huge.

She heard a shuffle. Sitting up, she listened. Was it her imagination, or was that retreating footsteps?

Managing to light the candle, she sat by its glow until her heart slowed to its normal rhythm. No other sounds came. After a while, she decided it must have been a nightmare.

She lay back down, but she didn't sleep again.

Chapter Twenty-One

The pups flourished and were frolicking within a few weeks' time. Helena sent a message to Chloe to bring her children round to see them, and it was a fine Wednesday afternoon when she arrived with Rebecca, ten, and Sarah, seven, the children of her husband's brother, whom she was raising as her own. In her arms she held Charles, her own son, who was just a year old.

"Are you certain you do not mind us invading you like this?" she asked with one of her infectious smiles.

"I invited you!" Helena declared with an easy laugh. "Come, girls, I want to show you the pups."

The girls were, she was tartly informed by Rebecca, partial to cats. They had two—one pet each—that lived in the nursery and ate cream from their tea saucers. They were spoiled rotten, Sarah said, chiming in happily.

Helena smiled at their busy chatter and held one of the puppies for young Charles, who stroked it very tenderly, with a look of awe on his face. "Isn't it adorable?" Chloe cooed, cradling the runt of the litter against her breast. "If Jareth wouldn't kill me, I'd take one." She looked up suddenly, as if a very unpleasant thought occurred to her. "Oh, Helena, they are not to be..." a glance at the girls assured her they were out of earshot, scampering after a rambunctious puppy "...*destroyed.*"

"Of course not. Why would you think that?"

Chloe raised her brows. "Oh, I am quite aware that many people do not think a life has worth unless it has a proper pedigree." She was referring to herself as much as the disenfranchised dogs. The world—especially her dour mother-in-law—had been scandalized when she'd married the Duke of Strathmere, because she was not of the proper social class.

Helena thought of another with the same lack of noble breeding, and yet Adam was the finest man she knew. "You should know me well enough to realize I would not feel that way."

"That is good. What has your father said? He cannot be happy to have one of his last bitches breeding mongrels."

Helena frowned. "Father doesn't hunt much anymore. He stays inside." Drunk for the most part, although she didn't say that.

"What a shame. Gerald is coming for Christmas and he wrote us how he was looking forward to bagging some small game."

"Adam likes to hunt. Perhaps he can take Father's place. He said he would be coming to Rathford Manor for the holiday."

"Yes. Adam will be excellent companionship." Chloe's knowing look made Helena blush and turn away. "We are very happy for you, Helena. Jareth especially. You know he always felt so bad about...well, everything."

"Nothing was his fault."

"Or yours. You saved my life. I will always love you for that."

Helena stood.

Chloe followed. "Why do you hate to acknowledge that

what you did was heroic? I know it must hurt you that your mother was ill, but she would have murdered two people if you had not stopped her.''

"It was a terrible thing to have to do," Helena admitted. "I—I've never spoken of it before. But…I think you are right. I'm just realizing, after all these years, that what I did…it…wasn't bad." She looked up, her eyes burning with questions. "Do you think my mother was ill?"

"Oui," Chloe said definitely. "Of course she was. It is the only explanation."

Helena shook her head. "You didn't know her as I did. It wasn't an illness that made her do all those awful things. It was the way *she was*. Always. Greed, drive, relentless ambition—they were a part of her." She broke off, turning away from the sympathy in Chloe's gentle eyes. "I don't think it was illness. I think some people just have an evil in them. She did. I don't think she ever really loved me. I was just a means for glory."

"Poor *petite*. I am so sorry you have suffered so. I wish I could do something to make it better."

Helena took Chloe's hands in hers. "You always tried so hard. I'm sorry I was so rude to you when you'd come to visit. I used to cry every time I sent you away. I wanted to accept your friendship, but it was too difficult, whenever I saw you, not to remember all the bad things that happened that day."

"I am pleased you have finally decided to let the past go." Chloe—who had never even attempted to master the reserve her title of duchess required—threw herself into Helena's arms. Taken aback at first, Helena returned the sisterly embrace.

Pushing her to arm's length, Chloe peered into Helena's face. "What made you change? Is it…oh, Helena! It is Mr. Mannion, *oui?*"

Blushing profusely, Helena shrugged and disengaged herself. "Chloe, I think I may be with child."

"It is so? Oh, Helena—that is wonderful news! I am so pleased for you, and it happened so quickly. It took Jareth and me the longest time to conceive Charles."

"What do you mean, it took a long time?"

"We tried for years to have a child. Surely you knew."

"Tried? You mean you didn't...that is...were you together?" She blushed. "You know."

"*Oui, mon ami,* of course we made love all the time. Didn't you say...?" Her eyes narrowed. "Why do you believe you are with child, Helena?"

Helena began to suspect she had made a terrible gaff. "Oh, Chloe, I don't know. My mother told me—" She broke off, covering her face with her hands.

Gently, Chloe peeled them away. "Helena, have you missed your monthly courses since the last time you were together?"

"No," she answered miserably.

"Then you are not with child, I am sorry to say. Sometimes it takes a great deal of...well, *trying.*" She smiled coyly. "But it can be very delightful, this trying, *oui?* If Mr. Mannion is coming home for Christmas, then he will have to do his best to get you with his child. It may take some time and some energetic lovemaking." She studied her companion and broke out in an eruption of giggles. "You should see the look on your face. *Mon Dieu,* you English are so *proper!*"

Helena had no idea what was so funny.

Chloe explained. "You don't look disappointed at all!"

Howard visited again, but claimed he had not seen Adam in the city. Helena was disappointed not to have any news. She looked forward to his return. He would be excited about the pups, she thought, as well as the new staff she had hired. The house looked so much better these days, although she still stayed very busy in the daily running of it. She was hardly a lady of leisure, but she began to enjoy long walks, often with Cain by her side. These she found cleansing, and she felt her spirit grow stronger with each passing day.

She felt as if she was just now awakening after a long, long sleep, and as soon as she had the thought, she laughed out loud. Adam had called her the Sleeping Beauty of Northumberland. What would he say, seeing her now?

There were only two spots of trouble. Her father seemed to be drinking more. He stayed in his study all the time now. Whenever she went to visit him, he seemed restless. She grew angrier each day he drowned himself in drink, and then she stopped going in altogether.

The other problem was the nightmares. As the dismal past receded from her daytime hours, it seemed to descend into the nights. She often woke chilled and perspiring at the same time, feeling mildly ill and knowing she had dreamed of that day at the inn, in that horrible room where her mother's blood had run crimson on the floorboards.

Helena did her best to shake off the tendrils of these disturbances and start each day with a positive view.

So different than before.

The weather grew frosty as the month passed and the holiday season grew nearer. Helena found herself counting the days until Adam's return. Even Kimberly's snide comments and evil glares couldn't dampen her enthusiasm.

She wondered if Adam thought of her, and if so, how often. She wondered when he would arrive, and if he were on his way already.

And then one day she was walking back from the stables

when he was suddenly there in front of her—a real flesh-and-blood man, not just memory, not just imagination, not just conjured from longing—looking dark and beautiful and taller than she remembered.

Chapter Twenty-Two

Adam wore that particular smile of his that crinkled his eyes and laid claim to every feature on his face. With his arms crossed over his chest and his feet braced apart, he regarded her with impish pleasure he took no pains to conceal.

Stopping in her tracks, she stared, holding her breath until she remembered not to. She let it out slowly, and as the air left her, she thought she might faint, her head felt so light. The urge to run into his arms with a great cry of joy was so hard to resist it left her body rigid and aching.

He raised a single brow in greeting. "Helena." Those deep brown eyes skated over her form, lingering enough in certain places to make her blush. "You look…absolutely wonderful."

She touched her hair, immediately thinking of a million reasons why this couldn't be so. She didn't take as much care with the sun as she should, so her fashionable pallor wasn't what it used to be. Having just come from a walk in the woods with Cain, she was certain her hair was mussed, and her dress was hardly the type one donned to entice a man. But it was one of her new ones, rather plain, but a pretty soft blue that tempered the iciness of her eyes.

At least that was what Mrs. Stiles had said, and she did have exceptional taste.

"Thank you," she managed to answer, correcting her posture and forcing the nervous hand to her side. "You, as well."

"What's that?"

She had meant he looked marvelous as well. He did. God, he looked so handsome. But she lost her courage to return the outrageous compliment. "I—it's good to see you, too, was what I meant to say."

"I heard you were out with Cain?"

"He's in the stables," she said inanely, pointing as if Adam didn't know the way.

His brown eyes were like liquid. "I heard he had a brood. Your father's not too pleased. The scoundrel." His lips twitched a bit.

She warmed at the half smile and countered, "He takes after his master."

He liked that. The laugh lines bracketing the sides of his mouth deepened. "You think so, do you? I hope you haven't taken it out on the poor creature."

"On the contrary. We've just returned from a brisk walk. He's excellent company." Too late, she realized that in light of her previous comment, she had just implied that *he* was excellent company. She blushed. "For a dog."

"Yes, well, sometimes that's the best sort of companion. Silent. Obedient." He cocked his head at her in a gesture that could only be flirtatious. "Loyal. When they roam, they always return. So, you and Cain, you've become friends, have you?"

It struck her how absurd it was to be conversing about a dog upon first seeing each other after so long a separation. It was as good a topic as any, she supposed, and was better than standing defenseless amid all of the tension crackling in the air. "Did you eat?" she asked in an effort to change the subject.

"No. I came straight to get you. Mrs. Kent said you were out here."

He had rushed out to see her? A tingling fluttered all the way up from the base of her spine to titillate the sensitive flesh at the nape of her neck, a feeling magnified by the way he kept looking at her. It was an expression she had once been accustomed to seeing on men's faces, but one she hadn't seen in a long time. Perhaps one she had longed to see on this particular face.

As if on cue, he said, "Really, Helena, you...you look...simply fabulous."

She locked her knees against the imminent possibility of their failure. "That is very kind of you to say so. Now, we should get you a decent meal. I remember well your...ah... appetite." She blushed and turned away, hoping he didn't pick up on the innuendo, knowing it was impossible he wouldn't.

He didn't mock her, however. "You know me too well."

She loved the way his eyes stared into hers, as if he were seeing everything without her having to explain or put any part of it into words. She said, "Come inside, then. I'll have Maddie fetch you some—"

His hand on her arm stopped her. "I've brought you something from London. Do you like surprises?"

"I...I don't believe I've had many surprises."

"It was supposed to be for Christmas." He reached inside his coat pocket to draw out a flat box. It was a jeweler's box, she saw, and her heart did a queer skid. "I'm terrible at waiting, however. Here, open it now."

She reached out for the gift slowly, apparently too slow for his liking. He withdrew the box, opened it himself and presented it to her.

"They are ear bobs," he announced, as if she couldn't see this for herself. She looked and saw two gorgeous clusters of stones, all varying shades of blue, from turquoise to azure. "I thought they'd look good with your eyes," he said. "You know, your eyes can be of these colors, depending on your mood." He looked at her doubtfully. "Oh, no."

"What?" she managed to query.

"They are darkening—your eyes, I mean. That is never good."

"No." She laughed at his troubled frown. "No, I assure you, it *is* good. I'm simply overcome."

He was pleased again. "Let's see them on you." But when she reached for the box, he was already wresting them from their hooks. Really, he was a most impatient man! She felt a rush of giddy joy come over her all of a sudden.

Adam frowned intently as he fiddled with the small article of jewelry. "How the devil—?"

"Let me," she said, reaching for it.

"No, I've got it." He didn't, but eventually he deciphered the clasp. "All right, come here." He stepped closer and tilted her head to the side. Warm fingers smoothed her hair behind the curve of her ear. She smelled the faint odor of soap on him, mingled with the musk from his horse. He must have ridden in, not taken the post or carriage. How like him. The indefinable scent that was *him* assailed her, sending her blood pumping in thick, rapid bursts.

"It goes like thus. I think," he murmured. Glancing up, she could see the sensuously curved mouth just in front of her. His strong white teeth pulled at his lower lip as his hands tried to unravel the feminine mysteries of applying an ear bob.

Helena started to smile. He leaned back and angled his

head, his brow furrowed in confusion as he tried valiantly. She found this inexplicably funny.

"Damn," he said softly, then he apologized. "This doesn't seem to be working."

She stayed obediently still. The brush of his ungloved hands against the tender flesh of her neck made her nervous, increasing the need to laugh, until she couldn't resist it. It exploded out of her.

He regarded her with grave puzzlement as she dissolved in a fit of giggles. She struggled to calm herself, but every time she nearly had herself under control, she'd only have to glance at his serious face and she'd be lost again.

She was bursting with happiness—that he was *here,* that he had brought her this gift, that he was being so solicitous and charming and absolutely *adorable* in his excitement. And in typically masculine fashion, he hadn't a clue what was so amusing.

He seemed a bit taken aback, perhaps even wounded, and she regretted her loss of control. Laying her hands on his shoulders, she struggled to get herself under restraint.

Then his hands slipped around her waist, pulling her tightly up against him. He wasn't put off by her outburst after all, she saw. His eyes weren't soft anymore. They were hard and intense and rich with something that sent shivers up her spine. Her laughing sputtered out.

The leashed hunger in his eyes curled her insides, made her fingers twitch with the sudden, irrepressible need to thread themselves in his wind-tousled hair. She felt ripples of sensation cascade through her with increasing intensity until she could stand it no more. With a whimper of resignation, she reached up and cupped the back of his head, pulling him down to her upturned mouth.

Without a shred of shame, she fastened her mouth onto

his and kissed him. He allowed her to have her way until she relaxed her grip and made to pull away.

Surging forward, he pulled her against him once again and took charge. With a slant of his head to one side, he twisted to the other so that her head was tucked nicely against the firm cushion of his arm. Trapped comfortably, she was then assailed with the exquisite persuasion of his mouth tenderly reacquainting itself with hers, possessing and enticing, sensuously playing until her nerves tingled and hummed. His tongue touched, then slipped through her softly parted lips. Gentle at first, it quickly became frantic and fierce, parleying their desire into a froth of uncontrolled need.

He stopped without warning. Her eyes fluttered open to find him staring off over her left shoulder. Drugged from his kiss, she didn't understand why he had ceased such lovely torment.

His face was hardened. His hands came to her shoulders, firmly gripping her as he set her away from him. She resisted weakly, wanting his closeness. Then he said, "I don't believe we've met," and it finally occurred to her that he had ended the kiss because they were no longer alone.

"Sorry," a strange male voice said. "I seem to have a knack for getting into awkward situations."

Whirling, Helena found herself facing a man she vaguely remembered, although full recognition eluded her. The ruddy face, the thick frame, the droll, sarcastic tone all tugged at her memory.

The man continued. "My cursed lack of manners, I suppose, but I don't see how it could have been helped this time. I just rode over for a quick hello, and there you, ah, *were.*" His merry eyes slid from Adam to a breathless Helena. "Hello, Lady Helena."

Yes, she remembered now. It was Gerald Hunt, Jareth's

cousin. Straightening, Helena took the time to pull her dignity into place. It was no small task, considering the circumstances. "Hello, Gerald. I'm afraid we didn't hear you."

"Understandable." He grinned, and although he was rubbing in the awkwardness of the moment, he did it with a twinkle in his eye.

Since meeting Gerald when she was being courted by Jareth Hunt, she had found him to be a strange man. He seemed intent on presenting himself as a scoundrel, but he was much too decent a person to convince anyone for long. She found she liked him despite herself, and his unconvincing show of suavity was more endearing than impressive.

Gerald, like her father, loved to hunt. Whenever he was visiting the duke and duchess, which he did several times a year, he rode over to arrange a run with her father.

Helena introduced him to her husband, and the two men exchanged a firm, assessing handshake. It was clear Adam was not going to be quick to forgive Gerald's intrusion, and Gerald was doing his smirking best to appear impertinent. Not a good beginning to a friendship.

"Have you been to see my father yet?" Helena asked.

"Just on my way in to do that now. How is the old boy these days?"

Helena couldn't keep the tightness from her voice. "Quite well." It was a blatant lie. Thankfully, Adam didn't say anything to contradict her.

"Well, I'll be getting on in, then," Gerald said, his eyes dancing. He added, "I'll do my best to finagle a dinner invitation, so perhaps I'll see you then."

Left in awkward silence after he swaggered away, Helena cast Adam a tentative glance from beneath her lashes, to which he gave a shrug and laughed. "We are married, after all."

"That is no excuse to behave disgracefully in public," she retorted. His eyebrows jerked up at her tone, which had sounded disturbingly like her mother's. That jolted her and, disconcerted, she turned on her heel and began to walk away.

"Helena," Adam called.

She paused and turned.

He held out the jewelry box, in which he had replaced the ear bobs. "Do you want this?"

"Of course," she snapped, reaching her hand out. "I'm so sorry."

He held it out of her grasp until she was forced to take a few steps closer. Snatching her chin in his fingers, he held her fast until she lifted her gaze to his. "*I* am sorry if you were embarrassed. We should make an effort to keep our disgraceful behavior private in the future. I would suggest frequent venting of these bothersome feelings, and since there's no time like the present, it may perhaps be best if tonight we begin the, uh, disciplinary process."

My God, he was suggesting he come to her bed. And he was doing it in such an amusingly charming way that all she could do was stare. Her heart lodged firmly in her throat, preventing any speech. Her brain became crowded with memories of his touch, of his body, of what they had done, and her flesh began to prickle.

The corner of his mouth curled in the most rougish manner and his thumb brushed her cheek casually before he released her and offered his arm. "Now, don't be angry with me," he prodded. "I've just returned home and a quarrel so soon after my arrival would be downright unwelcoming."

Of all the incredible things he had said in this short period, this was the one that stuck with her the longest. She kept recalling it as the day wore into evening, going over his exact words and marveling that he had, indeed, referred to Rathford Manor as his home.

She wondered if it had just been an oversight, or if he had truly meant it.

Chapter Twenty-Three

Gerald Hunt did stay for dinner. By then his devilish mien was slipping enough that Helena was able to relax and enjoy his companionship. He flirted outrageously with her, which she feared might anger Adam. But her husband tolerated the flagrant compliments and fawning attention paid her, perhaps sensing how harmless the chubby bachelor was.

The topic of hunting dominated the conversation and Adam's remaining reserve for their guest was swept away. By the time Helena left the three men to their afterdinner indulgences, they were all hotly debating the glories of the traditional fox hunt.

Sighing, she made her way upstairs. With herself as the only woman at the table, she might as well retire. Not to mention that she was as anxious to go to her bedroom to await Adam as a person could be.

As soon as she was in her room, she dismissed the girl she was training as her maid and sat alone at her dressing table. Surveying herself critically in the mirror, she noted her hair had improved since she'd been tending it more closely. Her eyes sparkled back at her, holding all the secrets of a woman in love—

She paused, sliding over that last thought again.

In love?

Was she in love with Adam?

The answer came readily and with a calm sense of self-assurance she would have never anticipated. Of course she loved him. She loved, and suddenly the beauty of that filled her with a flood of happiness.

She stared back at herself, noticing how her eyes were bright with the secret knowledge. Their brilliant color reminded her of what Adam had said, about how they changed color according to her mood.

When she had arrived in her room this afternoon, she had tried on the ear bobs several times. She had a sudden urge to see them again. She fetched the box out of the wardrobe and brought it back to the dressing table. Maybe she would wear them tonight. She had not done so for dinner because she had wanted to wear her most flattering dress, and that one was, alas, a pale peach that would have clashed hopelessly with the blue stones. But she had a delicate peignoir set that was a soft sea green and a perfect foil for the variety of blues.

She donned the lace-trimmed nightgown and slipped on a set of matching mules. Undoing her hair, she let it fall, brushing it out in long strokes until it gleamed. Then she opened the box slowly and reached for the ear bobs.

They were gone.

She frowned, blinking in confusion. She had put them away this afternoon. Thinking of every possibility, she searched her dressing table, got down on her hands and knees and examined the floor, turned her wardrobe inside out, all to no avail.

Panic set in and she wondered if someone could have stolen them. That made no sense, however, since she owned far more valuable pieces that were still in her jewel box.

An awful thought occurred to her. What if Adam asked to see her in them? It would seem as if she had cared nothing for his thoughtfulness if she admitted she had misplaced them. This was intolerable, since the complete opposite was true.

The sound of the latch on the door brought her quickly to her feet. A moment later, Adam entered. He stood for a moment, framed in the doorway. Helena rose.

His eyes narrowed. His mouth curled and he shut the door.

Adam opened his eyes the following morning to find himself still in Helena's bed. His immediate reaction was to reach for her. He found the place beside him empty. Lifting his head, he surveyed the room. Empty. He let his head fall back.

His body felt drained. Last night he had made love to his wife, just as he had dreamed of doing since the morning he had left her. He hadn't realized how much he had anticipated holding her in his arms again, sampling her particular blend of strength and fragility that made him feel protective and proud all at once. He could have loved her all night, except he hadn't wanted to push her too far. It still amazed him that she not only tolerated his plebian touch, but seemed to enjoy it.

Now he was fully awake, and fully aroused, and wondering where the devil his lover had gone to. It was about time Helena was initiated into the pleasures of making love in the daylight, he was thinking.

No sounds told him she was close by, so eventually he rose and resolutely put the idea from his mind. As he dressed, however, his body kept reacting to random snippets of memory from the previous night, and he was in a sorry state all over again. His mood wasn't dampened, however, and it was with a jaunty smile that he sauntered into the dining room less than three-quarters of an hour later.

Helena was there, as he'd hoped she'd be. She looked radiant. When he had seen her yesterday, he had been struck with how she had continued to blossom while he was gone. Her figure was beginning to fill out, her cheeks flushed prettily and the spirit in her eyes made them sparkle at him.

Those eyes had inspired the impulsive purchase of the ear bobs he had presented her with. He still hadn't seen them on her, he recollected. He'd ask her to model them for him the next time they were alone.

Which was something his nimble mind was already trying to maneuver as he took his seat. "Good morning," he said.

"Good morning." Her gaze skittered away from his. He grinned, knowing the reason for her discomfort. Last night, they had shared no small degree of intimacies. By the look of her today, she was experiencing a pinking of embarrassment at facing him. He wished he could take her in his arms and murmur reassurances in her ear.

The presence of his father-in-law checked that impulse. Choosing a safe topic, Adam took up the conversation begun last night after Helena had retired. Gerald, himself, and Rathford, all avid huntsmen, were planning to go out on a hunt. Adam planned to use Cain, to the ridicule of the other men. He had a guess that despite the dog's wretched bloodlines, his uncanny intelligence would make him an excellent tracker. Rathford scoffed at the boast, insisting that a dog's nose was in its breeding. Of course, Adam took exception to the snobbish attitude. He felt a kinship with the mongrel, being of no particular pedigree himself, and took it as a cause of honor to redeem the lowly born in a contest with the aristocratic snobs.

"Think you'll be riding today?" Lord Rathford asked with a twinkle in his eye. "It may be you could use the practice."

Adam grinned good-naturedly at the goading comment. "I can always do with a turn in the woods. Learn the lay of the land, so to speak."

"Take that worthless mongrel out with you, too, and see what you can teach him."

"Father!" Helena exclaimed, shocked at his rudeness.

Adam caught her eye and winked, signaling the competition between them was a friendly one. "You've offended Helena with your disparaging remarks about Cain. I'm afraid she's grown rather fond of us mongrels."

Their gazes held. In those few moments, time stood still and every flaming moment of the previous night came back to him, before she grabbed a tureen that had been set on the table and offered it to him. "Kippers?" she inquired, her eyes as innocent as a child's. He hiked his eyebrows at her, impressed that she could look so guileless when he knew damned well her thoughts had reflected his.

She, however, knew the persuasive power of his legendary appetite. And he loved kippers. He took the covered bowl and doled some out on his plate. Another dish followed. He peered inside. It was creamed beef. He ladled out a generous portion onto a few pieces of toast. Breakfast was a feast at Rathford Manor. Come to think of it, every meal was, and he enjoyed it fully.

Something caught his eye as he spread the sauce. Taking up his fork, he gingerly probed the suspicious mass, which appeared to be…an ear bob? One of the ones he had given Helena yesterday. It lay right now on his plate, covered in cream sauce.

Hooking it in a fork tine, he lifted it off his plate. "Helena?"

She looked up. "What is that?" Looking closer, her face registered shock when she recognized the object. "What…it can't be. They are in my room."

"Apparently not. Unless there are three of them instead of two." Taking his napkin, he wiped it clean and handed it to her. "Did you lose it?"

She stared at the piece of jewelry in her hand. "I don't understand. I put it in the box…yesterday."

So far, he thought the incident only slightly intriguing. He supposed the explanation would be that the thing had been loosely fastened and slipped off somehow when Helena had passed him the dish. But he saw now that she wasn't wearing the other one. It seemed rather a reach to think she'd lost both of them so early in the day. Besides, she insisted they hadn't left her room.

And then there was that little hitch in her voice. That was what really got his hackles up.

Lord Rathford interrupted. "Jewelry in the dishes?" He chuckled. "What's gotten into Maddie?"

Adam forced his voice to remain light. "Perhaps she's run out of spices."

"The devil you say," Rathford grumbled, and went back to his eggs with a shake of his head.

Adam glanced back at Helena. She stared at the piece in her hand. "How did it get in the food, Adam? And where is the other?"

Snatching up the tureen, she fished through the kippers, then went to the salver that kept the scrambled eggs warm. She froze for a moment and then drew out the mate.

"Someone's idea of a joke," he offered, taking it up to inspect it.

The look on Helena's face was stricken. "This is not funny," she said.

"I agree. But someone's sense of humor may be—"

"No." She set her jaw and gave a quick shake of her head. "It is cruel. Whoever did this didn't mean to amuse."

It sounded so far-fetched, to go through so much trouble just to annoy her, or him. "Forget it," he said, dropping it back into her hand. "As long as you've got them back, don't give whoever did this the satisfaction of allowing it to disturb you."

"I can't help it."

He wished she wouldn't look so worried. It was a prank, albeit a bad one.

"What say I go along with you," Rathford said loudly.

Startled, Adam turned toward him. "Pardon?"

"On that ride. It may be these old bones might need some practice. Don't want you getting an edge."

"Oh. Yes." He had forgotten about the ride. Suddenly, he didn't feel like going. There was something troubling Helena, something deeper than a joke gone sour. Her father, though sober so far this morning, was oblivious to the tension.

Rathford waved his fork imperiously. "Finish up, then, pup. Eat your fill and let's get going." Glancing conspiratorially at his daughter, he winked and added, "That is, if you've finished fishing my daughter's jewelry out of the beef—a peculiar game, child, and one that could cost a man a tooth if he wasn't looking closely at his plate."

Helena paled as her father chuckled and attacked the rest of his breakfast with gusto. Adam felt for her, but he was certain Rathford had no idea of the effect of his words.

Come to think of it, he wasn't at all certain himself why it upset her so.

Chapter Twenty-Four

"I know what you did." Helena squared off against Kimberly as soon as the servant closed the door to her bedchamber. "How dare you meddle in my belongings?"

The older woman held nothing back as she swung around to face her mistress. Her mannish body brooked no nonsense, nor did the arrogant set of her face. Her frizzled red hair stuck out willy-nilly from a limp mobcap and her small eyes gleamed with challenge. "I'm sure I'm not knowin' what yer talkin' about."

"I'm not interested in a battle with you, Kimberly. I don't need to be convinced of your guilt, I already am. It was a stupid trick and I will not tolerate you violating my privacy."

Helena was rather surprised at herself. After years of disrespect from this servant, it took a few pieces of inexpensive jewelry to get her to declare her emancipation. But the ear bobs were a gift. From Adam.

And with the thoughtful gesture, he had given her something more. Attention, notice. For *her*. How odd that it would mean so much to her. She'd never lacked for attention. In fact, she'd drowned in it. Always she'd been attended to, critiqued, instructed by her mother. She'd been complimented and fawned upon by hopeful, and ultimately thwarted, suitors, and had endured jealous glares from female rivals and their mamas. But this small notice, that the color of her eyes changed according to her mood, was more meaningful, more fortifying than all that combined.

The servant's eyes flashed. "I didn't take any ear bobs. I didn't know anything about 'em.''

"I am fully aware you make it your business to know *every*thing about *every*one in this house. Information is your weapon. You've used it to control me for years."

"Information," Kimberly echoed. "It is indeed a valuable thing, eh? I'm wondering what yer husband would do with…certain…information."

"You evil old creature," Helena exclaimed before she could stop herself.

Being reminded of her old sin had the power to stall Helena's show of fearlessness. However, she willed herself not to back down. "I do not want you in my bedroom ever again. If I find out you've disobeyed this order, or if I even suspect it, you will be dismissed."

The defiance in Kimberly's eyes communicated her conviction that Helena would not dare. Helena herself didn't know if she would. She wanted to believe in herself, but her fledgling courage didn't come from herself, but from Adam. Knowing love, feeling it alive and pulsing and brilliant in her heart for this man with his easy smile and unassuming manner, gave her something she had not ever possessed on her own.

But if he were to learn of her past, would he still gift her with pretty jewelry and bold, romantic flattery? Would he still hold her in his arms and bring her body alive with glorious passion?

Kimberly's face turned sly, as if she could smell indecision like curls of invisible smoke in the air. Picking up the ear bobs Helena had placed on the dressing table, she huffed with scorn. "He brings ye baubles bought with yer own money."

Helena snatched them out of her hand. Kimberly sneered and gave an ugly laugh. "He loves yer money, not ye, and he'll show kindness only to keep the golden goose content."

With a cry, Helena pushed Kimberly away. "Get out of my room!"

Smirking, Kimberly nodded. "As ye wish."

Helena watched her leave, then went to her dressing table. White knuckled, her hands gripped the edge. She stared at her reflection, then down at the ear bobs.

Bought with her money. It was true.

She knew she was foolish to allow anything Kimberly had said to take root inside her, but she had spoken truth. Adam had not married her out of anything close to affection. He hadn't even pretended it was so.

He'd never spoken a word of anything even close to love.

It was true he was a kind man, even a good man in some ways, for all his faults. He desired her, but that meant nothing. He'd bedded her out of simple lust, no mean feat for a man as virile as he. It meant nothing other than a night's pleasure.

Of course. Of course, she must remember the facts were so plain, so indelibly clear. She didn't need vindictive Kimberly to point this out to her. She should know better.

Her mother had taught her better.

When Helena began to feel ill one day the following week, she immediately thought of the possibility that she had conceived. Now that she was clearer on the specifics of how it worked, she knew the frequency with which she and Adam came together made it likely.

Her womanly courses started within a few days, and her hopes were dashed. The sickness increased along with a heavy dose of grief. She felt weak and nauseous most of the day, and head-splitting aches made getting out of bed impossible.

The village surgeon was of the opinion that these maladies were the result of poor blood. He called the leech and she was bled. The nightmares, which had so obligingly receded when Adam had come home, returned. She was afraid to sleep. She didn't eat.

Adam's concern knew no bounds. He talked of bringing surgeons in from York, but Helena said she didn't want any more bleedings or purgings. She pleaded so piteously that he relented, although it drove him to near madness to see how frail she had become in just a matter of days. He had never felt so frustratingly helpless, so insanely worried in all his life.

Then she began to recover and he thought the crisis had passed.

The wind blew cold in December in this part of England. It moved the snow into immense drifts. They covered the landscape like water, filling in gullies and concealing everything under the flat, dry, crystalline surface. Adam liked the view. It made everything appear different, obscured by the blanket of white—smoother, filling in the imperfections. The wintry fairyland was the most beautiful thing he had ever seen, Adam decided.

The thought surprised him. He was actually growing fond of this godforsaken north country.

It was warm here by the fire. He took another sip of the rum drink Mrs. Kent had brought him and continued to stare out the window. His brow was furrowed in worry, and his thoughts, although calmed somewhat by the scenery, were vaguely troubled.

Helena's recent illness had him uneasy, but she was recovering well. He shouldn't be worried, but he was.

He sighed. At least she was on the mend, and soon she'd be as good as—

Was that smoke? He looked harder at the scene in front of him. Out over the back meadow lay the stables. He could have sworn he had seen smoke rising.

Yes! There it was—ugly black smoke barely noticeable before the wind whipped it away. "Fire!" he yelled, racing out of the room. He yelled for the head footman. "Jack! Jack! Call the staff. Fire in the stables."

Through the kitchens, he shouted, stopping to grab Maddie and round up her assistants, getting them started with gathering cook pots for water. The scullery maids he sent off for the grooms, who were taking their midday meal in the servants' hall. Someone was dispatched to get Lord Rathford.

By the time they were gathered in the front hall, he already had donned his boots and redingote. "Let's go," he commanded, and they set off.

The snow made the going difficult. It was hip high at some spots, and they had to wade through. Adam's heart was pounding with both the effort of his movements and the panic blooming in his chest as they drew closer and he saw the boiling smoke spewing from the roof increase. He was thinking of the horses—Kepper, too! Where the devil was the man? Was he safe?

Adam tucked his chin in and strode on. He remembered Cain and his bitch and their pups, and gnashed his teeth at his slow progress.

The wind buffeted him, seeming to lift him up and carry him down the slope. The drift was thick here. He stumbled, went down on one knee, so the snow was up to his chest. He got up and pressed on. Behind him, the men who had come with him labored.

He reached the doors and flung them open. Heat hit him, knocking him back a step or two. The sound of the fire and the scream of the wind was deafening. Fire and wind—it was a bad combination. It would spread the flames fast within the building, although the thick blanket of snow should, hopefully, keep it isolated to the stables.

He shouted orders to the men, directing them to get the horses out. He ran to the unused stall where Cain and his brood slept.

It was empty. Looking around, he ran his hands through his hair in frustration. Cain was smart. He would have gotten the pups out. Adam raced down the aisle and began flinging open doors to the empty stalls. He had to be sure.

The thick smoke stung his lungs. He heard the shouts of the men as they yanked and pulled on terrified horses. The neighing was terrible. One of the beasts bolted past Adam, its head covered with a man's coat. Thankfully, it was heading for the open doors. A manservant chased after, smacking the panicked gelding on the rump to get it going.

"All out, sir!" Jack shouted.

"Kepper—is he safe?"

Jack nodded. "He was in the back. Out cold. We found him, sir, not to worry."

Drunk? Or was he hurt? Adam didn't have time to ask. "There were a litter of pups in here. Did you see them?" He could barely get the words out, his throat was so raw from the heat and the acrid smoke.

"No, sir. The water line is going. I'm off to help there."

"Let's go," he yelled, and the two men joined the effort to save the now evacuated building.

Adam selected a few men from the water brigade and

began packing the middle of the building with snow. They filled troughs with the white stuff and carted it in. The heat was intense, so the snow melted in moments. The resulting moisture created a barrier to slow the fire down. It might be possible to save at least part of the stables, they hoped. Up into the rafters they climbed, to drench everything in sight.

On the other side of the barn and outside, the men were having some success. The conflagration seemed to be lessening. Halfway down a loft ladder, Adam paused to catch his breath and survey the situation. If they had indeed weakened the intensity of the flames, they might just have a chance.

He saw something then, outside, on the edge of the woods. "Who is that?" he called down, pointing to the shape that wavered in the billowing smoke. Someone shouted an answer, something Adam couldn't hear. Another man, one of the footmen, was already moving toward the figure, gesturing wildly.

In a gust of wind, the smoke cleared, and he got a good view of the person. Adam started. Helena! She was dressed in a loose robe tied snugly at her waist. What did she think she was doing here, dressed like that?

But she was just standing there, staring off in another direction, as if unmindful of the tragic drama going on only a short distance away. What was the matter with her?

Adam jumped down, landing in the soaked hay littering the stable floor, and ran out the door toward her.

Chapter Twenty-Five

The door leading to the back gardens burst open and Adam came in, startling Mrs. Kent. In his arms, he held the unconscious body of his wife.

He stood in the entranceway, his eyes wild, his hair plastered to his head, dripping wet. His lips were drawn back in a snarl. Feet braced apart, he stood motionless for a moment when he saw the housekeeper.

His voice was sharp, urgent. "Get hot water, quickly, up to your mistress's room. She's drenched to the bone and frozen solid."

"My God!" Mrs. Kent lifted a trembling hand to her lips. "What happened?"

"She was down by the stables," he said, striding purposefully across the floor.

The housekeeper followed on his heels, beside herself with worry. "Was she in the fire?" she squeaked. "She isn't harmed, is she?"

"I don't think so. I have to get a better look at her." Helena's hair dragged on the floor as Adam took the stairs two at a time. "Please hurry, Mrs. Kent."

The housekeeper ran to the kitchen.

Upstairs, Adam laid Helena gently in the bed. She wa

very still. Too still, and he found himself fumbling against her clammy skin, desperately seeking a pulse. Ignoring the stabbing beat of his heart, he willed himself to remain calm.

Helena's eyes fluttered open. He leaned forward, his voice urgent. "Helena, it's me. Adam. Can you hear me?"

"Adam?" Her voice was so desperately faint. The slightest of furrows creased her smooth brow.

"What the devil were you doing out there? You were half frozen to death." He began undoing the buttons down the front of the dressing gown. There were a cursed lot of them and the damned thing was made of wool. "Why are you all wet?"

"The fire, Adam," she said weakly. He could barely hear her. "Cain..."

"Cain is out," he said, working to undo her buttons. He hoped it were true about the dog. "The pups, too."

"The horses..."

"All safe," he replied. The dressing gown was giving him a hell of a time. "What happened to you, Helena?"

"I saw the smoke."

She was out of her head, he realized, and gave up trying to get any information. Tugging at the garment, he finally got the thing open and began the arduous task of pulling the thick, wet wool over her shoulders. It clung to her skin, and it was very heavy. He grabbed bunches of her skirts and yanked, trying to work the garment down that way.

That was when he saw something fall out of her pocket. He reached down and picked it up. As he uncurled his fingers, the breath whooshed out of him in a rush.

Faggots. She had faggots in her pocket.

Mrs. Kent came in and he shoved the incriminating things in the back of his trouser waistband, then adjusted his coat. "Help me get these clothes off. They are wet and I can barely budge them."

"Dear Lord," Mrs. Kent exclaimed, putting down her burden and rushing to the bedside. Taking over, she made short shrift of the nightdress. "Go get the tea," she said over her shoulder. "It's on the tray I brought."

Mrs. Kent had Helena stripped and dressed in a fresh night rail and tucked under the covers by the time he had poured the water with shaking hands and steeped the tea, then fixed it with cream and sugar. He wasn't sure that was how she liked it, but damn it, he'd make sure she drank it.

Mrs. Kent was toweling Helena's dirty hair dry. "Do you have any idea how this happened?"

Adam shook his head. Helena's head lolled and her heavy-lidded eyes looked at him dully.

"Is she drunk?" Mrs. Kent asked quietly.

"I don't think so. Her speech is clear and there's no smell of anything. She does seem drugged, though. Does she...do you know if she's apt to use laudanum or anything else?"

"We've nothing in this house like that. She's not acted this way before. Of course, she has been ill. It could be a fever."

Adam didn't think that explanation adequate, but he had no other. He sat on the edge of the bed and brought the tea to Helena's lips. "Drink this, love."

She made a slight grimace and turned her face away. He wasn't going to be discouraged. "Come, Helena, drink it. It will warm you."

Mrs. Kent pushed his hand away and in one smooth motion brought the towel she had wrapped around Helena's hair to her mistress's face just in time. The sound of retching was muffled.

"She is ill," Mrs. Kent said with concern. "Perhaps the ague, and right after the other illness, it could have her disoriented. Send Jack for the surgeon."

A thin arm came up to flail somewhat wildly. Helena didn't turn her head. Adam understood. She was trying to reach out to him, to keep him from doing what Mrs. Kent had suggested.

Indecision tore at him. He knew Helena feared and despised the frumpy surgeon, and Adam was inclined to agree with her. The man seemed a sadist, always wanting to let blood or scourge the body to release the ill humors, he said. To Adam, it seemed only to weaken Helena. Her improvement had come when he had banished the stupid man from the house.

"Let her rest," he said at last. "If she's not better by evening, we'll call him."

Tenderly, Mrs. Kent wiped Helena's sweat-beaded face with the corner of the towel. "Poor thing," she muttered. "Maybe she can take some of that tea now, Mr. Mannion."

"Helena?" he asked, proffering the cup.

Helena sat back, managing to say in a squeaking voice, "Please, no."

"All right." He put the cup aside, taking her hand. "When you're ready, I'll make you a fresh cup. Go to sleep now."

She nodded, a slight bob of her head, and closed her eyes.

"I'll stay with her," Mrs. Kent volunteered.

"No. I will."

"You've got to get back to the fire, sir. I can sit with the mistress."

"It was well under control when I left to bring your mistress home." He looked down at his sleeping wife and fought the grip of anxiety that twisted in the pit of his belly. "Just...just stay for a moment while I go change. I'm stained with soot and I've gotten mud all over the carpets."

"Don't rush. I'll be here."

Adam exited the room, reaching behind him as he headed down the hall to his room. Extracting the pack of faggots, he gazed at them thoughtfully. There was an explanation. He'd ask Helena when she was feeling better.

Yet what answers could she give to put this matter satisfactorily to rest?

He thought of the ear bobs, and of her inordinate nervousness when they had turned up in their food. As he stripped off his stained clothes and quickly washed in the cold water still in the commode, he knew he had to accept the fact that something was very, very wrong with Helena.

Adam's worst fears were realized when a chill set in and Helena began to shiver. She was sweating profusely, yet calling for more blankets, a bigger fire. She began to speak nonsense, and he knew she was having delirium. He sat by her side, wiping her brow, holding her hand. At one point, he lay beside her and wrapped her in his arms, giving her his warmth.

The feel of her trembling body increased his terror. She could die if pneumonia set in. He listened anxiously to her breathing.

Mrs. Kent came up the following morning and he went to wash and change. On impulse, he ran downstairs for a moment to speak to Jack, the head footman, about the stables. He knew that the fire was out, and the damage must have already been assessed. Jack told him that the north end was decimated. Lord Rathford had already put out the order to rebuild.

Adam was more concerned with Kepper. He learned the groomsman was recovering. He had been taken in by one of the crofters to be tended by his wife. Adam was glad he wasn't in the hands of the village surgeon. He'd take folk medicine over that barbaric mule anyday.

The footman also told him that Cain and his brood had been found late yesterday afternoon and had been allowed into one of the cellars on a temporary basis. Adam went to check on them immediately, coming upon a maid who had brought them their breakfast and to cuddle with the pups.

Gesturing to the canine brood, she said, "I hope that's all right with you, sir. We didn't know where else to put them. It seemed cruel to turn them out in the snow, especially the wee ones."

"Of course it is. I would have done it myself," Adam assured her. They had been given a cozy corner where straw was heaped into a decadently plush bed. There, like a horde of four-legged princes, the fat pups lounged in luxury, tended by their content mother.

Cain held nothing back in his pleasure to see Adam, who gave him a good rubdown in return.

"You've taken good care of them," Adam said, examining each of the dogs closely for injuries. The bitch and the pups didn't have a mark on them, but Cain was streaked with soot. Grimacing at the odor of smoke that clung to him, he suggested the maid get a manservant to see to the dog's bath. Then he looked at his watch.

He'd been gone over an hour. Helena was probably sleeping, however, so he decided to go see Kepper.

The man was awake and propped up on a straw pallet when Adam was let into the small dwelling. "Mr. Mannion, sir!" he exclaimed in surprise.

Adam pulled up a stool. "Glad to see you are well, good man."

"Got me a headache near to split my skull, but other than that I'm not harmed."

"Did you fall?"

"I don't rightly recall, sir, and that's the truth of it. I'm thinking I heard something and turned around. But I wouldn't know the difference if I was whacked or if I walked straight into one of them low beams. It wouldn't be the first time I've done it, though not this bad."

Adam frowned, rubbing his fingers thoughtfully along his chin. "You said you heard something?"

"Barn noises. The horses acting up."

"Could something have gotten them stirred up?"

Kepper's eyes narrowed. "Could have. What are you thinking, sir?"

"Your mistress was found by the barn during the fire." Adam bowed his head and took in a deep breath. "Do you remember seeing her before you were hit?" Kepper raised his eyebrows and Adam amended with a lopsided smile, "Or walked into a beam?"

"No, sir. I didn't see the mistress. She's all right, isn't she?"

The question dammed emotion in Adam's throat. "I hope so. Kepper…if you recall anything else, have someone fetch me right away."

"Certainly, sir."

"And get some rest. We need you."

The groomsman chuckled. "Right-o. I'll get to mending straightaway."

Adam added with a grin, "There's plenty of work, so don't think I'll be letting you get off easy because you're wounded."

They said their farewells and Adam returned to the house to find good news. Helena's fever seemed to have broken, and she had awakened to take some weak broth. Mrs. Kent was ecstatic, and Rathford, who was hovering anxiously in the hall, pressed his clasped hands to his forehead as if in silent thanks.

Adam went to her side. She was sleeping again, but this time peacefully. Her chest rose and fell softly, and there was a touch of color in her cheeks that hadn't been there before. He cursed his luck. He'd been by her side from the moment he'd brought her home, yet she had regained consciousness when he had stepped out for just a few hours.

He sat for a long time. And he thought about those damned faggots and why she had had them in her pocket.

Chapter Twenty-Six

Sometime in the night, Helena raised her head off the pillow and peered at the window.

It was dark. She couldn't say what had awakened her. She felt strange. Achy in her shoulders, her arms. Her legs felt heavy and it was difficult to move them. She must have the ague, she thought.

Her head felt fuzzy as well. Thoughts came sluggish and slow, and she had difficulty perceiving her surroundings. She knew she was in her room; she recognized that much. But there was this pressing certainty that something quite specific had disturbed her dreams, though she couldn't think of what it was.

Then she heard it again. Someone was here—speaking to her.

Turning her head on the pillow, she listened. Was that a human sound whispering? It sounded like someone calling her name.

Fear curled a thin thread from her stomach to her chest before she quelled the reaction. It was ridiculous; she had nothing to fear, safe in her room as she was.

She was disinclined to worry about the sound. Sometimes night played tricks on the senses. It was the quiet, the utter darkness. It made one feel isolated, as if the nearest living being were fathoms away and all manner of unliving beings were right at one's elbow.

Fanciful stuff she usually had no time for. It must be the fever. She let her eyes close, which meant allowing the leaden lids to have their way. She fell back asleep almost immediately.

Adam roused himself out of the chair, wincing at the pain that shot from his shoulders to his spine. Damn, the blasted divan was like sleeping on a plank. He felt a hundred years old as he levered himself to his feet and rose in careful degrees.

Twisting his torso this way and that, he worked the stiffness from his limbs. A nice early ride would restore him, he thought, and decided to do it. Coming to Helena's bedside, he peered down at his wife. Her closed eyelids looked fragile, like the most delicate china. The only thing to name them human was the faint tracings of blue veins that showed against the translucent skin. Her cheeks were flushed, a sign of health, and her perfectly shaped mouth was slightly open, lips softly parted in too tempting a display. He bent over and touched them ever so slightly with his own. Straightening, he frowned at himself for the impulsive act. He had disturbed her.

She twisted around, and her head, half off the pillow now, was caught at an awkward angle. Gently, he reached under her and attempted to bring the pillow more in line with her head.

He made the adjustment without disturbing her any further. Something fell onto the floor. He stooped to pick it up. It was small, lumpy and soft. Holding it up to the light, he inspected it.

It was some sort of crude doll. Scraps of cloth were tied

with twine, and there was a rudimentary suggestion of a face on the flat surface of the top bundle. The printed material that wrapped around the torso area was vaguely familiar.

Then he recalled it was the ugly print pattern of one of the ill-fitting dresses Helena had worn when he had first come to the house. Since her new wardrobe had arrived, she had probably given it away or thrown it into the ragbag. He understood immediately what this meant.

The doll was a poppet. Crazy old ladies used them in the supposed dark arts of magic, and this one was supposed to represent Helena. He didn't believe in such nonsense, but the sight of the doll filled him with an unreasonable anger.

Someone who did believe in that balderdash was toying with Helena. Was it meant for good, or ill? He didn't know the answer to that question, but he did know where he could find out. There wasn't a doubt in his mind who was responsible.

Tampening his rage, he folded the vile thing in his fist. He glanced at Helena's peaceful face. Lifting his other hand, he touched her cheek lightly, then turned away and went to his room.

It was too early for the valet to come in. He hated having assistance in dressing, anyway, but it was expected here in Rathford Manor for him to behave like a gentleman. Except he wasn't planning on behaving like a gentleman when he saw Kimberly.

He sought out the enigmatic servant the moment he was downstairs. No one seemed to know her whereabouts, and it was clear they rarely did. He had already observed that the woman enjoyed a great deal of freedom. He set out to search for her. As good fortune would have it, when he exited the back of the house, he caught sight of someone in the herb garden. It was Kimberly, all right. He could see the frizz of her red hair just over the wall.

"Looking for ingredients for your spells?" he snarled, drawing up to her.

She tilted her head back and squinted at him in a most uncomely manner. Before she could reply, he shoved his hand out, dangling the grotesque poppet in front of her nose. "Keep this filth away from my wife."

The expression of surprise transformed in degrees to stony resentment. She didn't deny the thing was hers. Instead, she shoved out her bottom lip as she rose to her feet.

"Ye best put tha' back where it goes, young master. The spirits won't watch over her if ye don't."

"I'm not interested in your superstitious nonsense, and Helena has no need of it anymore."

Her look was sly. "Lady Helena knows the power of the spirits. She'd want ta' know she was being protected. Put tha' back where ye found it and she'll rest easy."

He couldn't believe the gall of the woman! The blood rushed to his face and the pulse in his temple throbbed so hard he could feel it. Clenching his teeth, he forced the words out with a snarl. "I'll assume you haven't been listening, rather than consider you've deliberately chosen to disregard my orders. Therefore, I'll repeat myself. Your pathetic rituals have no place in this house any longer. Either you control yourself and cease or I will have you put out of this house without so much as a second thought."

She glared at him. "Ye can't. Yer not the master here. Try gettin' rid o' me an' ye'll find yer not so high an' mighty as ye think."

"Do you mean to say you think you have more power in this house than me?" He was incredulous. It was difficult not to laugh. He didn't bother to conceal a mocking tone in his voice. "I assure you, I know my place in this house very well. I am Helena's husband, and that gives me every authority to forbid you from having any contact with her. If you cannot abide by my wishes, you will be let go. It is very simple.''

The sound of a throat clearing from the house diverted him. He turned his attention to Mrs. Kent who, by the look of her, had overheard enough of the exchange between himself and Kimberly to be uncomfortable.

''My lady is awake, sir. She's asking for you.''

''Thank you, Mrs. Kent. I shall go to her right away.'' He handed the poppet to Mrs. Kent as he passed her. ''Destroy this,'' he said, ''and let me know if anything like it is seen again.''

She gave him a look of approval. ''Of course, sir.''

He didn't go directly to Helena, as he had said he would. At the base of the stairs, he detoured into Lord Rathford's study.

The old man was sitting in the chair behind his desk, stiffly paging through a ledger. Adam registered a measure of surprise that he showed no signs of drinking at this early hour. Come to think of it, he seemed to be restraining himself of late.

This was a good thing. He wanted the man sober. Rathford had a tendency to become morose when in his cups.

''Why the devil haven't you put Kimberly out of this house?'' Adam demanded forcefully. ''She's a threat to Helena's well-being, you must know that.'' He drew in a breath and stopped at Rathford's raised hand.

Rathford's tone was rather sad. ''I hate the woman myself. But...she has a certain way with Helena. She calms her.''

''Calms her? My God, man, can't you see that she's cowed, not calmed?''

Rathford seemed confused. ''Helena's mother was very

close to Kimberly. The servant's 'sight' was irresistible to her. She elevated her to friend, and Kimberly did little in the way of chores. When my wife...died, she continued as Helena's confidante. I thought it gave her comfort.''

"Well, if you won't do anything about her, I will. I've given her warning to stay away from Helena. If she interferes with my wife, I will have her out of this house.''

Rathford blinked rapidly in surprise. "I'll dismiss her myself if she's doing anything wrong with my girl.'' He turned to the patiently waiting Jack. "Yes?''

"Mr. Howard has arrived, sir. I didn't know if I should send him in, or if you wished to continue your private conversation.''

"We're finished,'' Adam announced, heading for the door. "Helena is waiting for me.''

An urgent message from Mr. Darby, the solicitor handling Adam's investments, arrived, advising him that the investors with whom he had been wanting to meet were in London. Adam made swift preparations to return to the city.

Under different circumstances, he wouldn't think of leaving Rathford Manor. There were so many reasons to stay. The weather was bitter and unrelenting, making travel wretched. The hunt he and his new comrades had planned was nearly upon them. The snow had melted, but the ground was rock hard, making tracking impossible. It would be completely up to the dogs. If there was any wildlife out there. Personally, Adam doubted it. How anything could survive in this bitter cold was beyond him.

Repairs to the barn were already under way. Men from the village had come in to do it, and they needed to be supervised. And there was the invitation the Duke and Duchess of Strathmere had sent for a party at the end of

February. Helena's health was on the mend, but she wasn't fully herself yet.

Helena. Adam's wild rush of thought halted abruptly. What difference did all the rest of it make? It was only Helena that mattered.

Damnation, this trip came at an inconvenient time, but one had to seize these opportunities. Telling himself Helena would be all right, he grimly packed his things, eschewing the services of the manservant set aside for just these kinds of tasks. Adam very much relished his solitude as he mulled over dark thoughts while shoving badly folded items of clothing into a valise.

When his packing was finished, he went to Helena's room.

She was sitting up, propped with a plethora of pillows behind her. A tray was set before her, the kind used for dining in bed, with tiny legs straddling her lap. Upon it was a soup bowl, and she was idly skimming the silver spoon over the surface. Her night rail was fastened primly, tied at the neck with a girlish pink ribbon. Her hair was pulled back loosely, then left to fall over one shoulder.

There was nothing sexy in the picture she presented. It was decorous and demur and nearly angelic in its aspect...and yet the blood in his veins flared instantly hot.

"You seem improved," he said, and his voice, he was glad to note, sounded sufficiently detached.

"I feel much better." The thick ridge of eyelashes drifted over those cerulean eyes, veiling them and keeping their secrets.

This was the most frustrating part of the illness. For some reason, it had made her more distant. Not the heated animosity of their early days of acquaintance, not the tender blush of affection that had come upon them unexpectedly as their knowledge of one another deepened. These days, her eyes had a tendency to dart, as if she were wary all the time. She watched him, and he had the sense—although she never said anything to indicate it—that she was afraid.

Surely...not afraid of him?

This was the hardest part—feeling like he was abandoning her. It felt...wrong to go. Damn, he hated feeling helpless.

She played with her consommé, eyes lowered, her lashes fanned against the gentle blush of those impossibly defined cheekbones. "I am planning to dress today. I may even take a walk."

"I hope you will not push yourself too much."

"No. I shan't."

She wouldn't look at him. He wanted to make her.

Nervously, she laid her spoon down and smoothed her hair.

On impulse, he took a step forward. "Helena, I'm sorry I have to leave...." The stiffening of her shoulders stopped him.

"Yes. Mrs. Kent told me. About your leaving."

"Are you angry?"

She was so startled, she did look at him then. But only for a moment. "No."

It seemed an honest enough answer. Then what was the matter? "I'll return as soon as I can. There is the Strathmere ball next month. I want to be here for that."

"It's very kind of you." The words were spoken with not an ounce of irony, and yet it annoyed him all the more. He wasn't doing it to be kind, damn it all. He was doing it because it was what he *wanted*.

She turned, tucking her chin into her shoulder. He had the feeling he was being dismissed.

He had planned to stay, but felt awkward and dissatisfied all of a sudden. Making some excuse, he left.

She shot a quick glance at him before he turned away, and that look stayed in his mind's eye for the remainder of the day. It was likely his imagination, but he could have sworn it was ripe with a plea.

But a plea for what?

When he had gone, Helena lay her head back and stared at the ceiling. The hurt was on the fringes of her awareness, and she had the most foolish idea that if she stayed very still, she could keep it from rearing up on its hind legs like some rabid beast and devouring her whole. Rather, it crept upon her, stealing inch by inch until her chest ached and it was difficult to breathe. Her eyes stung and when she blinked, wetness spiked her lashes.

It was ridiculous to feel this way just because he was going to London to attend to business. Weepiness and clinging were certainly not qualities she was used to seeing within herself, nor ones Adam would consider attractive.

At that very unlucky moment, her father entered the room.

With forced brightness, she said, "Oh, Father. Any good news on the stables?"

He appeared distracted. "What? Oh. Yes, it's coming along nicely." He cleared his throat and asked, "I don't suppose...you haven't been to your mother's rooms lately?"

This caught Helena completely off guard. "Mother's rooms? No, of course not. Why?"

He frowned, muttering to himself. "Bettina must have imagined it."

Bettina was one of Mrs. Kent's helpers who'd come in from the village. She did most of the heavy labor, beating the rugs and polishing the floors, while the elder and more senior servant busied herself with the dusting and polishing.

"Someone was in your mother's rooms, it seems. Bettina said she saw someone—said it was you—coming out of them one day when she was going up to clean in there." He paused, glancing uncertainty at her. "It wasn't you, was it? Odd."

"No." She sat quietly, not proffering the obvious question: *Then who?*

"She's a silly girl," George Rathford said.

But Bettina was not at all the silly girl type.

Helena said, "I'll speak to her about it. It seems strange that she would be mistaken." Gazing up at her father, she saw a flash of something dark in his eye. A close, careful intensity as he gazed at her.

She might have heard his thoughts as clearly as if he'd spoken aloud.

She felt a cold finger trace a shivery path up her spine. Jutting her chin out, she forced herself to smile. It felt brittle and false, and she had the awful suspicion that her father wasn't fooled one bit. "I'm anxious to come and see the progress on the stables."

"Don't rush it, button."

The endearment rocked her. He hadn't called her that since she was a very small child. He smiled a bracing smile, patted her hand and chatted for several more minutes. Helena wished he would leave. As much as she craved time like this with her father, other thoughts, darker thoughts, pressed in on her, begging for consideration.

She was afraid. She was so very afraid.

It wasn't just this supposed mix-up about the servant girl thinking she'd seen her in her mother's old apartments. The nightmares...they were back, and they had grown terrifyingly real. Sometimes Helena thought they *were* real. Sounds so crisp, visions of shadows moving about her bed.

Also, there were all the things she had been misplacing

of late. The other day, she awoke to find a pair of slippers floating in the basin she used to wash in the mornings. No one had been in the room since she had slipped them off the previous night and left them on the hand-knotted rug by her bed.

She had stuffed them, sopping wet, into the back of the wardrobe, and when they were dried, she furtively threw them in the fire. Her hair ribbons were constantly going missing, then turning up in the oddest places. Something pinched her foot one night. She found it to be her mother's brooch tucked in the bed linens, one she hadn't seen for years. Not since…the accident.

After her father left, she closed her eyes and drew in a shaking breath. She tried to tell herself not to worry, that she was feeling stronger, and whatever malady had come over her was receding. By the time Adam returned home, she would be fully restored to her normal state. She had to believe that.

And for a while, she did.

Chapter Twenty-Seven

Adam returned to Rathford Manor on the fourth of February. Upon entering the house, he asked after his wife's whereabouts. Jack informed him, his lips rather set and stiff, that he believed Lady Helena was in the solarium.

There was a wealth of innuendo in the look the footman gave him, but Adam didn't take the time to inquire about it.

Helena was seated with the sun streaming in through the windows that stretched all the way from the floor to the twelve-foot-high ceiling. An opened book lay on her lap, ignored as she stared out onto the overgrown lawns that stretched in descending terraces all the way to the low wall of piled stone bordering the back of the property where the clearing met the woods.

He paused, taking in her profile, the lovely curve of her fine-boned nose, the high forehead unblemished by any lines of concern. Shadows delineated the hollows under her cheekbones. Her full lips were parted in relaxation.

She was so lovely. Something queer dipped in the region of his chest. He started toward her, his footfalls softly hollow on the slate floor. She turned at the sound. The serious expression she wore transformed into one of pleasure. Those perfect lips widened and smiled.

God. The effect of her reaction washed hotly through his veins. He wanted to sweep her into his arms. He almost did, taking a step toward her with his arms outstretched before the veil dropped over the evidence of her delight and her chin came up haughtily. He blinked, rethinking the impulse to hold her, and dropped his arms. He smiled a milder version of the delight that had betrayed him a moment ago. "Hello, Helena."

"Adam," she said, her voice a tad cool.

She was dressed in a pretty gown of a soft purple the color of grapes. It was trimmed in ecru ribbon. Her hair hung in loose curls from a topknot and splayed over her shoulders. She looked like an empress, he thought. A beautiful, untouchable, remote icon of Roman beauty.

"You seem well recovered." His voice, he was glad to note, sounded casual. "Your father told me in his letters of your rapid progress, but it is good to see for myself."

"Good as new," she said, lifting her hands. He saw they trembled a bit before she laid them back on her lap.

But she wasn't good as new. That haunted quality was still there, intangible and elusive and as impermeable a barrier as…as that wall down there that sheltered the tamed lawns from the wildness of the forest.

"What are you reading?"

She glanced at the book on her lap. "A romantic novel. Something silly to while away the time."

"You've been spending too much time in the house, I think." He pulled up a wrought-iron chair, scraping it rudely across the stones. "It must get wearing."

"Mrs. Kent won't allow me to do anything. I used to be so busy I didn't have time for anything else. Now, I'm bored to tears and reduced to reading this stuff." She glanced down and blushed. "Actually, I do usually enjoy Mrs. Radcliff's novels. I suppose it's just that I've had my fill reading, with no other distraction to break the monotony."

"Poor girl. I'll take you back out to the woods when the weather breaks."

Her aloof mien faltered and she almost smiled. "That would be pleasant."

Why did it feel as if they were strangers? And he had the strangest, most acute sensation that she was holding something back. More secrets?

He shook off the thought. He was back at Rathford Manor, with Helena, and he had thought about this moment every day for all the weeks he'd been gone. He wasn't going to let her inexplicable reserve ruin it.

He leaned forward, sending her a winning glance. "Let's have a game of cards, shall we? It will be more interesting than that novel."

She flushed girlishly, obviously liking the idea, although she tried valiantly to maintain her cool stance. "I suppose. What do you wish to play?"

"I'm not that versed in genteel games, so you choose."

Her eyes glinted mischievously, the first sign of her old spirit he'd yet seen. "I am wicked good at whist."

"Ah! A gambling girl, are you? I don't know if I should. I swore off laying money on cards."

She was genuinely shocked. "Did you? I hadn't known."

How odd. Did they know that little about each other, then? "Of course. The gaming tables haven't been good to me. My ineptitude at gambling is what brought me here in the first place, you know." Too late, he realized his error. Her eyelashes lowered and he cursed his tactlessness. He added, almost nonchalantly, "On second thought, perhaps the entire circumstance has been good. It all worked out rather to my liking in the end, didn't it?''

Her gaze slanted up at him, and again he was struck with how frightened she could look sometimes. What the devil was she so afraid of?

"Let's go into the parlor." He stood. "We'll have tea brought in.''

"Yes.'' She rose and he watched her covertly, studying her movements for any sign of lingering weakness. She seemed strong enough, even if the glance she shot him was uncertain.

Reaching out on impulse, he took her hand and pulled it through his, placing it on his forearm. It felt slender and fragile, like a small bird resting there. He covered it with his own, holding tight. "It's good to be home, Helena.''

"You are cheating!" Helena declared an hour later as he won another rubber.

"How dare you accuse me,'' Adam countered without a trace of indignation. He looked at her mildly. "You are merely being a poor sport because I'm winning.''

"Then you lied to me. You said you had no luck at card games.''

"I said I had no luck at the gaming tables. This is true. Whist, as you know, is a parlor game. It is not generally played for high stakes. All fours, now, that's a deadly trick, that one. No, whist is quite a different matter. As it happens, I am quite good at it.''

"You misled me,'' she said again with mock belligerence.

Adam shrugged. "I might have.''

Helena wanted to laugh. She bit back the impulse. Adam was being his utmost charming self, teasing her and dazzling her with his skillful handling of the cards—he could shuffle in the most amazing ways—and sleights of hand. It was impossible to stay angry with him.

He was trying hard to amuse her. And being quite successful at it. Why, he even looked happy to be with her. It showed in his attentive conversation, the affectionate glow in his dark eyes.

And she was so happy to have him here. It felt like an eternity since he had left her. Business. She hadn't known whether to believe him on that score. Had it been business or that plump morsel of voluptuousness, Trina, that had lured him to London?

If not her, then someone else, perhaps. It was true their marriage of convenience had developed into a pleasant association, but that didn't transform it from the reality of what it was. Theirs was a union based on necessity and a cordial understanding of Adam's need for money and her...her need...

Anyway, most men strayed. It was understood. Wives tolerated it and it was best not to dwell on it and spoil these light, enjoyable moments when he was so attentive and delightfully hers.

But...she didn't want Adam to stray. The very thought choked her, lying thick and heavy on her chest. And she couldn't forget it, either, or tolerate it in the least.

"That rubber goes to me." He was mockingly triumphant.

"This is ridiculous. How can one play a decent rubber of whist with only two people?"

"We modified the game nicely." He leaned forward, his liquid eyes gleaming. "*And* you agreed to the rules."

"That was with the understanding that you were no good at the game. You took shameless advantage."

"Of course I did. Isn't that expected?"

"I think it unfair."

"Ah, I see I shall have to make it up to you." He leaned back and folded his arms over his chest, looking like the genie in *Arabian Nights*—all mystery and otherworldly power.

Her heart skittered. A tight knot of desire twisted in her belly. Her attraction to him was nearly irresistible. He said, "I shall save it for a surprise. Speaking of surprises, I nearly forgot...." He fished in the breast pocket of his coat and handed her a small box. "I trust I'll not find this in the porridge," he added with a devilish expression.

She didn't know whether to be insulted or not. But the lure of the proffered gift proved too diverting. She opened the box.

"Oh. What a beautiful ring!"

Adam indicated the stone. "A fire opal. I thought it would become you." He took the box and put it aside. "It's mysterious."

She looked at him askance. "This romantic streak of yours is growing."

He looked horrified. "No need to insult me."

She didn't even try to suppress her giggles.

He indicated the ring. "Put it on. I guessed at the size."

It fit nicely on the middle finger of her right hand. "I like it very much." It was a pretty piece, much more to her taste than the gaudy, expensive pieces she had inherited from her mother. What's more, the fact that he had thought of her during his trip touched her. "But you don't keep having to bring me gifts every time you go away."

"I want to. It allays my guilt for having to leave."

Guilt? Was his guilt from the indiscretions he committed while away? The thought soured her pleasure and brought a recollection of Kimberly's goading words: *Buying gifts with her own money, to keep the golden goose content.*

Determinedly, Helena pushed the disturbing thoughts aside. "Thank you so much, Adam," she said.

"That is not a proper thank-you."

She looked up, taken aback by this. The way he was looking at her—the heat in his eyes—was impossible to misinterpret. Her insides curled like parchment singed by a close-burning flame.

The playing table was between them, seeming a daunting obstacle. Adam leaned on his elbow, spanning most of the distance, the corners of his lips curled with unspoken suggestion. Hesitantly, she came forward, too, closing the rest of the space until she could feel the soft brush of his breath on her cheek. His hand cupped her jaw, fingers splayed along her cheek and neck. They were very warm, stroking in a way that made her pulse jump.

He lowered his mouth. It was the gentlest of kisses he gave her, touching lightly, barely grazing his lips over hers. She stayed transfixed after that too-fleeting brush, eyes closed, wanting more. Waiting to see what he would do next.

His fingers tightened against the flushed skin of her cheek. She could hear his breathing, deep and labored. His nose nuzzled her, pushing her head back and to one side.

He kissed her again, and she turned into it. His hand crept up to cup the back of her neck and hold her steady. Working his mouth against her, he touched his tongue to the seam of her lips and she opened to him.

She had missed him so terribly, missed this—these feelings, this burning he could awaken within her. She was disappointed when his grip slackened and he broke off. "There." He smiled into her eyes. "A proper thank-you should always involve a kiss."

He leaned back in his seat and brought his attention back

down to their card game. Touching her throbbing lips with her tongue, she said nothing as she watched him make his play after a moment's concentration. Looking back up at her, he grinned. "I believe I've won again."

Chapter Twenty-Eight

"Did you see Helena?" Lord Rathford asked when he entered his study.

"Right off when I arrived." Adam was at the library table, pouring a stiff whiskey into a tumbler. He held up the glass in silent question. "We took tea together and played a rubber of cards."

Lord Rathford shook his head with a cross frown, declining the offer of a drink. "How did she seem?"

The question surprised Adam. "Well enough. Bored." He took a sip and moved to a chair. "Her illness is wearing on her."

"I meant her mood."

Sitting back, he considered the question. "Cool at first, but I don't think she understands why I had to go to London. To be honest, I can't say I had much appreciation for the timing. I didn't like having to leave her when she was just getting over all of that, the fire and the illness."

"That's right, you had pressing business to attend to." Rathford narrowed his eyes. "Did everything go well?"

"Very well, thank you for your interest," Adam answered mildly. He didn't want to brag, but "well" was as wild an understatement as there was. He had been able to join a consortium of investors who were acquiring interest in the overseas spice trade and reestablishing merchant lines with the colonies—states, he mentally corrected. They would be dealing with East Indies sugar, tobacco and cotton grown in the southern American states, metals from the northern ones, and the return journeys would bring the Americas Scottish wool, Oriental spices and French wines and textiles.

Rathford nodded with approval. "I'd like to hear more about it, but not tonight." He sat back and surveyed Adam as that one brought his drink to the leather chair. "I wanted us to adjourn in here because what we say is to remain private."

The glass halfway to his mouth, Adam paused. He looked up. "What is wrong?"

"I…I am concerned about my daughter."

"She is just lonely." Adam shrugged. "She was already improved after a rather haphazard game of cards." He remembered the kiss and the lively flush it had brought to her cheeks, but naturally didn't mention it. "Now that she is well, she will be restored to her old routines. This is all she needs to improve her."

Rathford was not mollified. His dark look remained fixed on Adam. "She's been behaving oddly lately. You remember the ear bobs? The stables?"

Adam shifted in his seat. "She was ill. Ill people are sometimes forgetful."

"She told Mrs. Kent there was an intruder in her room one night. Of course, there was no one. She…walks about when everyone is abed. The servants see her, yet she always denies it when asked later."

"What exactly is your concern?" Adam snapped. He knew his anger was unreasonable, but he couldn't control it. "That she has trouble sleeping some nights and had a nightmare that seemed so real she thought there actually was someone in her rooms? Perhaps there was. Were her rooms searched? Or it could be that ghoul—Kimberly. Get her away from Helena, and you'd have no more problems, I'll wager.''

Rathford gave his son-in-law a steely stare. ''She said the intruder was a man, and that he disappeared.''

''Then it was a nightmare, as I said. One that seemed real, but was just a dream all the same and nothing to fear at all.'' Adam heard the tightness in his own voice. In the silence that followed, he felt the very air around him thicken like some atmospheric aspic.

There clearly was something to fear. Rathford feared it.

''What is it?'' Adam asked urgently, unable to maintain his stance of unconcern.

The old man raised a trembling hand to his forehead to wipe the line of sweat that had appeared. ''I am afraid of madness,'' he said in a whisper that was at once both harsh and trembling. ''I am afraid that the madness of her mother has come upon her.''

He looked at his son-in-law, his face full of guilt. Then he couldn't look Adam in the eye any longer. His gaze fell and he said, ''There's something I have to tell you. The truth.'' He swiped away the sweat beading on his upper lip. ''It's time you knew the truth.''

It was strange how one moment could alter the world. Adam stood in his bedroom that night after the house had fallen asleep, and reflected that in the space of one quarter of an hour, everything had changed.

Rathford had, as promised, told him the truth.

And the truth was that his wife, Helena—lovely, ethereal, fragile, mysterious Helena—was a murderess. She *had* killed her mother.

Her mother had been mad, Rathford had explained with blanched face and glazed eyes. Mad with ambition for her daughter, whom she believed deserved nothing less than the Duke of Strathmere. So she had killed the elder brother and his wife, narrowly and miraculously missing killing their two children in the bargain. But as they were females and could not inherit, she didn't trouble to finish the job. When Jareth announced his intention to break his engagement to Helena and marry Chloe, the girls' governess, Althea had gone after the couple for revenge and to kill Jareth so that his cousin and heir, Gerald, would make Helena his duchess.

Helena, perhaps knowing by some intuition what her mother planned, had followed her that day, to find her mother had shot the duke and was pointing the second pistol at Chloe. Taking the spent flintlock, Helena had loaded it under her mother's direction, for Althea's first shot had only wounded Jareth. But only one more shot was fired that day. It was Helena's flintlock. She killed her mother to save the life of Jareth and Chloe.

The story Jareth concocted of himself shooting Althea in self-defense was told to deflect the stain of matricide from Helena. The constable had been doubtful, but the inquest proceedings had settled the matter finally.

The talk, however, had begun when Helena, out of her mind for a while after the experience, had spoken to the first few people to arrive, admitting her guilt. From there, the rumors could never be completely subdued, fed over the years by Helena's self-imposed isolation. It was easy to guess it was from shame that she, from that day forward, shrank from the world.

With trembling hands covering his face, Rathford had said he believed Adam would bring her out of that existence. It had been a desperate move, made impulsively because he believed himself to be dying. He had to make certain she was cared for, and he had hoped against hope that her marriage, even under such unlikely circumstances, would bring her happiness, wake her out of the stupor of pain and guilt she'd been locked in for five long years. So he had taken a chance on a fortune hunter, on Adam. But the madness had come, taking away a future that was beginning to look promising.

But Helena hadn't forgiven herself for firing that pistol, Rathford had theorized, even if it was to save two lives. Even in death, Althea's hold over her daughter was too powerful. Althea's madness had come to afflict her daughter as revenge for Rathford having tried to release her from the past.

Now, as Adam thought about it, he could laugh. Curses from beyond the grave—really. But in that library, under the force of Rathford's horrible conviction of what he was saying, he had gotten the shivers.

But he was a rational man and he put no stock in nonsense like this. Still, he felt betrayed. Murder was, after all, something a man likes to know his wife isn't capable of.

It was later still when he heard her playing. Without a moment's hesitation, he ran to the nursery tower and stood outside the doorway.

She sang so beautifully. The power of her song reached out to him, closed like a tender-fingered lover around his heart and squeezed emotions from him that felt foreign. Or perhaps it was just the confusion he had felt in the aftermath of Rathford's confession. The music was like a magnifying glass, bringing out everything that had been roiling inside of him all night, until he couldn't bear it any longer.

He opened the door and entered. Helena looked up and stopped.

"Don't stop, Helena," he said, and he could hear the gruff emotion in his own voice. "Please. I need to hear you sing."

She watched him, wary. She looked lovely. So lovely.

She wasn't mad, for God's sake. She *wasn't!*

"Please," he said again.

Taking in a deep, shaking breath, she bowed her head and began to play again.

He stood before her, arm resting on the curve of the instrument, leaning into it, leaning into the song to let it drench him and fill him and make him believe in her again.

She was beautiful. God, she made him ache. He watched her, not touching, but wanting to. And then he could stand it no longer and circled around the pianoforte and closed his hands around her wrist.

The song ended abruptly on a discord. She gazed at him, startled, and he pulled her to her feet and into his arms, and kissed her hard. She felt incredibly slight, no more substantial than a bird, he thought, but she kissed him back with a full measure of ardor.

No matter what she'd done, no matter what was happening now, he wanted her. It was like needing to breathe— as natural to him as drawing in air, part of him now. He had accepted it. And resisting her was like holding his breath. Fine at first, then a strain, increasing agony until at last, in control no longer, one gasps for air, filling one's lungs in greedy gulps until the need is sated.

He felt her body, too slender, yet utterly sensual. Her bottom had the most delicious curve, which he sampled with the flattened palm of his hand, and his chest, made ultrasensitive by his present state of arousal, knew the precise size and shape of her breasts. Even the tiny pebbled tips he could feel, and he wanted to touch them, test their hardness with his fingers, and his mouth.

He yanked her back over his arm and bent to her throat. He kissed the hot flesh, then quickly undid the buttons with his free hand and ran his tongue all the way down to the rise of her breasts.

She wasn't mad. She wasn't.

His hand cupped a heaving mound, squeezing gently. She moaned and grasped his head, arching into his kiss as he moved to taste her. His tongue teased her, whipped her into a state of wild desire. Straightening, he carried her quickly to the side of the room, where a small pallet lay.

He didn't stop to think. If he had, he might have wondered at the sense of doing what he was about to do in the place where she had been a child. He did know enough of his surroundings to register that this was unlikely to be her childhood bed. It was too plain, too Spartan—most likely a space for a servant to sleep upon during the governess's time off. In any event, Helena didn't protest.

He laid her on the bed. Face flushed, she looked up at him, breathing hard through softly parted lips. "I missed you," she said.

The words went straight to his gut, igniting the fevered sensations that churned there. "Helena. I want to make love to you."

"Yes," she answered breathlessly, and pulled him down to her.

He took his time removing her clothes. He touched her everywhere, lingering to arouse her nipples, tracing light patterns with his tongue over the flat of her stomach, tasting the supple moist flesh sheltered within her woman's folds, and teasing her there until she rocked under him with violent release.

He had himself stripped in no time, and he came over her, into her swiftly, needing to feel that heat surround him. He thrust and she welcomed him, wrapping her legs tightly around his flanks. She locked her fingers together at the base of his neck and kept her eyes on his. He braced himself over her, thrusting into her with rhythmic movements of his hips. Their eyes never left each other's. He saw every expression of pleasure and desire, and it was the most erotic thing he had ever experienced. His climax raged through him, shooting him quickly and immediately into incredible gratification that drove him on and on and on until it crested and finally ebbed.

Spent and weak, he curled up with her, holding her as tight as he thought she could stand. She didn't mind, he thought, for she clasped him back and fitted her head snugly in the curve of his neck.

He couldn't stop kissing her, tender little touches of his lips to her hairline, eyebrow or the smooth unlined skin of her forehead. She sighed, and he smiled up at the ceiling, knowing she was content. In this moment, all thoughts of trouble seemed not even possible.

He wished he could have slept. His body might have been given release, but his mind was more active than ever.

Surely, surely, all this talk of madness was just so much stuff and nonsense—fears being given too much credence by overactive imaginations. He simply couldn't believe those awful things, not when she felt this right in his arms.

After a while, he said, "Let me take you back to your room. It's almost morning."

They rose and dressed. He took her to her room, kissing her thoroughly on the threshold. Running a finger along her cheek, he murmured, "I'll see you in a few hours."

"Mmm," she said with a sultry smile. "Good night."

He laughed softly. "You mean good morning."

She shrugged and slipped inside. He stood staring at the door, grinning like a fool for a while before going to his bedchamber.

Chapter Twenty-Nine

Helena's beautiful euphoria lasted exactly five hours. After luncheon one of the new parlor maids came into the drawing room where Helena was making some notes on the menu to give to Mrs. Kent.

Expecting that the maid was going to tell her that Mrs. Stiles had arrived, Helena laid down her pen and rose. The dressmaker was working on a very special gown for the occasion of the Strathmere ball next Saturday, and had promised she'd bring it over today for a final fitting.

Helena looked up at the servant. "Is Mrs. Stiles here?"

"N-no. There's a problem, you see. Mrs. Kent has asked me to fetch you. Upstairs. She's upstairs." Round-eyed, the girl jabbed her finger at the ceiling. It wasn't hard to discern her distress.

"My goodness, of course," Helena said, picking up her skirts and rushing to the door. "Is she in my room?"

"No, miss." The maid paled. "In your mother's old rooms, miss."

Helena almost stumbled. She caught herself at the door, grasping the frame for balance. *Her mother's rooms?* No one went in there. The servants cleaned it, but otherwise it was untouched. All these years.

But someone had gone there recently. Someone Bettina had thought was her. Was that why Mrs. Kent wanted to see her there?

The first thing that greeted her was the housekeeper's pinched face. Clasping her hands, Mrs. Kent hovered in the hallway outside the closed doors of Althea's suite. "Oh, my lady, it's terrible."

"What? What has happened?"

"The rooms. They're completely destroyed. Everything is broken, even the furniture, and shredded…oh, my…the entire room. The draperies…and the counterpane…lord, it's a mess!" Wringing her hands, the housekeeper said, "I hope I did the right thing in calling you."

"Of course you did. Now, let's go in, Mrs. Kent."

The housekeeper opened the door and stepped back. Helena went past her and into…utter chaos. The entire room was nothing but debris.

"Bettina came in to clean, just as she always does. It was just a little while ago," Mrs. Kent explained. "She found it like this."

Helena walked into the room a little ways, looking slowly from right to left. Nothing was recognizable. Her feet crunched over decimated objects littering the floor, a carpet of shredded clothing, broken glass, fractured wood. "Who could have done this?"

The loud hiss of an indrawn breath brought them around to the woman in the doorway. Kimberly looked furious, eyes glinting and teeth bared as she looked at the ravaged things of her former mistress. Despite her newfound independence, Helena felt a stab of the old fear at the fearsome expression on the woman's face.

Gazing straight at Helena, Kimberly said, "What have you done?"

Off guard for a moment, Helena stammered. "What... me? I've not done this!"

Wailing, Kimberly grabbed two fistfuls of her own hair. "All her things—how could you?"

The wave of defensiveness that came over her was ridiculous, Helena thought. She looked to Mrs. Kent. Was it suspicion she read in those sympathetic eyes?

Adam's voice cut in. "What's going...oh, my God. What happened here?"

"I didn't do it!" Helena cried. She found Adam's gaze on her. It seemed a trifle too narrow, too pensive, as if he were actually thinking she had. "I didn't!" she cried again.

"Leave us," Adam commanded.

Kimberly started to say something, clearly too distressed to obey, but Adam shot her a look even she, brazen as she was, didn't dare ignore. With a parting glare aimed at Helena, she was gone. Mrs. Kent murmured her excuses and hurried out behind her.

She was not even out of earshot when Helena cried, "You think I did this."

"I didn't say that," Adam replied calmly.

"You are looking at me with accusation in your eye."

"Helena, why would I think that? If you wanted to destroy your mother's rooms, you've had five years to do it."

Yes. That sounded reasonable. Except...except sometimes lately she wasn't sure what was happening to her. All those misplaced objects, the oddities, the forgetfulness. The nightmares. Worst of all were the nightmares.

And Bettina had thought she had seen her in here not too long ago. Sometimes Helena found herself places and didn't remember how she had gotten there.

"Helena." Adam spoke gently, wading through the debris to wrap his fingers around her wrist and pull her out of the room with him. He closed the doors, then gathered her into his arms. "You're shivering."

Helena barely heard him. She let herself be pulled into the embrace.

"I want to ask you something," he began. His voice was slow, measured. Helena's fears raced faster. He pulled back to peer at her. "Have you had any times recently, like the time of the fire, where you found yourself confused, or disoriented, or maybe you woke up somewhere and didn't know how you had gotten there—"

She spun out of his grasp, backpedaling swiftly. "You think...oh, Adam!"

He held up his hands as if to ward off her accusations. "No. I didn't say that."

"Yes. Oh, yes, you did."

"Helena!" he called as she ran away from him. Down the hall she flew. She didn't stop, even when she thought she heard him coming after her. But when she arrived at her room, she was quite alone.

It was only a matter of time before Kimberly sought out Helena.

"Go away," Helena said, not looking up from the book she wasn't reading.

There was so long a silence, she looked up. Kimberly was smirking.

Helena narrowed her gaze at the woman. "I said leave me alone."

"How can I when yer mother calls to me from the grave to counsel ye?"

Those words, once chilling, only annoyed her now. Helena said through gritted teeth, "I desire none of your *counsel*. Now, get out of this room before I call John Footmar and have you thrown out."

Surprised at that, Kimberly seemed at a temporary loss. Then she tossed her head and said, "She knows it was ye who ruined her rooms. She's spitting angry with ye."

"Oh, stop it. My mother is dead. And I didn't do that to her rooms."

"No?" Her sly expression returned. "Perhaps ye just don't remember. It seems ye've been forgetting lots of things lately."

Helena stiffened. "I am one minute away from calling the footman."

Kimberly went to the door, where she paused and looked at Helena over her shoulder. "One question, my lady." She paused again for effect. "If not you, then who? It seems only ye have cause to hate her."

"I don't hate my mother."

Kimberly raised her head and said loftily, "Well. She hates ye. She'll have her vengeance yet for what ye done."

And then she finally did leave, but Helena thought about what she had said long after. It wasn't anything to do with the ghoulish predictions Kimberly made, or the macabre references to her mother.

It was that sometimes she felt as if she were losing her mind. She feared that Adam might be wondering a very similar thing....

When Adam and Helena arrived at the Strathmere's ball, they were greeted exuberantly by Chloe, who exclaimed at the sight of them and rushed forward to take Helena into her arms for a quick hug.

Helena accepted the greeting with a tremulous smile. She was very nervous. The urge to turn on her heel and run out of the ducal residence was overwhelming. She hadn't wanted to come, but Adam wouldn't hear of a last-minute cancellation. She was frightened of the crowd, of facing down all the stares. She hated it when she knew they were all whispering about her behind their fans. However, instead of fleeing, she murmured, "Your grace."

Chloe held Helena at arm's length and surveyed her. "My goodness, Helena, how do you manage to look so flawlessly lovely all the time?"

"You are too kind, your grace. It is your presence that lights up this room and makes everyone turn their heads."

"Really?" Chloe asked, breaking into a brilliant smile. Leaning forward, she hooked her arm through Helena's and led her away from the receiving line, an appalling breach for anyone but her. "Does it show so much?"

"What?"

Chloe giggled and squeezed Helena's arm excitedly. "I am with child again."

Happiness flooded through Helena and she almost—almost—snatched her friend back into her arms. "I am so happy for you," she said.

"Thank you. Please come visit me soon. Oh, Helena, I *am* so pleased you have allowed us to become friends."

The effusive sincerity of this unconventional duchess touched Helena. Something broke open within her and she laughed. She suddenly was not feeling so afraid. She said, "You should go see to your other guests." Chloe left with a final squeeze of her hand. That was when Helena saw Adam, standing a ways off, staring at her with a half smile on his lips. His eyes were dark and shiny like the sea at midnight, and he was looking at her intently, as if he knew that she had just cracked open her protective shell a little bit wider.

Emotion caught in Helena's throat. He looked so handsome, and just seeing him filled her with a deep sense of...*rightness*. His presence seemed to fill every corner of the room. He came to her and took her hand in his. There were still people staring, just as she'd dreaded, and as Adam moved with her through the throng, he nodded and greeted each gawking face so that people either turned away, embarrassed, or blinked in surprise and nodded back, a smile replacing their calculating expressions.

His mischievousness was so offhand, so casual that no one seemed at all put out. As always, his presence lent her courage. They danced a waltz together, a giddy whirlwind of movement with Adam's arm around her, his warm palm burning through the barrier of kid that sealed hers with proper modesty. They drank—perhaps too much—and she laughed. She laughed with abandon, not the ladylike titters her mother had taught her to produce.

The men kept trying to draw Adam off into their haven of cigar smoke and political talk. Finally, Gerald managed to pull him away with enticements of meeting more of the neighborhood hound-and-hunt lovers. Adam went with open reluctance and an apologetic look over his shoulder at Helena.

She was content, however. So different than she had anticipated, the evening was turning out to be rather enjoyable. Adam, of course, made all the difference. Moving to where some chairs had been set up, she found an empty one and sat, content to be alone for a moment and watch the crowd.

The woman seated next to her turned. When her eyes focused on her new companion, they widened for a moment and the mouth that had been pursed and ready with a greeting fell open. Her hand clasped over it, as if to hide the evidence of her shock.

Feeling quite unlike herself, Helena chuckled softly and pulled the woman's hand down with a gentle tug. "I know," she said lightly, "it is quite unexpected to find me here.'' She held out her hand. "It is clear you know me, but I have not made your acquaintance."

The woman shook her hand while her mouth tried hard to work, opening and closing a few times, before her name came forth. "Lady Germaine."

"A pleasure, Lady Germaine. Are you having a good time?"

"Indeed, yes." The woman finally seemed to recover. "Yes, I am."

"The duchess is such a wonderful hostess."

"Oh. I thought…that is—"

"Yes, most people assumed there would be hard feelings between us, but I can assure you, I am as charmed by her grace as anyone."

Was this her, laughing freely, chatting with strangers, making jokes of the rumors circulating about her?

Thawing by degrees, Lady Germaine relaxed back in her chair. "She is a dear, and she and the duke are so happy. And now you have been recently married."

"Yes." The glow of joy burned bright on Helena's cheeks. "My husband has just been abducted by the men."

Lady Germaine laughed. "I saw him. He's very handsome, and so attentive to you. How nice that you've found someone at last…. Oh! I'm sorry, my dear."

"Please don't be. I couldn't agree with you more."

The conversation progressed easily. Some of the braver, or more curious, guests ventured closer. Biting back her nervousness, Helena looked each one in the eye as Lady Germaine made the introduction. Before long, she realized she was all right. She was holding her own, and the knowledge of that made her confidence swell.

Then her eye caught a familiar face and she felt a jolt of pleasure go through her. Adam.

He was speaking to someone, a woman. Helena couldn't

see her face, but she could see her husband's. He had his head tilted forward in that way he had, making it seem he was intent on every word. The woman laughed at something, laying her hand on his arm, and Adam broke out in one of those grins, eyes crinkling, whole face transformed.

The woman tossed her head in a gesture Helena marked as flirtatious. And Adam seemed to gobble it up. At least he wasn't in any hurry to leave. A slow, hard burn worked its way up from Helena's chest to her throat. Heat replaced the light, airy feeling of only moments ago. She kept a surreptitious eye on her husband, noting how he greeted another young woman who came up to him. As she was presented, Adam gave a bow. So gallant. This was Adam—all devastating charm. And apparently he didn't reserve it exclusively for her.

The magic was gone out of the evening in an instant. She stayed on, conversing lightly, pretending to listen to boring stories as the men and women who came to meet her gushed on and on—nervous talk as they seized this moment to get a close look at the elusive Lady Helena.

She made certain she won them over. If she concentrated on their conversation, she didn't think so much about the bevy of ladies fluttering around her husband like a swarm of rabid moths before a single candle flame.

It was Jareth who came for her, extricating her with his usual grace and tact. But when he had her alone, the facade of pleasantness fell away abruptly. "Where is your husband, Helena?"

Helena felt as if she'd been punched. "He's...here."

"Go fetch him this instant. Do you want more talk?"

"I?" For the first time ever, she was angry with Jareth. "What do you suggest I do, race over and drag him away from his...his admirers?"

"I expect you to use the skills any lady of breeding is

taught, and make certain that idiot doesn't incur any more damage. The talk about him already is wild. Did you know he told the parson and his wife that he had been abducted as a child and raised by aborigines?''

"He meant it to amuse, not to be taken seriously."

Jareth's dark, elegant gaze was reproachful. "That sort of sport might be diverting for a man from Adam's background, but we are trying to put to rights the shadows of the past, are we not?''

"What sort of sport is diverting for a man of my background?''

Jareth and Helena snapped their heads around in unison to face Adam. His tone was calm, his face deceptively mild, but Helena did not mistake the fire in his eyes for anything but fury.

Jareth, however, was not chagrined. "A man who doesn't understand the delicacies of high ton, Mannion—''

Adam cut him off. "Oh, I didn't realize this was to be a lecture. I abhor lectures. I am tired, in any event.'' Helena gasped at his rudeness. Jareth's chin came up, a sign of challenge.

Continuing in the same cordial tone, Adam said, "Come, Helena. It is time to go home.''

The undercurrent of tension was thickening by the moment. Jareth took a protective step in front of Helena. "Lady Helena is upset. Perhaps if we adjourn to a private parlor, we can—''

Adam interrupted a second time, looking directly at Helena. "Now, please. It is time we leave.''

Jareth stood indecisively for a moment. Laying a hand on his arm, Helena murmured, "It's all right, Jareth. Thank you for inviting me. I've had a…it was a lovely ball.''

Stiffly, the duke accepted her good night.

It wasn't until they were in the carriage that Adam exploded.

Chapter Thirty

"Can you kindly explain what the devil *that* was all about?" Adam demanded. "My God, I can't understand why everyone insists on treating you like some fragile piece of porcelain. It's ghoulish!"

"Jareth was quite rightly worried about gossip." Helena looked at him with accusation in her eyes. "With you pandering to all of those little misses, he was concerned that it might make a bad situation for me."

"Pandering?" He nearly choked. "Is that what he told you? Christ, he wants trouble between us in the worst way."

"The trouble was with you, the way you fawned all over those girls. I—" She broke off, mortified by what she had said.

His expression changed all of a sudden. "You're jealous!"

"I'm humiliated," she said defensively. "My husband spent the entire evening chasing skirts in front of every curious gossipmonger in the shire."

"Your husband," he said quietly, no longer amused, "spent half of the party right at your side. The rest of the time I spent making the acquaintance of some gentlemen who share my love of hunting. When I returned from their company, I found you surrounded by the very members of society who intimidate you, and you had them in the palm of your hand. It was your moment, Helena, and I stayed away to let you have it.''

She sat in the silence he left, suddenly awkward. Her throat felt horribly dry. When she swallowed, it was with some difficulty. As far as dressing-downs went, that was as fine a one as she'd ever heard.

The distance between them lasted through the next several days. Adam was adamant he was not going to relent until he had an apology from Helena. Helena's reasons for avoiding him were a mystery to him. It puzzled him, as she had never impressed him as the type to hold a meaningless grudge. On the third morning, John Footman came into the drawing room where Adam was going over his correspondence. ''Sir, ah, if you would...it is the mistress.''

Those words, and the urgent tones in which they were spoken, brought Adam immediately to his feet.

Jack said, ''Her room. Please hurry.''

Adam dashed past him, and Jack trotted behind, reporting what little facts he knew. ''Kepper brought her in just now. She was outside, behaving as if she were sleepy, and saying strange things. She was weeping.''

Adam reached Helena's room and burst in without bothering to knock. His wife sat slumped on the side of the bed. Her lips were blue and she was shivering violently. She looked up at him, the expression in her eyes ripping a chill through his taut body. ''I'm cold,'' she said in a small, thin voice. ''My head hurts.''

''Hush. I'm here now, sweetheart.'' He turned to the servant girl. ''Find Mrs. Kent. Have her fetch a tonic for your mistress.'' Kneeling before Helena, he took both of her hands in his and rubbed briskly. ''What happened?''

''I don't remember.'' She blinked, as if just remembering something. ''Adam, you are speaking to me. Does this mean you aren't angry with me anymore?''

He silently cursed himself and his blasted pride. He had planned to teach her a lesson, had he? It seems he was the one receiving a lesson—in regret. ''Oh, darling, no. I'm not angry.''

''I was just jealous.''

''It's all right.'' He took her shoes off and rubbed her cold feet. ''Why were you outside without boots? It's freezing outside!''

''I...I'm not sure. I don't remember going outside. I just was there.'' She frowned. ''They were so beautiful.''

''Who?'' He stripped off her stockings.

''Those girls.'' She yawned sleepily, her head beginning to loll. He tore the counterpane off the bed and wrapped her snugly to still her shivering. As she was bundled, she mused wistfully, ''I was once beautiful like that.''

''You are more beautiful than they.'' He pushed her back on the bed, leaning over her with a hand braced on the pillow on either side of her head. ''I don't have a single idea why you would be jealous of them. They were silly and unpleasant. You are exciting and challenging and...and more woman than all of them put together.'' The fervor of his voice surprised him. It did her, as well. Her eyes rounded, becoming large. The irises were a clear, startling cerulean blue for just one moment.

She smiled slowly, as content as a cat. ''That is lovely. Thank you, Adam. I hope I remember that you said it.''

He kissed her nose. ''If not, I shall remind you.''

''I think there is much we need to tell each other.'' She yawned.

"Not tonight. Sleep, love." He paused, then added in a voice rough with frustrated emotion, "Be well."

When Helena awoke the following afternoon, she had only a vague sense of what had happened. She thought she must have been outside, which she confirmed when she saw her ruined shoes. Also, the sense of coldness—deep, penetrating cold, remained distinct.

There was a suspicion that Adam had been with her, shown her kindness. If this were true and their argument over with, then she was greatly relieved. But it was a thin victory in the face of the fact that she had, apparently, had another "spell."

He came in to take tea with her late in the afternoon. "You seem better," he said with forced cheer. He wasn't so good of a liar as he supposed.

"I feel well." This awkwardness that remained was so very frustrating when she wanted to curl up on his lap and have him hold her. She needed that reassurance so much.

"Cards?" he asked, bringing forth a deck from the inside pocket of his coat.

"You do not have to entertain me."

"Tea or chocolate?" he offered, undaunted.

"Neither. I'm not hungry."

His tone became infuriatingly patronizing. "Helena, we've discussed this. I won't have you refusing to eat when you are upset. You need your strength—"

Without knowing that she was going to, she whipped the covers off the bed and leaped to her feet. "Stop it!" she screamed. "I can't stand this…this coddling! I'm not a child. Or a lunatic."

He came to her side, placing a solicitous arm around her shoulders. "Don't get upset. Come back to bed."

"I'm not getting in that bed!" She whirled on him, fury and pent-up terror mingling, making her wild. "You want to put me to bed, then do it as a man, not a nanny. I'm weary of this, Adam. I don't—'' She broke off with a sob.

His eyes stared at her, holding horror and fear. Oh God! Oh God, he thought her mad. He did. She could see it. "Helena," he said gently. He held out his hands to her. They were large, broad of palm and blunt of finger. Callused hands, made so by his work to restore the barn. They were the hands of a man, and they had touched her and made her feel loved, cherished, beautiful. Now they reached for her again, not to caress, not to stir, but to tuck her into bed like an invalid.

She ran from the room, pausing at the door after he had barked her name like an irate governess. "Leave me alone!" she shouted, and ran down the hall.

A servant, a new one whose name she couldn't recall just now, stopped and stared at her, and Helena groaned. Yes, mad Lady Helena, running about midday in her night rail, fleeing her husband, whose tender ministrations only the insane would refute.

She ran to the tower, up to her pianoforte. Restless, she sought her music as reflexively as her father sought the bottle. She reached the schoolroom and crossed it in long, angry strides. Her gaze caught on the beautiful dolls lined on the shelves just as she was about to enter the maid's chamber where her instrument was kept.

Stopping, her breath caught in her throat, she stared. Those dolls. Those damned, blank-faced, ghoulishly placid dolls. As a child, she'd loved them—she had wanted to play with them, but Mother never allowed it. They were too costly, her mother had admonished when Helena had cuddled one close and mussed its hair. Too precious.

And she, obedient, tractable child that she was, had placed them gently on the shelf and looked to her mother, waiting for the nod of quiet approval. She had fed off that grudging, silent praise like a suckling drinking poisoned milk, until she had become like those dolls. Precious, costly, not to be held. Not to be loved.

She took up one of the dolls, held it, looked at it. With all of her might, she flung it to the floor. The gorgeous china face smashed, showing the dark cavity of its hollow head.

They were empty. All empty inside.

She picked up another one and cast it down. Then another, not stopping until every last one was destroyed.

Chapter Thirty-One

Adam didn't stay around after Helena went up to her tower. He needed to be alone as well. Heading for his rooms to change, he donned his well-worn boots and a pair of riding trousers. On his way out of the house, he overheard a pair of servants whispering none too subtly about her having one of her "spells."

Not bothering to chastise them, he went to the tack room, selected a saddle and bridle, and fitted it to one of the Rathford stable horses, taking no note of the glare from his gelding. The animal hated to be ignored, considering himself far superior than his barnmates, but Adam made it a rule to take turns exercising the horses. He whistled sharply for Cain. Within moments, the exuberant dog came bounding around the side of the house and took up a trot behind the horse.

Heading out over the back meadows, they entered the woods, where the denuded bracken grew thick and the tree trunks clustered together like beggars huddling for warmth against the cold winds.

The land here was so utterly desolate, and yet it contained a primitive beauty that was beginning to feel comfortable, even welcoming. Adam hadn't thought he'd ever want to live away from London. He'd hated the long summer months, when everyone fled the city for more restful climes, and the social season moved to country estates and the seaside resorts, especially Brighton, which the Prince Regent had made so popular. It wasn't London—the seat of the 'Change, the hub of investment activity where he planned to make his mark—and so it hadn't interested him very much.

To his surprise, this place had proved very different. It felt raw and wild, a challenge of some sort, as if there were untapped resources inside of him that rose up and met the savage beauty around him. He was rather obsessed with learning the lay of the wilderness in these parts, not missing a day of riding and exploring. His interest in the barn had resulted in his taking a major part in the refurbishing designs. He knew all the horses by name, their dispositions, their favorite treats and just how to scratch each one of them to elicit a nicker of sublime contentment.

His mild interest in hunting had blossomed into a full-fledged occupation. Next week, he was traveling to meet a man about buying some hounds. The growing circle of like-minded acquaintances in the neighborhood had welcomed him, already inundating him with plans for the fall season.

A brook ran along the path as it turned. He led his horse to the edge and let her have a drink. Cain sniffed, tail wagging excitedly, then began the arduous canine task of marking territory. He snuffled around every tree and shrub, investigating thoroughly.

Adam watched him for a while, then tilted his head back to bask in the glory of the day. He could have been content but for the unease that sat with him. Worry about Helena felt like a weight on his shoulders, but he staved it off, wanting to avoid that Pandora's box and just…relax for a moment.

Cain's furious barking broke him out of his thoughts. The dog was out of sight, but the gruff barks emanated from deep in the brush. Swinging down from the mare, Adam walked along the loamy turf and called, "Cain. Come, boy."

The dog only barked louder and more anxiously. Adam went toward the sounds. He stooped and swept aside a spiny branch, stepping into the undergrowth. "Get out of there. Come on."

Cain stopped barking, and in a moment, Adam saw his mottled head poke up, ears cocked. Adam slapped his thigh and clicked his tongue. Cain crouched and began barking again, throwing his head back to give full vent.

With a resigned sigh, Adam entered the dense copse. Holding on to low-lying tree limbs for balance, he picked his way gingerly. Branches clawed at his clothes like condemned souls grasping for aid. They tore at his skin, leaving deep scratches on the back of one hand and his right cheekbone. He cursed out loud but didn't turn back. Cain's barking was urgent.

The dog better not be showing him a rabbit warren, Adam thought, and then stopped dead in his tracks.

The foot was the first thing to come into view. It was sticking out of a gorse bush, shoeless, its black wool stocking in shreds around a beefy leg ruined by purplish veins. The exposed flesh gleamed in the low light, drawing him against his will. He reacted violently when a prickly finger of berry vine dug a light trail along his neck.

Using a gloved hand, he shoved the bush aside, ruining the fine leather and not giving it a thought. Cain had quieted, and the silence was more unnerving than the barking had been. The dog's bright eyes questioned him, his triangular head cocked to one side.

Adam braced himself, fighting instinctive reluctance as

he worked to reveal the body hidden by the thick under-brush. It was a woman. The material over her ample bosom was covered with blood. It was stiff and brown, testifying that the fatal wound had been delivered some time ago.

He pushed back the stubborn bracken until he saw her face. A wave of reaction ripped up from his stomach. He had to force himself to look at the round eyes that stared straight up, sightless in death. Kimberly's frizzled red hair lay all around her in the dirt.

She had been stabbed—that was apparent, as the handle of the murder weapon still protruded from her neck.

Adam's heart stopped for a moment as he focused on that instrument. He blinked, trying to clear away what was surely a trick of his eye…. No. God, no.

He reached for the knife and pulled it out. It slid easily, with no gush of blood or a single sound other than a crisp gliding noise. It lay in his hand, the thin blade encrusted with rust-colored stains. The distinctive handle, however, was unmarred.

He recognized it. Anyone would. It was an exquisite medieval dagger that usually resided on the desk in the drawing room, the one at which Helena sat to see to her household duties or attend to her correspondence. It was kept as a seal breaker for letters. He himself had seen Helena wield it several times.

Cain's whine broke the preternatural quiet of Kimberly's unhallowed grave. Adam started, his head snapping up. Sweat soaked his body, plastering the linen shirt to his back and clammily grasping at the woolen riding breeches so that they clung to his thighs. With less care than he had entered, he backed out of the bush.

He still held the knife in his hand. It felt like it weighed a thousand stone. Straightening, he looked at it for a long moment before slipping it in his pocket.

He had no idea what he was going to do with it. He only knew he didn't want it lying around for discovery when they came for Kimberly's body.

"I'm glad you're feeling better," Lord Rathford said to his daughter. He looked at Helena a bit balefully, and she assumed it was because he had heard about the dolls. She'd smashed them all. No doubt this confirmed everyone's certainty of her insanity.

Raising her chin a notch, she replied, "I feel wonderful."

"Good. Good." Rathford frowned, not at all pleased. "I, ah, I wanted to talk to you, button. About Mannion."

He was nervous. That alone raised Helena's interest. "Yes?"

They were in the library. Her father was seated behind the large mahogany desk. He now drew a folded piece of paper from beneath the blotter. "There is no gentle way to tell you this. Would that there were." He paused, then held up the paper. "I received this from Howard."

Helena held out her hand and her father gave it to her. "You can read it for yourself, but apparently Mannion has made inquiries into getting control of your trusts."

"What?" Helena exclaimed, hurrying to open the letter.

Rathford nodded regretfully. "Howard tells me he's been pressuring the trustees of the banks to relinquish guardianship of the money."

"That's absurd. That money is mine, protected from my husband under the terms of the trust. He knows that."

"I was told that he…" Rathford shifted uncomfortably in his seat. He gave a shrug, then winced. "He, ah, he says he has grounds to declare you incompetent."

"How so?" she demanded with indignation.

"He claims…you're…insane. That is the basis of his case."

"How does Howard know this?"

"One of the bank trustees isn't as discreet as he could be. Someone talked, and Howard's heard tell of your...eh, condition. *Supposed* condition."

"It can't be...."

Rathford sighed. "I could make other inquiries, speak to the trustees myself. Perhaps Howard heard wrongly...."

It was too humiliating, the desperate platitudes she heard in her father's voice. "No. Please, don't involve anyone else."

Rathford's voice was gruff when he spoke. "Helena...I know you hoped he'd be more. Christ, I hoped... Ah, bloody hell, it doesn't matter. He's a fortune hunter, plain and simple. He never claimed to be anything else."

"Then you believe it?"

Rathford seemed to struggle with an inner war. "Do you?"

Her gaze fell, and as the breath left her body, all the strength fled as well. "It doesn't seem like Adam. He's always been so forthright about his motives."

"That we know of," Rathford amended.

Brow creased, Helena allowed the comment to stand. "I suppose I should ask him."

"I'll do it," Rathford said, a gleam of violent anticipation in his eyes.

"No." Helena came to her feet, ready with more to say, but paused as Rathford made to rise as well. He suddenly stopped. He seemed to be in some pain. "Father?"

Then all at once, his features collapsed and he reflexively threw his hands out, grasping for something to hold on to. Helena acted swiftly, coming to tuck her shoulder under his outstretched arms. She braced her legs to bear his greater weight. "Father! Father, what is it?"

"Damnation and bloody hell!" he exclaimed. "Get me to the divan."

"Lean on me," she urged, hobbling under the weight.

"Christ!" he groaned, doubling over and nearly dragging Helena to her knees. "Get my medicine."

"What medicine? My God, you are ill?"

"It's...ah, hell, child. Let me lie down here and just call Charlie and Philip."

Helena's coolness of a moment ago was gone completely. Her voice came, high and shrill with burgeoning panic. "You are in terrible pain."

His voice was strangled. "Not this bad before. The medicine, girl. Now. In the desk. Go."

She turned on her heel and fled to do what he asked. Tears ran, scalding hot, down her cheeks as she fumbled with the drawers, finally finding the laudanum.

Laudanum. She remembered someone asking her—was it Mrs. Kent?—if she'd taken a tincture of opium, that her symptoms had at times put one to mind of someone taking laudanum—sleepy, disoriented, headachy and nauseous. She remembered replying with the observation that there was none in the house.

She pushed the thought aside and rushed back to her father. She administered the dose with shaking hands, calling for the menservants her father had requested. When the medicine was given and her father borne up to his bedroom, cursing and gasping with pain in turns, Helena pulled a chair up to his side and took his hand.

"I'm dying, button," he said to her in a quiet voice.

Tears sprang to her eyes. "Don't say that, Father."

"I've known for some time. The pain started months ago. Drink dulled it for a while. Then it seemed to make it worse." He turned his head on the pillow and looked at her softly. "It always made you so angry when I was drunk."

"I thought...I thought—"

"I know," he replied. "You thought I ceased to care about you. I tell you, I've never stopped loving you more than my very own life. You're my child, my little daughter." He stopped. Helena saw the muscles in his throat contract. "I had hoped Mannion would take care of you for me. When I'm gone. A father likes to know his child is being provided for, loved. I didn't want to leave you alone in the world."

"Oh, Father. Is that why you chose him?"

"It was the only thing I could see to save you from this cursed life you were determined to live. He did seem to do it, too, for a while." His face turned bitter in an instant. "Now I want to wring his worthless neck. I never thought he'd steal from you, hurt you like this. How can I bear to leave this earth when I know what he's done?"

"Please don't talk like that. You are not leaving. I've sent for the surgeon."

"Bah. The man's an idiot. One thing Mannion did right was banish him from you when you were ill."

A strange, nagging thought niggled at the edges of her awareness. She didn't have time to search it out.

Rathford drew in a pain-racked breath. "Let us say our goodbyes now, Daughter. I don't want you to remember me like this, helpless, an invalid."

"I won't go."

"I'll have John drag you out if you don't." He tried to sound stern, but he was too weak. "Now say farewell."

"I won't go," she cried, clinging tighter to his hand.

"Helena," he said gently. "Leave me my dignity."

There was a short silence. Then quickly, before she could change her mind, Helena got up and quit the room.

Chapter Thirty-Two

When Adam entered the house, he was greeted by Mrs. Kent, who asked to speak to him in the family withdrawing room. With his hand over the murder implement secreted in his coat, he followed her lead, only half paying attention.

"Lord Rathford has taken ill. He refused the surgeon."

The news caught his attention. "Is it serious?"

"Indeed, sir, I know he is in a great deal of pain and..." She swallowed, and continued in a thin voice. "Well, sir, he expects to die. He has said as much."

Adam ran his hand through his hair, fingers digging into the scalp. "Good God. I'll go see him immediately."

"He wishes to see no one, but says he shall have a final letter for you. He is working to put his affairs in order."

Adam shook his head, pinching the bridge of his nose. "Where's Lady Helena?"

"The master sent her out. She's terribly upset, sir. She's in her rooms."

"I'll go right away to check on her."

"Oh, no, sir, not there," Mrs. Kent said quickly. "Not in her bedroom suite. She's up in the old nursery and schoolroom. Playing the pianoforte, I suppose."

But Helena wasn't playing, Adam discovered when he

entered the tower rooms. She was standing against a wall, arms wrapped around herself. He made to go to her, and as he crossed the wood floor, his eyes caught the heap of debris in the corner.

"What happened?" he asked, detouring to inspect the mess. He paused, then looked at Helena. "Did you do this?"

"I did it." She looked at him, sullen and angry. "My mother is dead. I don't want to live for her anymore. I don't want to be like those dolls."

He approached her cautiously. "Of course not."

Her eyes flashed. "Don't take that tone with me. Or look at me like that. I'm not insane. I didn't destroy those dolls in a fit of lunacy, Adam. I did it because I was angry. I was furious. Do you know how many of those dolls I held and cuddled and played with as a child? Do you know how many of them even had a name?"

He stood mute, not sure of her all of a sudden. He had been prepared for her to be disoriented, as she had been before. However, she was looking directly at him, speaking sharply, clearly, and not at all confused.

"None," Helena continued. "Not a one. They were trophies, beautifully crafted and meant only to look at, not to love. And that was how I was raised to be."

As the words registered, he felt a dawning sense of horror. She looked so lovely, so fragile. The welling tears in her eyes made them look luminous, and the sight of them produced a physical ache in his arms to hold her.

She dragged in a staggered breath and said, "And my father was the only one who didn't treat me like one of those dolls. He loved me. He didn't always show it, he wasn't always strong. I wish he had stood up to my mother. I wish things had been different. But…but he did love me. It's only now when I'm going to lose him that I realize that.'' Her face collapsed and her hands came to cover her mouth. ''Oh, Adam, what am I going to do without him?''

Helena wasn't thinking about the letter. With all that had happened with her father falling ill so suddenly, with his terrible talk of dying, she had forgotten the explosive revelations. However, she recollected the facts all at once as she saw Adam coming toward her. She held up her hand to ward him off.

''This should please you,'' she said sharply, moving backward until she collided with the wall. She leaned up against it, letting it support her.

Again, that wary, suspicious look. Oh, he was a master, all right. One might think he actually cared. ''Helena, what are you talking about? Your mood is so capricious.''

''Father dies. Then you can enact your little plan.'' She waved her hand at the broken dolls. ''Look, I've even furnished you with more proof. Lunatic Helena went off on one of her wild tantrums. And you didn't even have to drug me this time.''

He made to step toward her, but she flung up both hands. ''Keep away from me. I will scream, and there are still servants in this house who are loyal to me and will help me.''

''What exactly are you accusing me of?'' His voice sounded so steady, so reasonable.

''Howard heard of your plan from one of the loose-lipped trustees.''

''What trustee? What are you talking about?''

''You play the innocent well, Adam. In fact, you make a very convincing devoted husband.'' She tossed her head loftily. ''You almost had me fooled. But you got greedy, and that always makes a man sloppy.''

He crossed his arms over his chest and regarded her steadily. ''Are you going to tell me what this is all about?''

"Your little tricks with the laudanum. And the jewelry always coming up lost. You wrecked my mother's rooms." She stopped, her hand coming to her throat. "Good Lord, did you even set the stable fire and leave me out there, hoping I'd perish?"

"Did I...? What the devil has gotten into you? The stable fire? I was the one who sounded the alarm. I brought you in, stayed with you the whole night. This is—"

"Crazy?" she asked. "Yes. It does sound crazy. You've done a thorough job on that account. If I go to anyone to tell them about this, I'll seem like an utter madwoman."

"Are you telling me that you believe someone is trying to make it seem as if you are going mad? And I take it this someone is, in your mind, me?"

"No. Not *somebody*. You, Adam. No one else has any cause."

He surged forward and demanded through gritted teeth, "And what exactly is my 'cause'?"

She thrust her chin out, bringing her nearly nose-to-nose with him. "The money," she answered bitterly. "The trusts that are in my name alone, protected from you."

His eyes flared, then narrowed. "I see."

"Yes. The only way you'll get your hands on them is if I'm declared..." She swallowed.

"Mad," he finished for her in a soft voice. "Christ, Helena, I don't want your money."

"Oh, really. This from the self-confessed fortune hunter."

He looked affronted. "I never denied my motives for coming to Northumberland. But you surely understand how things have changed. I can't believe you think me capable of this."

"Then what is the explanation? Tell me." There was more than a hint of desperation in her voice. Yes, she wanted to hear him give her another possibility, a thread of hope, anything not to believe he wasn't what he seemed.

"God," he muttered. In disgust, he turned away. At the door he paused, peering at her over his shoulder. "I don't have any explanations. I have nothing to tell you except I'd never do anything to hurt you. Never, Helena."

"I'm leaving," she announced. "I'm going downstairs to await word about my father."

"I'm coming with you."

"Please don't," she said curtly.

"I *am coming with you.*"

In the drawing room, she kept her distance, sitting over by the large window. Adam went directly to her desk. She sneaked a look over her shoulder to see what he was doing. She saw he had her dagger, the one she used for opening letters. He seemed to be looking at it, then put it back in its place. When he turned, he saw her eyes on him.

"That is a lovely antique," he said. He was staring at her most intently. She pursed her lips and glared briefly. He shrugged, then sauntered over to a divan, collapsing upon it with an artless grace she never failed to find appealing.

"By the way, Helena, have you seen Kimberly lately?" he asked as he examined his fingernails.

Shaking her head, she sank back into a seat. She had lost interest in him for the moment. Her worries for her father were taking over again. She began to weep, this time silently and all alone. Adam sat on the divan and watched her.

The news that Lord Rathford wasn't going to die came just after dawn the following day.

Mrs. Kent threw open the doors to the drawing room, the sound like a clap of thunder in the silence. Adam, who was still draped loosely over a divan, half in a doze, jumped a foot at the noise. Helena was slumped in a chair by the roaring fire. Sitting up straight, she asked, "Is there word, Mrs. Kent?"

Mrs. Kent clasped her hands together. "My lady, your father is much improved! Oh, he had a terrible time of it. The ailment was acute, but he seems to have passed the vile poisons out of his system."

"What's this? He's improving?" Adam queried.

"Oh, but the illness, it was beastly, sir. I've never seen the like, not even with a woman in childbirth, but thank goodness it's over now. He's resting."

"I want to see him," Helena and Adam said in unison.

"Certainly, right away. Come, then."

They went swiftly up to Lord Rathford's room. It was a Spartan space, the wood furnishings dark with age, and battered. He had no care for style or comfort, giving the place a utilitarian atmosphere. Even his bed looked uninviting and small, barely holding the large form of the master of the house.

Rathford was sleeping. Disappointed, Helena turned to go. Adam grasped her by the upper arm. "Does your father believe what you do about me?" he whispered fiercely.

She blazed a challenge back at him. "He was the one who told me."

Adam frowned. He released her. "Damnation," he muttered. "I can't figure what the devil is going on here. I've got to speak with him."

"He needs his rest."

"You go. I'll wait." He turned away, dismissing her.

Helena disliked leaving him with her father, but saw no reason why he couldn't stay. Besides, she was exhausted, a condition she hadn't realize until just now. With the news that her father was going to recover, the tension that had kept her taut as a tightly strung harp string drained out of her and she felt as if she could sleep for ages. She headed for her bedroom.

"My lady," said the maidservant, Cathy, who was just coming out of her boudoir, "I've turned down your bed. Do you want me to help you undress?"

"No, thank you. Just make certain I'm not disturbed."

Once alone, Helena's mind churned over the events of the past few hours. Only a single day had passed, and yet so much had happened. With her father well—and thank heaven for it—she soon settled on the subject of Howard's letter. And Adam. He'd tried to get her trusts. He'd argued that she was mad....

No. She wouldn't believe it. Her first reaction had been defensive, true. It seemed very easy to blame Adam, think the worst, but she didn't really think that now. Perhaps she should not have confronted him. Even if it were true, what proof did she have? And if it weren't, then she had hurt him deeply.

Oh, God, she'd even accused him of trying to make her believe she was going insane. What had made her say that? She hadn't ever thought of herself as a victim of a plot. In the heat of the moment she'd blurted it out, but now...now she wondered if she hadn't finally hit on something. It was finding there was laudanum in the house. It made the possibility that her "madness" had been staged, that she'd actually been being drugged all along, shockingly real.

Sinking onto the window seat, she drew her legs up and hugged them to her chest. Yes, it was obvious. Now that she was able to think clearly and not be so afraid, she could see it. Someone was playing games with her mind. She refused to believe Adam had been behind it. If it made her a fool, than so be it, but it wasn't Adam. It wasn't.

Someone else, then. An enemy who was unknown.

As she rose to her feet, she found she was trembling. She could hardly believe what she intended to do. Going down to the library, she headed straight for the cupboard situated between two tall windows, and drew out a large box. Laying it on the desk, she opened it. Two elegant flintlocks lay on the blue-velvet-covered casing. She picked one up.

Load that one. We'll need it to finish him off. He's not dead.

The cold, curt voice of her mother, telling her to put in the powder, then the plug, then a lead ball. Helena had followed the orders while her mind was thinking that it really wasn't happening, that it was some misunderstanding or a terrible jest.

And then it had struck her that it *was* real. Her mother had fully intended to kill Chloe and Jareth and there was nothing to stop her.

But Helena had. She'd stopped her mother.

Now, holding these flintlocks in her hands was like touching fire.

She knew where her father kept the powder and balls. She fetched them and loaded each pistol, then carried them upstairs in their box, removed them and slipped them under her pillow.

Enough doubt remained to keep her from going to Adam tonight. She would wait and see, let the dust settle on all of this, and go to him in the morning if she was still of a mind to. Her emotional state, after the night of worry and the previous evening of high tempers, could hardly be trusted. If anything happened, she had the pistols. Just in case.

Chapter Thirty-Three

It was just after tea that very afternoon when the magistrate came.

Adam had given up waiting for Rathford to awaken. The man was doing well, he'd been told, and had roused from sleep briefly to eat some thin broth, but absolute rest was the best thing for him, and Mrs. Kent meant to see he received it. Seeing the gruff old bear in this unaccustomed weak state, Adam hadn't the heart to go against the prescribed regimen of peaceful repose to tell him about Kimberly. Or ask about the ridiculous accusations Helena had made.

By late that afternoon, however, he had tired of waiting and began to think that Rathford wouldn't appreciate being coddled. This was a matter of murder, after all.

That was precisely the moment the magistrate knocked upon the door. From his place on the landing, Adam watched as the man was shown into the center hall, heard the officious voice announce his name, followed by his title.

They were here for Helena, then. The bottom fell out of his world and he gripped the banister for support as he watched the guests below shown to the parlor. Adam spied four men in all. All wore serious faces. One was carrying a length of rope he didn't bother to conceal. Adam understood its purpose—to subdue anyone who might not feel inclined to be cooperative—

They were not going to *tie* her, for God's sake. He'd not let them do that to Helena!

With a heavy tread, he went into the parlor, thinking it best to do this on a friendly basis and avoid an ugly scene. The introductions were made stiffly. "Mr. Mannion," Theodore Tandy, the constable said. "I shall come directly to the point. There's been a murder. A member of your staff here at Rathford Hall. Her name was Kimberly O'Banyon."

Adam looked from one dour countenance to another. The man with the rope twisted it restlessly. Another man moved to block the doorway.

Returning his gaze to the magistrate, Adam felt his heartbeat begin to race. Could it be he had come to the wrong conclusion?

The constable said, "We'd like to ask you a few questions."

It was some hours later when Cathy shook Helena awake with the frantic words, "They are arresting him, ma'am. Please wake up."

Helena sat up, alarm flooding her in an instant. "What is it?" She shot to her feet. "Who? Arrested? Who has been arrested?"

"Mr. Mannion, ma'am. The constable says he murdered Kimberly."

"Kimberly... My God, Kimberly has been murdered?" She pushed her hair away from her face. "Mr. Mannion is with the constable, you say?"

"Indeed, ma'am, they're about to take him. He sent me to fetch you. He's terrible frantic, he is. They..." The poor girl looked like she was about to cry. "They tied him, ma'am, because he kept saying he had to get to you, and he wouldn't cooperate when they wanted to take him away. Oh, it was awful."

Deep cold flooded her in an instant, and she stood uncertain in the middle of her room. Why would the authorities believe Adam had killed Kimberly?

In the clear rationality that comes after a refreshing sleep, she knew he was innocent of any wrongdoing. Her momentary doubts of the day before, fed by exhaustion and worry over her father, plus the shock of Howard's letter, had calmed.

And she had remembered something late last night, something simple and ridiculously obvious. When she had been speaking with her father, he had observed that the town surgeon was an idiot and that Adam had wisely kept him away from Helena during her "spells," as he'd be likely to do her harm. It had occurred to her, then, that if Adam had been against her, why would he keep her from the incompetent surgeon, whose bumbling and painful methods would only have aided a nefarious cause?

Adam had protected her from him, as he had from all danger. That was the reason he'd disliked Kimberly. But he hadn't killed her. He'd had no reason to, for he'd succeeded in keeping the strange servant out of Helena's way and nullifying her demented influence.

So how could they possibly have any evidence whatsoever to accuse him of such a thing?

Slipping swiftly in a gray morning gown, her hair undressed, her feet stuffed into slippers without benefit of stockings, she raced downstairs.

But she was too late. John Footman—whom Adam had taken to calling Jack—stood in the hall, a stricken expression on his face. Helena skidded to a halt and stared at him. "Where—?"

"They've taken him, my lady," he said in a stunned monotone.

"Oh, my God." Helena rushed to him, forgetting propriety, and grasped his arm. "Why did they arrest him? On what grounds, Jack?"

"They spoke to the staff," Jack explained. "They didn't want to say anything to cast blame on him, madam, but it was no secret that Mr. Mannion disliked that woman."

"Kimberly had many enemies, any one of whom could have killed her."

"But they said there was a witness, that someone had come forward and said they'd seen Mr. Mannion do it."

Helena felt her knees weaken. "Who would tell such lies?"

"They wouldn't reveal who it was. The constable said the man was afraid for his life, that he'd be the next victim if he didn't keep his identity a secret until the trial."

"Can they do that? I mean, is it legal?"

"I don't know, my lady." He lifted his hand to indicate the drawing room, then let it fall. "They searched a bit, found a knife on your desk. They said that was the one he'd used to kill her. They found blood in the pocket of his coat. They say he carried the knife home in it, and it stained his clothes."

"I don't care what they found. My husband would never kill anyone. Didn't he tell them that?"

Jack's brows drew down. "That's what has me so confused, ma'am. He didn't say anything. He didn't deny it. He just let them take him."

"That's absurd." Her head reeled. She had to blink several times to steady her vision. "He didn't kill her, Jack."

"I know it, my lady. Then why…"

But Helena knew.

By the way, Helena, have you seen Kimberly lately?

Her mind had been too clouded with useless suspicions to recognize the same in his tone. He'd watched her reaction closely, tension making his voice curt—a tension she had misread as goading.

He believed she'd killed Kimberly. He'd somehow known the Irishwoman was dead and—

Helena's memory shifted. The knife! She'd seen him pick up the antique—but what if he'd been putting it back? He'd known it was hers. He'd taken it, placed it back in its regular place, to protect her—in his mind, he was taking the blame in her place. He thought she had murdered the woman!

"Jack," Helena began, trying to keep her voice calm, "was the knife they took the antique dagger I keep at my desk?"

"Why yes, my lady. It was indeed."

"Then how would anyone know it was that precise knife used to do the murder?"

"That witness, they said."

"No. Not a witness. The murderer himself, who has cleverly ensnared my husband to take the blame for it. And Adam won't say a word against the accusations because he thinks he's protecting me."

"I don't understand, ma'am."

"Fetch the carriage and come with me to the constable's office. I'll explain on the way."

Adam found himself in the old gatehouse to Kennibank Abbey, a small retreat now in ruins and overrun with trees and brambles. The gatehouse, however, was used as the village jail. They put him in a small chamber with a thin pallet, a stool, and a table upon which sat a lamp, as well

as a tray of congealed stew and a crust of stale bread. Th
constable apologized, muttering something about his wif
not being a very good cook. This was difficult to believe
as the man had an impressive belly. However, Adam mad
no comment. He took the three-legged stool provided an
sat upon it, politely replying that his appetite was not u
to snuff tonight. The constable had nodded as if he under
stood, saying he'd leave the supper for him, in case he grev
hungry later, and then he had left Adam alone.

It wasn't so bad a place. Adam supposed men had bee
incarcerated in far worse. But it felt like a slice of hell. Hi
whole body rebelled with pent-up frustration when h
thought of Helena. She was alone, unprotected...and
killer was on the loose tonight.

No doubt she wouldn't listen to him, even if he coul
speak with her. Already she regarded him as a maliciou
opportunist. Why not believe him a murderer?

He stretched out on the pallet trying to think. He had th
strangest nagging sensation in the back of his brain, a sus
picion that he'd forgotten something.

The rattle of the lock surprised him. He had supposed h
would be left alone for the night. When a slender figur
entered, he shot to his feet.

Helena wore a cloak with the hood up. When she en
tered, she pushed the cowl off, and the pale shade of he
hair caught the glow from the candle and threw it bac
with a flourish. He felt a knot in his throat, a momentar
damming of joy and desire.

She paused inside the doorway for an instant. "O
Adam," she cried, and ran to him.

The shock was pleasant, easing instantly into a wonderf
warmth that drenched him all the way to his toes. "What'
this?" he murmured hoarsely, emotion nearly choking him

"I thought…well, I thought you were quite cross with me."

"I don't believe you've done any of the things you've been accused of."

He closed his eyes for an instant, thanking God for her change of heart. "It's about time we believed in each other."

She looked up at him. "You understand that it was someone else, don't you, trying to make me appear mad?"

"I believe you are as sane as I." He considered the statement and cocked a speculative brow. "That's not saying much from a man accused of murder."

"Falsely," she amended. She lowered her voice. "You found Kimberly's body, didn't you? My dagger had been used to kill her, and you put it back. I saw you, although I didn't realize what was happening at the time. You thought I'd done it."

"I thought…I'm sorry, Helena. I admit I thought the worst. It was wrong of me, but the facts…well, they seemed so logically to implicate you and only you. I thought perhaps in one of your spells you might have… God, I am so sorry."

"I've had my own moments of doubt about you. Whoever is doing this to us is manipulating us quite cleverly."

"Why have you decided to trust me?" He ran his hand along her arms.

"I love you," she said in a soft voice. "And I suppose that if I trust you enough with my heart, I should trust you with my life."

He was too stunned to speak. His hands stopped moving and he couldn't think of a thing to say.

She smiled, tentatively at first. Reaching up and tilting her head to the side, she held his face in her hands, bringing it within reach of her mouth. Her kiss was sweet, searching, an offering as gentle and lovely as the lady herself. He took it, returning his ardor in lieu of an answer, holding her closer, tighter, and she reached up and wound her arms around his neck.

The door opened. They broke apart, awkwardly pulling themselves together with an effort. "That's all the time I can permit," said the constable.

"Please," Helena said softly over her shoulder to the man, "we have hardly yet spoken."

"The magistrate will have my hide, my lady. I shouldn' have let you in at all."

"Helena." Adam spoke softly but in a firm voice. "Go ahead, love. We can talk tomorrow."

When she turned back to him, he could see the anguish in her eyes. "There's so much I want to say to you," she murmured. "I haven't had a chance to tell you even a little part of what—"

"I know. I... There's much I have to tell you, too. God knows we've kept too much held back from one another, which is most of our trouble. But now isn't the time." He cast a meaningful glance at the hovering constable. "Go on. We'll sort all this out on the morrow."

She took a moment to deliberate before giving a reluctant nod. "First thing in the morning, I will be back." She paused and touched his cheek. "I'll have Maddie pack you a fine breakfast."

Adam gave a baleful glance to the cooled dinner sitting on the table. "You are a wife beyond measure," he said dryly. His face composed itself in sober lines. "Take great care, Helena. Someone has committed murder. Whoever it is isn't done yet. There is danger. Great danger."

Wordlessly, she nodded. He kissed the back of both her hands before releasing her. She slipped through the door past the uncomfortable constable.

After she'd gone, Adam was more restless than ever.

She loved him—that was what he kept thinking about, and although the idea was thrilling, he had far more urgent matters to untangle. Still, it settled warm and right into his heart and made the uncertainty of their present circumstances all the more acute.

He felt the danger around them, sensed it was going to strike. How much more neatly could the murderer have put Adam out of the way than he was right now? And Rathford was still ill, making his slow recovery. Helena was unprotected.

Adam had to get to his wife—this he knew with the silent urgency of inflamed instinct. The very smell of threat, metallic and acrid like blood, curled in his nostrils and filled his head.

He called for the constable. There was no answer. He called louder, kept at it for nearly an hour, until his voice was almost hoarse. Accepting the futility of such efforts, he settled down to sort through the facts.

Kimberly... Why had she been killed? This puzzled him greatly. Had she been an accomplice in the plot against Helena, or an innocent bystander? Searching his mind, Adam went over everything he knew in fine detail.

He remembered what Helena had said to him the night her father had taken ill, and shot to his feet. Pressing his thumbs to the bridge of his nose, Adam tried to recall Helena's exact words.

Oh, God. The identity of Helena's tormentor came to him in a blinding flash of insight.

How had he missed realizing it before? The madness—the madness should have been the key. He had been so afflicted by his own fears for Helena that he hadn't taken

the time to analyze how it fit in so strategically in a large
plan.

Running to the door, he began pounding and shouting a
the top of his lungs for the constable to come immediately
It was a matter of life and death!

Chapter Thirty-Four

The storm rolled in around midnight, throwing rain savagely against the shuttered windows and whipping the wind into a frightening fury. Inside her room, Helena sat hunched on her bed, wishing it would stop.

She had been to see her father earlier. He was resting comfortably and in good spirits, and it eased her to know this. She didn't tell him about Kimberly, or about Adam's arrest. Kissing him on his cheek, rough and unfamiliarly stubbled, she had told him she loved him and begged him to get well soon. She needed him, she had added silently. She was very afraid.

Sleep seemed impossible, but drowsiness crept upon her steadily until she doused the light. She lay stiffly on her back, not at all certain she could give up her vigilance enough to close her eyes. Surprisingly, she succumbed, slipping into dreamless slumber just as the clock out in the hall tolled one o'clock.

When a noise awoke her, she thought at first the shutter on her window had come undone. In the groggy state of half sleep, she sat up. She froze, listening as another sound came. This time, being awake, she could tell quite distinctly that it was outside the door. A tide of numbing terror took hold of her and for a moment she didn't know what to do

Then she remembered the flintlocks. Fumbling under the pillow, she had them in her hand when the bedroom door opened. The room was dark, but for a lamp turned down low, which the intruder carried.

In one move, she brought up both her hands and aimed at the man who had come into her bedroom.

"Helena!"

The face, the voice—she saw it was Adam! Here! She leaped out of bed and went straight into his arms.

Wet and chilled from the storm, he nevertheless felt wonderful—solid, large. She laid her cheek against the damp fabric of his coat. He held her tight with his free arm and set the lamp down on the bedside table. "What are you holding? Dear Lord, pistols. Good girl!"

She drew back and stared at the two weapons she held "I almost forgot." He placed his hands over the muzzles taking them from her. Helena said, "They are primed. Take care."

He placed them on the floor gently, then tucked her under his arm once again. "Thank God you are safe. I was near frantic with worry."

"What has happened, Adam? Why did they release you?"

By the dim light, she saw that familiar, beloved grin "Well, they didn't. I rather took unfair advantage of the constable. To my credit, I tried to reason with him. He left me with no choice. It was easy to catch him unawares. The fellow is in the wrong line of work. Far too trusting."

"You didn't."

"If you are meaning to scold me, I should tell you that you don't sound horrified at all. In fact, you sound rather pleased."

"Oh, I am. I'm so glad to have you here. Adam, I was terrified."

"And I for you. I just thank the Lord you had the presence of mind to protect yourself. Come over to the bed. You're shivering."

"It's from excitement, not cold." She paused. "You know, they will come here when they discover what you've done."

"Maybe. I was hoping you and I could apply ourselves to something avoiding that circumstance."

"How?"

He gave a low chuckle. "I hadn't come up with anything just yet. You?"

"The only thing I can think of is for us to give them the real killer."

He gave her a penetrating look. "And just who do you think that is?"

"I haven't figured it all out yet. I do know one thing— it has to be someone close. Whoever it is knew us well enough to feed our worst fears in order to separate us from one another."

"Yes." He sounded as if he were pleased with this reasoning. "For example, your father's fear that you would exhibit the madness that had infected your mother. Once Rathford was convinced, he confided in me, lending credence to the suspicions your behavior had already roused." Adam touched her hair, his eyes soft and radiating some blend of emotion that drew her to him. "And then when you heard I had tried to gain control of your trusts, you believed it because of the circumstances of our betrothal, known only to those very close to you."

"I am sorry I didn't have more faith in you," she murmured. "But then, when I thought about it, I knew you wouldn't do such a thing."

"I don't know why you wouldn't believe the worst. I've given you little enough reason to think well of me."

"It's not true," she declared. "You've been nothing but kind to me from the first." He raised his brows and she amended with a smile, "Well, maybe not the first. But Adam...can it be you don't realize all you've done for me?"

"Done for you? Forced you into marriage, a marriage you hated, all for the sake of money—that's what I did."

"You sound regretful," she observed ruefully.

"Of the circumstances, but certainly not the outcome."

"Oh, Adam—do you mean that?"

"Of course I do. How could you not know how I felt? Lord, Helena, have we been that bad to each other that we are doomed to misunderstanding?" He pushed his hand into his thick dark hair with impatience. "God knows what you think of me, what ideas you must have of why I needed that money. I never explained all of that, did I?"

"You never told me much of anything about your past."

"It's rather embarrassing, that is why. My father left me with a very small inheritance and a great deal of debt. I know many members of the ton don't feel it necessary to make good on certain bills, especially to tradesmen, whom they consider beneath them, but I couldn't condone that. I took the little bit of money I received, doled it out carefully to the most pressing creditors, and then I did a very foolish thing." He drew in a long, deep breath. "With the arrogance of youth, I thought I could turn to gaming to get myself out of trouble. It was a crazy plan, but it worked for a while. Luck is fickle, however, and my losses mounted. I had to admit that I was not very good at being a profligate and wastrel."

His voice was gentle, as was the hand that smoothed her hair. "I came here to use you, and you had every right to hate me for it. I'm ashamed to admit that I was that callow. I was ashamed even at the time, but too arrogant to show it. That shame made me determined not to depend on Rathford money any longer. I began to participate in a far more sophisticated game of chance—an investment pool formed of London investors. I've always had an interest in business, you see, and it seems that I might have a talent for the game of commerce. My initial investments have paid off. I was hoping I could surprise you very soon with the news that I wouldn't be taking my portion any longer. I believe by Christmas next I shall be independent of Rathford money, and will pay back everything, with interest.''

''You don't have to. That's my dowry. Every man expects to receive a gift from his marriage.''

''But I have received a gift.'' He paused meaningfully, and she flushed with pleasure. ''I am sorry, you know, for how we started. I thought about those regrets in that room tonight. That is, when I wasn't worried half to death for your safety. If the constable hadn't come in, I think I could have torn the place apart, mortar and stone.''

''Oh, Adam, I was worried about *you!* I can't lose you,'' she cried, pressing her body up against his, burying her face in the curve of his neck. She could smell him, the stirring aroma of man and sweat and rain all mingled together, and she felt as if she was going to weep.

He jerked her chin up and kissed her, and she hung on, opening to him, offering everything. It was as if he, too, laid bare a part of himself in that kiss, pouring out passion and tenderness and desperate need all in one.

Breaking away, he touched her reverently, fingertips tracing her features, his eyes sweeping lovingly over her face. ''Nor could I ever bear to lose you. I love you, Helena. I love you very much.''

Helena closed her eyes, savored those words. ''I love

you," she answered. "I won't let them take you away from me."

His expression changed. "Listen to me, Helena. I believe I know who killed Kimberly. The key was in something you said to me when we argued last. Just now, you said that the person would have to be someone who knew us quite well."

"True. I would suspect Kimberly, naturally, or perhaps she was a part of it."

"My thoughts exactly. Oh, my love, I am afraid it may come as a shock to you, but it is your cousin, Howard, whom I suspect."

"Howard? Why, how could it be him? He was not even here. He stays in London."

"Curious, but when I traveled to London, I saw nothing of him. Do you recall how he made such a point of dropping all the names of premier personages of the beau monde? One would think he existed at the pinnacle of the ton, don't you agree? And yet I never saw him once at the gentlemen's clubs, or any other place of fashion."

"But I know he does father's business transactions. He must go to London."

"Yes, but not as frequently or for as long as he has you think. I have a notion he stays close by, and has been keeping an eye on things here. Besides, he would know the layout of the house well, wouldn't he?"

"He used to come frequently as a boy. His father and mine were close before Uncle Randolf died. That was his father. It was that fondness between the brothers that fostered the close relationship between Howard and my father." She shook her head, confused. "But what was it I said to make you think of him?"

"He was the one who wrote your father of the supposed rumors about me. When I realized that the men he claimed were speaking ill of me were many of those I was involved in with my business dealings, I knew this gossip could not possibly exist. Therefore, the rumors had to originate with Howard. From there, the rest of it made sense.''

"Yes. He knows the family well, knows the secret about my mother's death. And my father's fears for me.''

"Don't forget that he knew the tension between us was about your inheritance. That makes it easy to prey upon that sore subject, to turn you against me. It also is significant that he seems to be the only one to benefit. He is, after all, your father's heir.''

"But then how was Kimberly involved with his plan?'' Helena frowned. "She must have been, but why would he kill her?''

"Because she was in the way, dear coz, just as you are.'' Helena and Adam turned in unison and faced the man who had entered the room. It was Howard.

And he was pointing a pair of pistols at them.

Chapter Thirty-Five

"Your deductions are astonishing, Mannion. I applaud your powers of reason. They do not surprise me, however. You struck me from the first as a bit too clever for your own good. Of course, that was part of the problem." As Howard stepped farther into the room, his grim face came into view. "If only you'd been the conscienceless gambler you seemed to be at the first. It needn't have got so damned *serious* if you hadn't had such a keen mind."

Adam stood, gently setting Helena away from him. "I apologize for the inconvenience."

"Very sharp at the repartee, you are."

"Howard, why are you doing this?" Helena asked in a dismayed voice.

"Why, the oldest reason in the world, coz, all that wonderful Rathford money. You never needed it, not before Prince Charming here showed up. After that business with Aunt Althea, you went into hiding. Wonderful circumstance for me, especially when Uncle George became a recluse as well, and it all fell on me to handle the family business. But then you had to go and get married." He looked to Adam, and said with a heavy dose of resentment, "I didn't begrudge you your slice at first—at least not too much.

After all, the Rathford fortune is deep. I mean, a bad gambler might even be an asset, if certain…inconsistencies in the books ever came to light.''

''How flattering. You saw me as a scapegoat.'' Adam's voice was droll.

''Not after I met you, I didn't, and then heard the talk around the Town that you were making quite a go of it on the 'Change. I mean, really! You were a no-luck fortune hunter, for God's sake, and then suddenly you were having all this success. That was when I realized you were shrewd. Uncle George was dying—he had told me that—and I ran the risk of exposure after he passed on, should you get involved with the family finances. With you in the picture, I began to realize I might be in a bit of a jam.''

''Howard, you are my father's heir,'' Helena protested in confusion.

''I inherit only that which must be passed on through the laws of entailment,'' he said sharply, his tone full of vinegar. ''Your father's estates, the heraldic arms, the incomes tied to the lands he owns—all of this comes to me. But it all requires a great deal of management for relatively little income compared to the great pots of money coming to you, little coz, without any effort needed at all.''

Adam said, ''The madness was just a game, wasn't it, Howard? It was supposed to make Helena look unbalanced, but you weren't after her. The plan was always to murder me. Then blame Helena.''

''Oh, I see I was right about you.'' Howard smiled coldly. ''Far, far too clever. Well, it was a good plan. After all, she'd murdered before. With a little help making her look all scrambled up, who wouldn't believe she'd kill again? And she'd be so potted at the time, she'd not know any different herself. A little laudanum, a few other things mixed in to keep it interesting. It was ridiculously easy.

When you eventually showed up dead, Adam, we wanted it to be very clear who the main suspect should be.''

"Helena would take the blame, especially with the handy little motive you supplied, putting it out that I'd been trying to pry into her trusts.''

"We didn't fall for that trick, Howard.'' Helena lifted her chin and bestowed an arrogant look on him. "You aren't as great as you think. I suppose Kimberly found you out somehow. That's why you had to kill her.''

"She saw me one time, the time I came in to have fun in Aunt Althea's rooms. She wasn't certain if she wanted to help me or turn me in, no doubt weighing which course of action would bring the best advantage to herself.'' He snorted. It was an ugly sound. "You have already deduced how little I like to share. Altogether, I couldn't see any reason to keep her around. As for Helena being the one to take the blame for it, it was merely an insurance measure. If or when the body was found, all that evidence pointing to Helena would simply strengthen the suspicion of her when Adam showed up dead.''

Howard shook his head, as if he disapproved of them. "Then, when the knife was taken out and returned to its proper place—your doing, I'm guessing, Mannion—I could no longer proceed with that tack. However, I got a better idea. *Adam* hangs for Kimberly's murder and you, coz, take your own life in your grief.''

Helena gasped. "How can you be so cold?''

"Cold? That's rich, coming from you. You, who had everything so perfect all your life. You were always safe and secure in your fabulous wealth, never having to worry about paying off the tailor or the shoemaker because they refused to advance you any more credit and the new styles from France were in and your old clothes were absolutely passé.''

Helena was breathless with rage. "You were going to take away my life, my love, steal every bit of happiness I've ever had in my life...just so you could more easily afford an extravagant way of life?"

Howard looked at her blandly. "You've put it quite succinctly. And don't bother insulting me over it. I assure you I am quite immune." He waved his pistol. "Now, I want the both of you over by the bed."

Adam stepped in front of Helena, slipping her protectively behind his back. "There's no way for you to get away with this now."

"Don't be silly, of course I will. Your being here doesn't change much. Let's see, all I have to do is put my mind to it and I shall think of a way to turn this to my advantage— wait! I have it. Oh, this is grand, this is just grand." He waved the pistols happily. "Oh, wonderful. You see, it will seem as if you were, indeed, Kimberly's murderer, and because you had gotten caught and your life was, for all intents and purposes, going to be over, you came back home because you couldn't bear to leave your beloved. You kill Helena so that she and you can be together in the afterlife, then take your own life. Oh, it is too good!"

Helena grew chilled. It was frightening to think how well it all might work. She was suddenly infused with a raging determination that Howard would *not* get away with this. After fighting all her life for a chance to live—really live— she would not let this greedy worm take it from her. Not now, not ever.

Then suddenly Adam made a strange movement, drawing her interest. His foot grazed one of the flintlocks. Very steadily, he maneuvered it with his heel until it was directly behind him, and right in front of her. Shielded from Howard's view, it lay within her reach, if she could only find some way to bend down to retrieve it.

Inspiration hit her, and without stopping to consider the wisdom of such a move, she sank to her knees. "Adam, Adam!" she said in a faltering voice. "I am afraid I feel quite faint."

In the billowing cloud of her lawn night rail, she moved her hand swiftly, grasped the flintlock and secreted it in the folds of the full skirt. She wanted to give it to Adam, but Howard barked at him to step away from her, and Adam complied swiftly.

Catching his eye, she saw a grim expression on his handsome face. He slid his gaze to Howard and gave a quick nod. He made no move to come close to her. He didn't seem to want to take the weapon from her.

No. Oh, God no.

"Get up. No tricks, do you hear me?" Howard was shouting, his face red with anger. Helena saw immediately that her cousin wasn't going to tolerate any disobedience. That was why Adam had backed off immediately. He knew the man's nerves were nearly at their limit.

Narrowing his eyes, Howard jerked the weapons to indicate she was to move. "Over there. Face each other, and keep on opposite sides of the bed."

Helena looked at Adam. He gave another nod—quick, nearly imperceptible. She wanted desperately to slip him the loaded flintlock—thank God she had primed the pistol earlier!—but he was moving farther and farther away from her.

He swung on her cousin and said in a loud voice, "Just how do you propose to get away with this? The staff will hear the shots, you know. They'll be in here in moments."

Howard addressed him. "I've gotten quite crafty at slipping in and out of these rooms undetected. Consider that the staff is abed. They'll hear the noise, sit up, ask themselves what the devil they just heard. By the time they decide it was a gunshot and spring into action, you'll both be dead, and I'll be halfway down the old tower stairs nobody uses any longer.''

Helena saw him glance at her, then run his tongue nervously over his lips. Adam spoke again, diverting Howard's attention, and that was when she realized what her husband intended.

Howard's plan was to position them so he could shoot from the correct angle—a detail that was necessary for the deception he planned to explain the murders. He would fire one flintlock near where Adam stood, close enough to make it seem as if Adam had done the murder, then shoot him with the other at close range to simulate suicide. Howard was also trying to get himself as close to the door as possible so he could make good his escape.

And Adam was being cooperative so that he could use Howard's careful positioning to draw her cousin's attention from her. When Howard turned toward Adam, he faced away from Helena.

Adam struck a defiant stance and laughed. ''You are a fool, Howard. You are forgetting one very important detail.''

Howard's eyes grew wide with surprise...and concern. He faced Adam, Helena momentarily forgotten. ''What? What are you talking about?''

Adam chuckled. ''That's for you to figure out.''

She raised her arm and pointed the pistol.

Oh, God. Oh, God.

A tide of panic swept over her.

She looked to Adam. There was sweat on his brow. He didn't look at her, but she could tell every line of his body was taut with tension. He was waiting—waiting for her to save their lives.

The room at the inn...

Howard began to turn his head, as if somehow sensing the threat. Adam said something quickly, trying to draw his attention back to himself, but Howard had seen the gun. His face registered fear for a split second before she fired.

The sound was deafening. The smell of burnt powder singed her nose, and a flood of sickness came over her as she remembered that terrible scent from all those years ago.

She fell to her knees, gulping in air. Head tucked in, she grasped her stomach against the waves of nausea slamming into her. Somewhere in the direction of the two men there came the sound of a scuffle, then the hideous crunch of a closed fist meeting bone.

She must have missed. Oh, Lord, how could she have failed?

She must have missed!

Scrabbling on the floor for the other flintlock, she closed her hand around the handle and brought it up in a quick motion.

"Whoa!" Adam barked, holding his hand up to stop her. At his feet, Howard lay unconscious. She could see crimson on the felled man's thigh.

She hadn't missed, after all. And she hadn't killed him, either. She'd shot Howard in the leg.

Coming forward slowly, Adam gently took the pistol from her hand, then knelt down beside her and pulled her into the haven of his arms. "My poor girl," he murmured softly. "My poor brave girl. I'm sorry, my love. I'm so sorry."

"It's over," she said dully.

He pulled back to look at her. There was a smile on his lips. He seemed surprised to hear her speak so clearly. She touched that sensuous mouth of his and said, "It is over, isn't it?"

"Yes, love, it's over. It's all over. I'll never let anything like that happen again."

"I love you."

"I love you," he replied, his voice a soft hush of a whisper. "Madly, insanely—oh, that wasn't a wise choice of words, but there's no help for it, is there? It's the way it is."

She laughed suddenly. Imagine, finding anything funny in this room, freshly snatched from the bony grip of mortal danger and an unconscious Howard lying so close. But then, Adam could always make her laugh. "I suppose there are some acceptable ways for one to lose one's head. Falling in love is certainly one of them."

"What here!" a new voice demanded.

Adam twisted and looked at the manservant who stood at the door, a lone candle flickering in his hand. "Jack. There's Kimberly's murderer, and very nearly ours, lying on the floor. It is Master Howard. Get him locked up someplace, will you? Oh, and see that his wound is tended. Your mistress has gone and shot him."

"Master Howard?" the man cried, incredulous.

"The very same," Adam drawled, turning back to Helena.

His eyes shone with love as they swept over her features. Placing his hands gently on her face, he ran his thumbs over the magnificent cheekbones, down the smooth cheeks, touching gently the delicately formed mouth. Ignoring the sounds of the head footman struggling to drag Howard's dead weight out of the bedroom, he bent to kiss his wife.

He paused and lifted his head. "Oh, Jack?" he called.

The footman puffed hard as he looked up. "Yes, sir."

"Make certain that wound is tended."

"You told me that, sir."

"In fact, call the village surgeon. And tell him we will

need him to specially apply all of his prodigious skills to heal the dreadful bullet hole.''

Wearily, he replied, ''Yes, sir, of course...'' Jack stopped, then grinned as he got the meaning. More crisply, he said, ''Of course, sir. And rest assured the staff will execute each and every one of his instructions with precision...and enthusiasm!''

A pair of other menservants arrived then, and Howard was born out between their brawny shoulders.

Helena tilted her head at her husband as he turned back to her. Adam let loose one of those devastating smiles and laughed with her before he took her in his arms for a kiss.

After a moment, they broke apart. ''Why was I so afraid to love you?'' he murmured against her lips. The soft texture of his mouth against her flesh sent ripples of pleasure all through her. ''I don't think I truly knew what living was until I met you.''

''Do you feel that way really, Adam?'' she asked, surprised. ''I rather thought it was the other way around.''

The corners of his eyes crinkled and the bottom fell out of her heart as she lost herself again in his gaze. ''Then it's mutual.'' His eyes darkened, becoming deep pools of pitch. ''You know, I feel rather a cad, given everything that's gone on tonight, but you see, I am overwhelmed with the most powerful urge to make love to you right this moment.''

She took his face in her hands. ''It wouldn't be right.''

''No, of course not.''

''Not with Howard, you know...''

''Right.''

''And the constable is bound to come for you soon.''

Adam frowned and scratched his head. ''Well, he might be indisposed for a good while....''

"The staff is probably waiting for us to make an appearance, explain the shots they heard."

"Indeed, I had thought of that myself. That is why I think it wise that we cease this discussion and get things under way as quickly as possible."

Then they laughed, rose and hurried to the bed.

Epilogue

M<small>RS</small>. Featherston peered through the lenses of her jewel-encrusted lornette at the couple who had just entered the room. This drawing room was far enough away from the dancing at Helding's ball that the strains of music were faint, making it possible to converse easily.

Next to her, Lady Whitesby leaned in close and whispered. "Who are they? Why, she's magnificent. Look at that face, and that hair—when have you seen such a color?" Lady Whitesby placed a fluttering hand over her spare breast. "And him...oh, my. Dark eyes, dark hair. And that smile. Goodness."

"He looks familiar, although I cannot recall where I've seen him before." Mrs. Featherston frowned. "They could possibly be the Mannions...yes, I'm sure of it now. I had heard all the talk. Well, well...*that* is the Sleeping Beauty of Northumberland. Even those exaggerated rumors didn't do her justice."

"Oooh! Is that him? Adam Mannion? Oh, Lord Whitesby was telling his friends just the other day about the fortune he made on the 'Change. Shipping, I believe."

Mrs. Featherston sniffed. "Well, new money and all."

"Of course, of course." Pausing, Lady Whitesby added

tentatively, "And yet he seems most…charming. Look at how he looks at his wife." Her fan snapped open and began to flutter wildly. "Goodness gracious, he's absolutely… well, *devouring* her."

Leaning forward with impertinent disregard for subtlety, Mrs. Featherston gasped. "Dreadfully unfashionable. Imagine, demonstrating that kind of…affection for one's own spouse!"

"Indeed, and she's no better. Why, she might as well be in her boudoir with the way she's—oh, gracious, Clara, did you see that? Oh, did you?"

"Calm yourself, Irmegard, he merely kissed her hand." Still, the older woman wrinkled her nose. "Scandalous, certainly." She cocked her head. 'Yes, that was what I heard of her…some sort of scandal…oh, yes, I remember now. She was a recluse or something. Her mother had been murdered and she took it so hard, poor thing. Locked herself in the country." Both women, avid social parasites, paused to shudder at the thought of the slower-paced life outside of Town. "What was her family name? Oh, yes, Rathford. Filthy rich, they were. Old money, quite a distinctive family." She was completely delighted with her powers of recall, and sat back in her chair with a satisfied expression on her face.

"Oh, poor dear," the smaller woman fussed. "I suppose he rescued her from that dreary life."

"They have a son, I believe, and he's to inherit both fortunes. Imagine the catch he will be when he comes of age. We shall have to warn our granddaughters!"

"Oooh, how delightful. Oh, look, Clara—what are they doing now?"

The larger woman leaned forward, lornette ready. "He's bidding her to play the pianoforte. And she's doing it."

Helena Mannion sat down and placed her fingers on the

keys. She looked radiant, with her glossy blond hair piled artfully on her head, a few coy locks curling seductively along the graceful curve of her neck and against that flawless brow. In London only a fortnight, she'd already attracted a few admirers. They were gathered around her now.

Adam didn't mind the glut of male attention. He beamed at her from his spot off to the side, and never took his eyes from her even when the Duchess of Blenheim came up to speak to him.

At the urging of the men gathered around her, Helena began to sing. It was a sweet song. Over in the corner, Adam spied the two biddies who'd had their heads together since the moment he and Helena had entered the room. One heaved her ample bosom as Helena's glorious voice gave the song life, and the other dabbed at her eyes.

Adam turned his attention back to his wife. She was truly beguiling, he had to admit. He'd lose patience with these impertinent bucks who flocked around her eventually, but for now he couldn't say he blamed them.

How very glad he'd be to get home to Rathford Manor. It *was* home, the place where his whole life was centered. His son had been born there, his friends were there, the growing pack of hounds he had raised were there, already earning him a reputation as a fine breeder. His whole life, which he'd come to treasure. He'd gone looking for treasure, hadn't he? Well, he'd found it, a wealth beyond imagining.

It wasn't the same here. Although Helena had been good enough to accompany him on this trip to London for business, their son and staff in tow, she belonged with him in Northumberland, where they'd walk or ride together almost every day. He could see her in his mind's eye, supervising the restoration of the great house, overseeing large dinner parties or small routs with their close circle, where she could laugh easily and come and tuck herself in the crook of his arm if she liked. Mostly, he liked to think of how she looked with their son, Stephen, defying all convention and caring for the tiny boy herself without benefit of a nurse.

She looked up at that moment and caught Adam's eye. He smiled, and she gave him that tender, melting look that never failed to make his insides quiver and his body take notice. He'd make her pay for that look, he mused as he sipped his champagne.

With a darting look about, she ascertained that no one was looking and mouthed three words to him: *I love you.*

He raised his glass and mouthed them back.

Over in the corner, the two biddies began to fan themselves so wildly he feared they might take flight.

He had business to see to with a consortium of men ensconced in the library. When he finally emerged, suppressing his impatience, he headed directly for his wife. He extricated her from her conversation without too much trouble. "Are you having a good time?" he asked.

She turned toward him and inadvertently—or was it by chance?—brushed her right breast against the back of his hand. His entire body stiffened. Lifting her cool gaze to him, she murmured, "Take me home, Adam."

There was no mistaking the look in her eyes.

They raised a few eyebrows with their rushed farewells, but in the carriage ride home that evening, they most certainly didn't give it any thought.

* * * * *

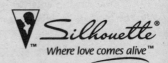

Harlequin truly does
make any time special. . . .
This year we are celebrating
weddings in style!

A
Walk
Down
the Aisle

WEDDING CELEBRATION

To help us celebrate, we want you to tell us how wearing the Harlequin wedding gown will make your wedding day special. As the grand prize, Harlequin will offer one lucky bride the chance to **"Walk Down the Aisle"** in the Harlequin wedding gown!

There's more...

For her honeymoon, she and her groom will spend five nights at the **Hyatt Regency Maui.** As part of this five-night honeymoon at the hotel renowned for its romantic attractions, the couple will enjoy a candlelit dinner for two in Swan Court, a sunset sail on the hotel's catamaran, and duet spa treatments.

Maui • Molokai • Lanai

To enter, please write, in, 250 words or less, how wearing the Harlequin wedding gown will make your wedding day special. The entry will be judged based on its emotionally compelling nature, its originality and creativity, and its sincerity. This contest is open to Canadian and U.S. residents only and to those who are 18 years of age and older. There is no purchase necessary to enter. Void where prohibited. See further contest rules attached. Please send your entry to:

Walk Down the Aisle Contest

In Canada	In U.S.A.
P.O. Box 637	P.O. Box 9076
Fort Erie, Ontario	3010 Walden Ave.
L2A 5X3	Buffalo, NY 14269-9076

You can also enter by visiting www.eHarlequin.com
Win the Harlequin wedding gown and the vacation of a lifetime!
The deadline for entries is October 1, 2001.

HARLEQUIN®
Makes any time special ®

PHWDACONT1

HARLEQUIN WALK DOWN THE AISLE TO MAUI CONTEST 1197
OFFICIAL RULES
NO PURCHASE NECESSARY TO ENTER

1. To enter, follow directions published in the offer to which you are responding. Contest begins April 2, 2001, and ends on October 1, 2001. Method of entry may vary. Mailed entries must be postmarked by October 1, 2001, and received by October 8, 2001.

2. Contest entry may be, at times, presented via the Internet, but will be restricted solely to residents of certain geographic areas that are disclosed on the Web site. To enter via the Internet, if permissible, access the Harlequin Web site (www.eHarlequin.com) and follow the directions displayed online. Online entries must be received by 11:59 p.m. E.S.T. on October 1, 2001.

    In lieu of submitting an entry online, enter by mail by hand-printing (or typing) on an 8½" x 11" plain piece of paper, your name, address (including zip code), Contest number/name and in 250 words or fewer, why winning a Harlequin wedding dress would make your wedding day special. Mail via first-class mail to: Harlequin Walk Down the Aisle Contest 1197, (in the U.S.) P.O. Box 9076, 3010 Walden Avenue, Buffalo, NY 14269-9076, (in Canada) P.O. Box 637, Fort Erie, Ontario L2A 5X3, Canada.

    Limit one entry per person, household address and e-mail address. Online and/or mailed entries received from persons residing in geographic areas in which Internet entry is not permissible will be disqualified.

3. Contests will be judged by a panel of members of the Harlequin editorial, marketing and public relations staff based on the following criteria:

    • Originality and Creativity—50%
    • Emotionally Compelling—25%
    • Sincerity—25%

    In the event of a tie, duplicate prizes will be awarded. Decisions of the judges are final.

4. All entries become the property of Torstar Corp. and will not be returned. No responsibility is assumed for lost, late, illegible, incomplete, inaccurate, nondelivered or misdirected mail or misdirected e-mail, for technical, hardware or software failures of any kind, lost or unavailable network connections, or failed, incomplete, garbled or delayed computer transmission or any human error which may occur in the receipt or processing of the entries in this Contest.

5. Contest open only to residents of the U.S. (except Puerto Rico) and Canada, who are 18 years of age or older, and is void wherever prohibited by law; all applicable laws and regulations apply. Any litigation within the Province of Quebec respecting the conduct or organization of a publicity contest may be submitted to the Régie des alcools, des courses et des jeux for a ruling. Any litigation respecting the awarding of a prize may be submitted to the Régie des alcools, des courses et des jeux only for the purpose of helping the parties reach a settlement. Employees and immediate family members of Torstar Corp. and D. L. Blair, Inc., their affiliates, subsidiaries and all other agencies, entities and persons connected with the use, marketing or conduct of this Contest are not eligible to enter. Taxes on prizes are the sole responsibility of winners. Acceptance of any prize offered constitutes permission to use winner's name, photograph or other likeness for the purposes of advertising, trade and promotion on behalf of Torstar Corp., its affiliates and subsidiaries without further compensation to the winner, unless prohibited by law.

6. Winners will be determined no later than November 15, 2001, and will be notified by mail. Winners will be required to sign and return an Affidavit of Eligibility form within 15 days after winner notification. Noncompliance within that time period may result in disqualification and an alternative winner may be selected. Winners of trip must execute a Release of Liability prior to ticketing and must possess required travel documents (e.g. passport, photo ID) where applicable. Trip must be completed by November 2002. No substitution of prize permitted by winner. Torstar Corp. and D. L. Blair, Inc., their parents, affiliates, and subsidiaries are not responsible for errors in printing or electronic presentation of Contest, entries and/or game pieces. In the event of printing or other errors which may result in unintended prize values or duplication of prizes, all affected game pieces or entries shall be null and void. If for any reason the Internet portion of the Contest is not capable of running as planned, including infection by computer virus, bugs, tampering, unauthorized intervention, fraud, technical failures, or any other causes beyond the control of Torstar Corp. which corrupt or affect the administration, secrecy, fairness, integrity or proper conduct of the Contest, Torstar Corp. reserves the right, at its sole discretion, to disqualify any individual who tampers with the entry process and to cancel, terminate, modify or suspend the Contest or the Internet portion thereof. In the event of a dispute regarding an online entry, the entry will be deemed submitted by the authorized holder of the e-mail account submitted at the time of entry. Authorized account holder is defined as the natural person who is assigned to an e-mail address by an Internet access provider, online service provider or other organization that is responsible for arranging e-mail address for the domain associated with the submitted e-mail address. **Purchase or acceptance of a product offer does not improve your chances of winning.**

7. Prizes: (1) Grand Prize—A Harlequin wedding dress (approximate retail value: $3,500) and a 5-night/6-day honeymoon trip to Maui, HI, including round-trip air transportation provided by Maui Visitors Bureau from Los Angeles International Airport (winner is responsible for transportation to and from Los Angeles International Airport) and a Harlequin Romance Package, including hotel accomodations (double occupancy) at the Hyatt Regency Maui Resort and Spa, dinner for (2) two at Swan Court, a sunset sail on Kiele V and a spa treatment for the winner (approximate retail value: $4,000); (5) Five runner-up prizes of a $1000 gift certificate to selected retail outlets to be determined by Sponsor (retail value $1000 ea.). Prizes consist of only those items listed as part of the prize. Limit one prize per person. All prizes are valued in U.S. currency.

8. For a list of winners (available after December 17, 2001) send a self-addressed, stamped envelope to: Harlequin Walk Down the Aisle Contest 1197 Winners, P.O. Box 4200 Blair, NE 68009-4200 or you may access the www.eHarlequin.com Web site through January 15, 2002.

Contest sponsored by Torstar Corp., P.O. Box 9042, Buffalo, NY 14269-9042, U.S.A.

PHWDACONT2

MONTANA MAVERICKS HISTORICALS
Discover the origins
of Montana's most popular family...

On sale September 2001
THE GUNSLINGER'S BRIDE
by **Cheryl St.John**
Outlaw Brock Kincaid returns home to make peace with his brothers
and finds love in the arms of an old flame with a secret.

On sale October 2001
WHITEFEATHER'S WOMAN
by **Deborah Hale**
Kincaid Ranch foreman John Whitefeather breaks all the rules when
the Native American dares to fall in love with nanny Jane Harris.

On sale November 2001
A CONVENIENT WIFE
by **Carolyn Davidson**
Whitehorn doctor Winston Gray enters into a marriage of
convenience with a pregnant rancher's daughter, only to
discover he's found his heart's desire!

MONTANA MAVERICKS
RETURN TO WHITEHORN—WHERE LEGENDS ARE BEGUN
AND LOVE LASTS FOREVER BENEATH THE BIG SKY...

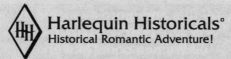

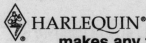